Praise for *The Ball*

I was hooked immediately by the narrative voice, which I would describe as utterly kickass, take-no-prisoners in tone. The combination of hyperbole and hilarity throughout is what I would call High Hillbilly in the purest form.

—Chuck Kinder, author of
Honeymooners and *Last Mountain Dancer*

Such writing as we find in *The Ballad of Trenchmouth Taggart* is rare these days. So much of what we normally get—about rural life—is slick, shallow, and overtly sentimental. Glenn Taylor has cut to the bone and written an elegant story that tells a truth about his people and place, a kind of truth occasionally found—when we're lucky—in a novel. It's a testament to Taylor's craft as a writer that this story is so detailed, present, and personal, yet covers so much time—a hundred years or so. It's as if we were there, marveling at something in danger of being lost.

—Clyde Edgerton, author of
Walking Across Egypt and *The Bible Salesman*

Part *Rip Van Winkle*, part *Professor Seagull*, part *O Brother, Where Art Thou?*, part *Matewan*, *The Ballad of Trenchmouth Taggart* is picaresque, legendary, epic, and outrageous, and in spite of all that, I can't help but wonder if maybe it isn't also more than just a little bit true. And with a narrative voice so confident, so compelling, so arresting and pure, the conclusion I came to is that Glenn Taylor must have channeled the whole damn thing.

—Sara Pritchard,
author of *Crackpots* and *Lately*

THE BALLAD OF TRENCHMOUTH TAGGART

THE BALLAD OF TRENCHMOUTH TAGGART

by M. Glenn Taylor

Vandalia Press

MORGANTOWN 2008

Vandalia Press, Morgantown 26506

© 2008 by West Virginia University Press
First edition published 2008 by Vandalia Press

Printed in the United States of America

13 12 11 10 09 08   9 8 7 6 5 4 3 2 1

ISBN 978-1-933202-31-0 (alk. paper)

Library of Congress Cataloguing-in-Publication Data

The Ballad of Trenchmouth Taggart/M. Glenn Taylor.

p.   cm.

I. Title. II. Taylor, M. Glenn.

IN PROCESS

Library of Congress Control Number: 2008927388

Printed in USA by Thomson-Shore

Vandalia Press is an imprint of the West Virginia University Press

AUTHOR'S NOTE

This novel is a work of fiction. The places are real, and some of the events and individuals depicted herein were in fact real, as can be further studied in any of the excellent historical sources listed in the acknowledgments. However, the author has taken great liberties in the writing of this novel. Thus, all characters, their actions, and their speech are the product of the author's imagination and in no way represent any person, living or dead.

Cover images: Top, Hoover Light, Hawkins County, Tennessee. Photograph by Kenneth Murray; Middle, Harmonica by Richard Holden, http://www.flickr.com/photos/ richardholden/; Bottom, Abandoned Sawmill and Lumber Plant, Trace, Mingo County, W. Va., courtesy of the West Virginia and Regional History Collection, WVU Libraries; Snake drawing by Bryn Perrott.

This one is for Margaret

I have gulled the pith from a sumac limb
To play a tune that my blood remembers.

—Louise McNeill

PROLOGUE

On December 3rd, 2010, the old man sewed his mouth shut with saltwater-rated fishing line. The sores and the throbbing were back. It was his 108th birthday, and it was the day *Time* magazine sent a reporter to his home in Warm Hollow, West Virginia. This was on account of the old man's reputation, and on account of Pearl Thackery. Pearl Thackery was the oldest living West Virginian and had died the week prior, leaving the old man, a one time inventor, snake handler, cunnilinguist, sniper, woodsman, harmonica man, and newspaperman, as the oldest living Homo sapien in the state.

He'd left a small, pinto bean-sized hole unsewn, so that he could ingest chicory coffee and spruce needle tea through a straw. So he could speak if he needed to. And so he could smoke his Chesterfields.

When the *Time* magazine reporter sat down across the kitchen table from him, the old man broke his vow of silence and mastered, in minutes, smoking and speaking simultaneously. It was a speech difficult to discern, but it was talking nonetheless. The reporter pushed the record button on his miniature, steel voice recorder. A red light the size of a tick lit up. The old man marveled at this invention. He stared at the little red circle until it went blurry there on the kitchen table. It entranced him. He spun a blown-glass ashtray with his plump-veined, purple-blotched hands. His skin was thin. A full white head of hair. His eyes and ears, though drooped and wrinkled, were still keen. He farted freely.

The reporter got down to business. "I'd like to ask you about your life, if I may," he said.

The old man leaned back in his split wood chair, then forward again. "You want me to bend your ear?" he said. "I'll do it. But the bend I put on it won't never heal. You're liable to go deaf." He pronounced "deaf" like "deef." It was a lot of voice from a little hole. He said, "I feel like that big small fella the Jewish actor played. Hoffman. Small Big Man. You seen it?" He lit a cigarette and stuck it in the hole. Pulled white paper red. "Was a time I had but two talents," he said. "Back then it was speaking in tongues and pleasin women by way of their nether-regions."

The reporter cleared his throat.

"I come up with the phrase, 'I'd rather have a bottle in front of me than a frontal lobotomy.'" This was a bald-faced lie. He said, "You may have heard along the way somewhere that I killed men." He considered the younger man, his hands and the way he held them on the table. His eyes. Then the old man bent his ear.

·

BOOK ONE 1903–1921

Let any man shoot me with cannon or gun.

—Cap Hatfield

CHAPTER ONE

THE WOMAN COULD CURE AILMENTS

When Early Taggart was baptized in the Tug River in 1903, he was two months old. His mother, whose husband had left her a week earlier, had got religion. She believed it right to bring lambs to the fold before they could crawl or sit up on their own. Before Satan could fill their little blood vessels with the seven deadly sins. It was these sins that had caused her husband to run off, that she now preached on to her twelve pound boy while he breastfed.

But it was February when she decided to baptize him, and no preacher would agree to it. "You'd have to break through the ice down there," the Methodist man said, "and that boy ain't old enough to get wet in the head anyhow." So Mittie Ann Taggart did it herself. She punched through the inch-thick ice with her shoe heel and held her baby boy by his thighs. She dunked his head like wash. He came up screaming.

She claimed he spoke to her then, spit water at her cheek. "Pretty as you please, pretty as you please," is what he said, according to Mittie Ann. Then he said, "Devil's got a hold on God."

She dropped him on the ice. He cracked through, went under and rode the current for a quarter mile. Then he kicked out onto the banks where a woman had melted through the ice washing a cast iron pot. This woman, Ona Dorsett, picked the boy up and blew her air in his mouth. She smacked his back until he colored up again, until he spit out the gray water through his nose holes. She wrapped him tight against her breastplate under a bearskin coat and took him home.

Mittie Ann Taggart went to the mayor. She demanded he call on all the preachers in the county to renounce Satan with a single cry of "Down with Beelzebub." When the mayor surmised she had dumped her newborn child in the river, he ordered her confined. The boy was at first presumed dead. There was talk of lynching Mittie Ann in public for what she'd done, hard talk considering she was a woman, and a white one at that. Then somebody said the widow Dorsett had the boy, was healthifying him like she had the other young one who lived with her up back of Warm Hollow. This was enough to calm the lynching talk, and Mittie Ann Taggart was transferred by horse and buggy to the Home for Incurables in Huntington. When she walked from the jail to the buggy, folks spat on her.

The widow Dorsett was thirty-one years old. A tall, dark-haired woman, strong-boned and plain. She had a three-year-old girl living with her. Girl's name was Clarissa, and she had come to Ona Dorsett by way of a raped teenager who could not handle her situation and was running off to Charleston to get citified. Ona Dorsett had lost her husband in a mine cave-in in 1899. She'd never been able to reproduce. She'd spent her days tutoring children on how to read and write. That, and she helped her husband tend his moonshine still. When he was gone, she did less tutoring, more moonshining, and baby Clarissa was a welcome presence in her home.

The home was modest if not hazardous. A pioneer farmer had built it without the advantages of a permanent settler's dwelling. This was a cabin of unhewn logs. Its mass of cracks was filled and refilled with grass and mud. The roof was clapboard. The cookstove kept the space warm, and the fireplace sent smoke up and out through a cat-and-clay chimney hand-laid with stones.

It was here that Early Taggart would grow into a boy and then into a man. Here with Ona Dorsett, a woman who could do most anything, it seemed. A woman whose livelihood was the sale of moonshine, though she used a middleman on a small commission since woman moonshiners were not taken seriously. As far as she knew, she was the only woman shiner in the state. And she was certainly the only woman able to ride her dead husband's gelding of seventeen hands as if she'd been born equestrian. Ona Dorsett had once loped across uneven hill terrain and dropped a black bear on the move as it watched her, unaware that such a sight was possible. She'd lined up her Winchester rifle and sunk a shell in the beating heart of a three hundred pound animal, all while posting bareback and calculating trees, distance, the movement of the horse below her. She skinned and filleted the animal, cured his meat. With this, and the meat of deer, turkeys, pheasants, and squirrels, she was able to feed her two adopted children. Though she did not particularly enjoy it, she hunted regularly for them and took pride in her efficiency.

The woman could also cure ailments. She made fever-killer drinks from dogwood bark. If rheumatism visited her children, she bathed them in water she collected every year from a stream before sun-up on Ash Wednesday. For double rheumatism insurance, she'd turn their shoes upside down before bedtime. For coughs, she had procured a respectable stockpile of Virginia snakeroot. Hacking coughs meant swallowing the unmistakably bitter bears-foot tea. Inflammation of the chest required horseradish and mustard poultices to aid in breathing, and she could wrap these in such a way as to provide instant mother-comfort.

Ona Dorsett took care of the two children given to her by chance. She fed and clothed them and fixed all their ailments, save one. The boy was afflicted with a mouth disease so early on and so strongly, that the Widow could do nothing for him. A week after she found him in the river, now fully recovered and wrapped tight in heavy cotton blankets and the skin of a deer, Early Taggart began to scream through the night. He worked tirelessly at busting through his heavy wrap. The Widow couldn't figure it out until his gums were caught momentarily in the light of her lantern. The gums were bloody red, swollen and full of holes like anthills made of skin. She had the doctor come in, a man who had known her husband well, a man who drank a good bit of her moonshine. Doctor Warble said the boy had calcium overloads, that he was actually sprouting teeth at two and a half months, five ahead of schedule. But this was not all. The doctor surmised that the gums had already split, that the boy had already been teething, at the time of his attempted drowning. He further surmised that coal sludge in the water had infected the openings. This infection had somehow evolved into what resembled an incurable oral disease in older folks, a disease that left gums eternally rotten and bloody, teeth decaying and odorous. Such a sight reminded Doctor Warble, who had been a medic with the Rough Riders at the battle of San Juan Hill only five years prior, of the mouth disease he'd encountered among Spanish soldiers, dead and agape in their trenches. It was beyond explanation that this disease could occur in an infant, but it had. The boy had Trenchmouth.

CHAPTER TWO

HERE CAME A MAN

The mouth was a curious orifice. When it ailed a body, its throb was merciless as a hammer in the hands of John Henry. Headaches were mere discomforts—nagging, small pain otherwise ignored. But this disease of the tooth and gum that had afflicted the baby boy, this was oral torment. It was evident to Ona Dorsett that Doctor Warble's pain powder would not do. She took to singing to the baby boy, calling him by the word Doctor Warble had used: Trenchmouth. She decided he'd keep his given surname. She also took to dipping a finger in the house moonshine jug, rubbing that finger across the little one's gums and fanged teeth. When she did it each night, his agonized wails subsided. He was quiet. He was asleep. This became ritual.

Dorsett's moonshine was of no ordinary hill recipe. The dead Dorsett man had cultivated a process begun by his father before him. Ona had further enhanced the still, its capabilities. She had thrown in some new ingredients. The results were what some would call miraculous. Men paid top dollar for that shine, though they knew not where it originated. The middleman who sold it to them had taken an oath of holy secrecy to the dead Dorsett's widow, and he intended to keep it. It was said a drop of the stuff could spin your brain like a top, feather-tickle your pecker hard. This mule-kick possessed no odor.

Ona took it herself, once at Trenchmouth and Clarissa's bedtime, once at her own. She'd long since realized her blend had none of the unfortunate effects other blends had. On the contrary, Dorsett shine caused her to read at night, fortified her vocabulary. It made things clear as the new glass windowpanes town folks had. Headaches and slurred speech were not part of the bargain. The only physical change an observer would take note of occurred in the eyeball. Pupils, upon first swig and for a minute thereafter, spread wide to the edge of the iris. Exploded like perfect black planets. This gave the drinker a look of animal capability. It was beast-eye.

Ona Dorsett sat at her kitchen table on a Saturday night in May of 1903, her pupils gradually rescinding to normal. By lantern light, she read a book called *Following the Equator* by Mr. Samuel Clemens. It was near eleven o'clock when a knock came at the door. She looked up to the loft where the little ones slept sound, then rose to answer. On her way to the door, she took her Remington Double Derringer out of a big empty flour tin. She held it behind her back when she answered.

A man stood before her. He was dirty, his clothes nearly worn past their life expectancy, all tears and patches. Ona's dress and the fabrics she put on her children were not without flaw, nor were they contemporary, but this man was something else. His beard had last been shaved two weeks on the right side, a month on the left. When he smiled there were cigar-wrap pieces the size of cockroaches in his yellow teeth. "How do missus," he said.

"What can I do for you?" Ona said softly.

The man looked behind her into the house. His eyes rolled left, right, up, and down like he wanted to gain his bearings but would never remember them. A habit of the sharp-eyed gone sour. "You got your youngins up there in the loft, I reckon?" From where he stood outside, he looked up where he couldn't see.

"What can I do for you?"

"You can drop whatever pea shooter you got tucked in your spine bone there." His smile widened. There was sweat under the brim of his brown slouch hat though it was cold outside. "Just put it off on yonder floor there. I ain't lookin to take it from you," he said.

Ona pulled the gun out to her side, feigned dropping it for a second before she swung it around to his neck. He caught her wrist with his left hand before she reached his shoulder. She did not fire. The man reared back and slammed his forehead against the bridge of her nose. Bone crunched like thin cornstalk. Ona hit the floorboards.

While the man regarded the pistol and rubbed at his forehead, she fought blackness and the little popping stars that broke through it. He was re-positioning his hat when she got most of her sight back and pulled a stag-handle knife from her felt-button boots. She came up off the floor like the serpent's strike and had the eight-inch blade buried in his neck before he could discern the occurrence. She was silent as she pulled and pushed the handle made of deer antler, maneuvered it so that it nearly went in one side and came out the other.

His knees never gave. He stood there, gun dropped to the floor, one arm limp at his side and the other touching his neck and the thing piercing it like a kabob. He gurgled a little. Said something to her that she couldn't quite get. He was only one foot inside the door when she put her boot sole against his stomach and forced him backwards onto the dirt. She put the pistol back in the flour container, took a belt off the house jar, and went outside. She stood over the man, dead now, a wide stream of blood traversing down the incline beneath his head. She said nothing, though she had an unexplainable urge to spit in his eyes. Instead, she went around back and got the shovel.

Ona lashed heavy rope around the mule she had to smack to make move. The other end wrapped the base of the outhouse. The mule, called Beechnut, strained his old, nicked haunches and pulled the outhouse a good six feet away from its designation over the hole. Ona told him good boy. The hole was half-filled. Two months worth of shit and piss. The Widow had her work cut out. Widen it by four feet, deepen it by three. She began digging the man's grave.

It was just the time of spring when the earth was finally diggable.

Before she rolled him into the hole three hours later, she went through his pockets. A half dollar and a mouth harp, silver and worn, but well-made. Cheap cigar and kitchen matches, loose, no package. A folded photograph of a woman in a lace-fringed dress and fur hat. She tossed the photograph of the woman into the grave, then rolled the man in on top of it. He went still at the bottom, belly up. There was loose dirt on the end of her shovel. She held it above his face, dropped half on one open eye, half on the other. "I know you," she said. The man looked like he had on straight temple spectacles, the glass lenses tinted mud black.

He'd rolled easy into his new home five feet below the outhouse basin. The earth went smoothly back to where it originated, patted down without much trouble like it had never moved. Ona re-dug the waste-hole and Beechnut hefted the outhouse to its original location. She gave him an apple which he ate with finick.

Inside, Ona climbed the ladder to the loft before washing her hands. The two of them were there, the baby boy in his wicker bassinet, the three-year-old girl on the horsehair mattress. The Widow stared at them for ten solid minutes before she descended the stairs and washed up with cold well-water over the tub. She put on a sleeping gown that had been her mother-in-law's, ascended the ladder again and slept between her two children, marking the patterns of their sleep breathing in her mind, smiling when the inhales and exhales matched up. Matching her own to theirs.

CHAPTER THREE

CLIMBING AND DIGGING CAME NATURAL

By the spring of 1906, it was evident that three things separated Trenchmouth from the ordinary two-year-old. There was of course his oral ailment, which required higher doses of nightly moonshine as his weight swelled. But the other two things were remarkable in an entirely different manner. The boy could climb and dig in such a way that only boys thrice his age had mastered. He scampered up hillsides like a Tibetan antelope, and his hands dove into mud like a posthole digger. "Climbin and diggin is what comes natural to boys," the Widow Dorsett would say, "and this one here is more natural than any."

Trenchmouth buried things. Found things too. An 1859 Indian Head penny. The skeletal structure of a barn cat with a .22 hole in its skull. Seventeen clay marbles.

On a warm, overcast day in early May, the boy did what he often did while he was supposed to nap. He pulled himself up and out of the crib the Widow had made, and he descended the ladder from the loft to the main floor. Two-year-olds shouldn't—and most couldn't—

do these things, but such was the boy's stock, determined. His mother and sister were out knocking tomato worms off newly sprouted yellow Hillbillies. Trenchmouth reached up for the front door latch, opened, and ran for it.

He was a big boy at two years and four months. Long since off the diaper and expertly outhouse-trained. On this day, he felt the morning's oatmeal churning so he headed for the backhouse, as Ona called it. The half quarter moon cut-out was lined with cobweb. Inside, the seat was two-holed, big for the Widow, small for Trenchmouth and Clarissa. He perched himself. Afterwards, like he was taught, the boy reached in the scoop bag and dropped lime down the hole, on top of his business. Something always caused him to run out of there afterwards, some stench he could not place.

He could heave rocks. While Ona and Clarissa tended plants, Trenchmouth stood in the barn and threw rocks and dirt clods at Beechnut the mule. The animal swished his tail and rocked his head side to side. He generally didn't care for being hit with such things, but he took it. Blinked his eyes. Snorted. The boy laughed and clomped his way to the tack room. He knew the Widow kept a paper sack of sugar cubes in a saddle bag high up. That climbing came in handy.

Out back of the barn, the boy sucked on a cube, then set it down and watched the flies come to it. The flies only landed on licked sugar cubes, never dry. Little Trenchmouth could already figure such things as useful somehow. He buried more clay marbles in a quick-dug hole next to another hiding the jawbone of a fox. He'd come back for all these in time. They'd all have their uses.

When he walked up to them, they were bent at the waist, Ona strong and middle-aged and wiry, Clarissa a miniature version of all these things. It was as if they were blood kin. Their dresses were made from old window curtains.

"Get to bug knockin," the Widow told Trenchmouth. She'd long since stopped scolding for naptime escapes.

"Get to bug knockin," Clarissa said directly. She liked to mimic her mother. She was tall and thin, not quite grade school aged, but already taller than the first and second graders, girls and boys both.

Trenchmouth made a noise at them not unlike a cat's call before a fight. Deep and verging on howl. The boy was gifted physically, and he could figure the way things worked quick, but he could not, or did not, speak a lick. Just moaned and howled and grunted, and, when he really got bothered, smacked his own head on both sides with little open palms.

He began knocking worms and bugs with his little squared-off fingernails. He bent at the knees. Concentrated. Licked his rotten gums and teeth and stared wide-eyed. But something bad got in the wind again and he stood up, sniffed. The smell made his lip quiver. It was too much for his olfactory to take, something awful he'd not caught wind of so strong before. The Hillbilly tomato in front of him went blurry, filled his vision with red, and his ears went to ringing. Terror took him, sudden and unexplained. He spat and grunted and ran for his mother, clinging to her rough-stitched muslin skirt until the gray hem ripped and she shook him loose like a wet dog does water.

CHAPTER FOUR

FRANK DALLARA FASHIONED A TOOL

Once every three months, Ona Dorsett took her children to the Wholesale Grocers in Williamson for evaporated milk, navy beans, sardines, table salt, and toilet soaps, among other things. Once, she'd bought them a nibble of Mungers Fancy Chocolate because the shine business was especially good in winter months.

Just before Thanksgiving 1909, the three of them made a trip. Some folks had Model T's by then, but the Widow and her two children rode in a canopy-top horse wagon.

Trenchmouth was nearly six, his sister nine, and they couldn't have been more different. She was in school, he wasn't yet. She was brave of speech to adults and peers alike, while he spoke as little as possible. This was due not to any lack of intellect, but instead a desire not to show folks the inside of his mouth. So it came to be that when he spoke, he did so with his lips curled over the swelled gums and crooked teeth. A mumbler, some would say. An otherwise good, handsome, brown-haired boy who spoke like someone had soldered his jawbones in such a way as to prohibit full opening.

In the grocers, Clarissa handed her mother items for the sack while Trenchmouth sprinted the aisles, his boots leaving marks when he turned corners. He wasn't looking where he was headed on one such turn and ended up with a face full of pantleg. From his seat on the tiled floor, he looked up to see who he'd plowed into. "I'm sorry sir," he mumbled.

The man said nothing. He was tall and thin, and though not yet thirty years old, his face housed wrinkles rivaling a bulldog's. He stood stooped. His hands carried the permanent black residue of an undergrounder, a miner, just as his father's had before him. His father had been born in Italy, and it would be another generation before the last name morphed pronunciation, quit carrying the unpleasant ring of an outsider. When he smiled at Trenchmouth, his teeth looked nearly as bad off as the boy's, and this was comforting. "You're liable to outrun a coal train ain't you son?" he said. He was pulling pieces of smooth carved wood from a sugar sack. The wood pieces were lashed with rubber.

Trenchmouth watched him place his wares on the store's shelf, one by one, lined up.

"Slingshots," the man told him. He looked at the sling shot in his hand for a moment, thought, then handed it to the boy, who had stood back up. "Go knock Goliath on his behind," he said. Trenchmouth wanted to take the weapon, but he didn't. Until the man took the boy's hand in his own and placed it there. Then the man, whose name was Frank Dallara, finished putting his goods on the shelf. "They bring in a nickel from most boys. You got a deal on that there."

"Thank you sir," Trenchmouth said.

Frank Dallara stared at the awkward mouth, the way it hid its own parts. Then he looked the boy in the eye and said, "I'd bet my last dollar you'll be a dead-eye with that weapon in one week. I can see it in you."

The Widow came up behind him, Clarissa beside her. "Frank," she said.

"Missus Dorsett," he said and tipped his hat. Something or someone had taken a bite out of the brim. "I reckoned this one was yours. Grow like weeds, don't they?"

"They do."

Dallara turned his attention to Clarissa. "My boy Frederick is in your class isn't he young lady?"

"Yessir he is," Clarissa said. "He doesn't say much, but when he does it's not mean like some other boys."

"Well, glad to hear it. He speaks highly of you."

For once, Clarissa had no response. Her cheeks went a little pink.

"You're selling goods Frank?" Ona said.

"I'm out of the mines, done for good with it. Too many gettin killed for one contraption foul up or another." He looked at her and then at the floor, like he shouldn't have said such a thing in the presence of a mine widow. "I sell these for a little extra, but I'm framing construction over at the Urias Hotel in Matewan."

"Well, good. I reckon that's safer."

Trenchmouth pulled back on the rubber and extended his arm. He squinted one eye like he'd lined up this shot a hundred times before. He didn't let the rubber snap back, just stood there still as a statue.

"I told him I could see it plain as daybreak," Dallara said. "This boy's a dead-eye. A crackshot if I've ever seen one."

CHAPTER FIVE

BEAST EYE AND SOMETHING ELSE

1911 was to be a bad year for the isolated, hill-spiked terrain of southern West Virginia. Death and discovery of the unpleasant would visit more than one family in the coalfields, and Trenchmouth, aged eight years, would be shaped by all of it.

A third talent had gotten in his bones, natural as the digging and climbing, which he still practiced daily. Frank Dallara's words had come to fruition, and Trenchmouth could knock a crow off a sugar maple branch from sixty feet using nothing but his eyes and that little wooden wrist rocket he'd picked up at the grocers.

Frank Dallara took the boy out on weekends for practice. "Ancient man couldn't always carry a bow and arrow or a spear," he said. "They needed something lightweight." Accuracy was studied through repetition. "David protected his sheep with the same contraption you got in your hand, except Mr. Goodyear give us cooked rubber to work with," Frank Dallara liked to say. "Old David slew a giant with it too." You could find stones anywhere, in any size. Small, smooth ones for line drive precision. Big, heavy ones for high-arced momentum.

Dallara was a miner and a carpenter by trade, but he should have been a physicist the way he tutored Trenchmouth on velocity, gravity, and inertia.

He'd put his arm around the boy after a particularly good shot, as if Trenchmouth were his own. Like most, he called him "T," but it sounded better somehow. It didn't seem like much to Frank Dallara, but to the eight year old, it was everything.

The boy was taught on guns too. The Widow taught him safety first, everything else second. She schooled him on a hammerless 10 gauge that had been her husband's. Frank Dallara let him get used to a .22 rifle belonging to his boy Frederick. The three of them went squirrel hunting on Sundays, and afterwards, each and every time, Clarissa and Frederick, by then almost twelve, made eyes at one another. Talked by themselves on the porch for a while.

This made Trenchmouth a little mad. There were three reasons why. The first was a natural propensity for protecting his sister, younger or older did not factor. The second was a distaste for the bland nature of Frederick Dallara. He had no fire in him. Was good in school, but never hopped a moving train. When other boys caught and skinned blacksnakes or threw bullfrogs at the Model T's in town from hidden launching spots, Fred Dallara always got quiet and went home to study. He was a bore, and Trenchmouth didn't like bores. He wanted to be in it anytime and everywhere, and he had the scars to prove it. The third reason Trenchmouth was bothered by his non-blood sister's flirtations with the other boy was simple: she was non-blood, and this meant *he* could be there for her the way Fred Dallara wanted to be. Trenchmouth was a little bit in love with Clarissa, as much as an eight-year-old can be.

One Sunday evening in winter, standing by lantern light on the Widow's front lawn, Trenchmouth, Frank, and Fred cleaned the four fox squirrels they'd bagged that afternoon. They cut them around the middle and peeled back the skins. Inside, Ona heated up some bacon drippings on top of the black Acme cook stove. Clarissa watched from a window until the squirrels were halved and quartered and so on, then she came outside. It was the kind of cold out that creeps into you, takes you by surprise. "Y'all need help?" she said.

"We've got her just about done," Frank Dallara said.

The almost twelve-year-olds made eyes. Trenchmouth watched them.

When he and Frank Dallara took the little legs and abdomens inside to rinse and remove buckshot, Fred and Clarissa stayed put in front of the house. From inside the kitchen, the boy could see them. They kissed.

Trenchmouth was up and toward the door like he'd sat on a tack. He didn't slow once outside. He took the bigger boy down by driving his right shoulder into the hips. Once on the ground, while a confused Clarissa looked down at them with her hands to her mouth, Trenchmouth straddled Fred and commenced to fist pumping. He was like an out of control oil drill, swinging away, up and down, and when Fred Dallara finally grasped what was happening and threw the younger boy off, his nose and lips were split and leaking crimson fast. They both sat on their butts. Clarissa was about to lean down and check on the boy whose lips she'd just kissed, and Fred was about to lurch at his attacker, when Trenchmouth, squatting now like he might come back for more, squinted his eyes to almost nothing, pulled back his forever-covering lips to reveal the mess of sores and bulges and sharp crooked calcium, and hissed. In the low light of the lantern, he made a sound reserved for mountain cats with their backs against a rock wall. Then he shot forward like one and sunk his diseased teeth into the left cheek of Fred Dallara. The boy wailed something awful.

Trenchmouth ran for the woods.

He didn't come back until they were gone. Until the Widow had made a wet snuff poultice wrap for Frederick's face. She and Frank Dallara didn't speak a word while they tended to him. Fred choked back a confused cry. And Clarissa went to her bed in the loft and stared up at the wood beams.

Frank Dallara did speak one thing before he left that night, and from his hiding spot behind the outhouse, Trenchmouth heard him. "Your boy ought not to have done what he did," Frank told Ona Dorsett. "I like him, treat him like my own, but what he done here is something else." The something else he spoke on was more than protecting a sister from puppy love.

The Widow said nothing. Trenchmouth could hear the disappointment in his mother's silence, in the voice of the man he regarded as his Daddy, and it got to him.

They all read the newspaper. The Widow had made sure her two little ones were plenty literate by six years. A man called Orb brought the *Williamson Daily News* to them every Thursday. He was seventy-four years old and he liked to climb mountains and descend into hollows, but only if he had a destination, a nickel coming his way for delivering goods. On an early January Thursday, they'd heard most of what was coming to them already from folks walking by, looking to gossip about death. But, when old Orb rapped at their door that evening, none of them, not Ona, Clarissa, or Trenchmouth, expected those words on the page.

Trenchmouth's reading needed the most practice, so he read aloud to the other two while they strung half-runners. The first two stories weren't much more than the tragedy that had come their way in breezy gossip the day before. "Eight killed," Trenchmouth recited.

"Thacker. Eight miners are dead—two Americans and six Italians—as the result of the derailing of a mine car in the Lick Fork mine of the Red Jacket Coal Company." The derailing had knocked mine props loose and unleashed a precipitation of heavy slate on the men. The article ended by giving the mine owner's name, and lamenting that the mine itself was "badly wrecked."

Clarissa stood up, holding her dress in her fingertips like a satchel, weighted down with the throwaway ends of beans. She walked gingerly like this to the pail used for hog slop, dumped them in. Trenchmouth read the next one. "Cables Broke. Bluefield. Eight men were killed and two seriously injured on an incline in a mine near here. The men were . . ." he'd come upon a word he couldn't sound out, but he was a determined boy . . . "ascending the incline in a coal car when the cable broke allowing cars loaded with coal to shoot down the plane and crash into the ten men. Eight of the victims were buried beneath tons of coal and instantly killed."

"Eight men in two separate accidents. That's something," Clarissa said.

The Widow did not look up from her stringing. "Don't make something out of nothing, Clarissa. There isn't no plan in such filth."

"Moonshine charge," Trenchmouth read. His mother looked up at him. "Huntington. Mrs. Caroline Carpenter, 50, of Burdette, Putnam County, said to be the only woman distiller in West Virginia, was arrested and lodged in jail to await the action of the next federal jury. It is alleged by federal officers that Mrs. Carpenter operated on a place at her home that was the only oasis in the Putnam County district, and from her illicit sales of liquor netted a large sum during the past few months."

The Widow stood and dumped her bean heads as her daughter had done. She wiped her hands together. "Some folks don't keep their money close to their skin, I reckon," she said. "But children, we've got to be more careful than ever now. Got to let them keep on thinking there's but one woman shinin in the state." She told them to look at her and they did. "It's time to tombstone it again for a while." This meant whiskey headstones. It meant hiding moonshine in a hollowed marker of the dead at the Methodist Church cemetery where the bootlegger would pick it up.

Trenchmouth looked down at his paper and read silently. When his mother told him to look back up at her, he didn't. She hadn't spoken her full mind on the seriousness of the change coming down on her livelihood. "Boy," she said, "you'd be smart to listen."

Still, he read the ink. "Disastrous fire at Matewan," he said. "One man dead." Tears were coming up now. It was hard to read, but he did. "Soon after passenger train number 2 left Matewan about 6:30 a.m. Wednesday, fire was discovered in the Urias Hotel, inside the saloon building owned by Anse Pilcher, just across the street from where the recently burned Belmont Hotel stood, under reconstruction. Frank Dallara (Italian), forty, was burned to death after entering the Urias Hotel from across the street, where he was working as a builder. George Bowens, another worker burned considerably about the arms, said Dallara was attempting to save a child that was unaccounted for." The boy did not read on aloud. Only to himself. None of it mattered from there anyway; the child wasn't in the building, folks' wounds were dressed at the Y.M.C.A. hospital, the entire town burned to the ground, and so forth. But Trenchmouth had read the words about the man who'd taken him in, looked at him real, and been disappointed by his savagery just four nights prior. And now he was dead.

The boy ran out the front door.

When the Widow found him, he was under a birch tree, shaking from the kind of cry that has no sound. She'd brought with her a small luggage bag filled with jars of moonshine. A woman sat in jail for this juice. It was time to clear the house stash. From the bag she pulled a small canning jar. It was half full of the strongest moonshine she had. For a moment, she just stood over him. He couldn't look up at her, knew it wasn't for boys to cry like this. She bent and brushed at the hair on his forehead, her fingertips working in such a way as only a mother's fingertips can. "Tonight you'll sip a little extra for your pain," she said, unscrewing the lid.

Through his shaky inhales and exhales, he managed to swallow a little, and it calmed him. The Widow kept at rubbing his face, his cheeks, his neck, until he nearly fell asleep on the spot. She took back the jar, nipped it herself, and pulled him up by the hand. "Let's get to the cemetery before nine," she said. "You don't have to go to school tomorrow."

Once there, they worked. There was no time for crying. You had to look out for the law, for folks visiting their dead. You had to find the four foot tombstone marked with the name Mary Blood, dig under it a little, and unearth the hollow metal casing awaiting its delivery. It was paranoid work, the best kind to put a mind off sorrow.

But sorrow always came back. That night, long past midnight, long past the pain-numbing effect of the shine, Trenchmouth stirred in his bed. It seemed to the boy that the world was burning, that men were being pulled to its center to die, and that he somehow was responsible. It also seemed that the air inside the house was unbreathable. So he descended the ladder and went outside. He wore nothing but his nightclothes and socks.

It didn't take long for another scent to embed itself in his nose. It was the same one he'd gotten hold of that day knocking bugs in the garden so many years before. On this night, with the miners dead and Mr. Dallara burned alive, he almost recognized it. The smell of rot and regret. Of meeting the maker unnaturally.

He tracked it liked the Widow had taught him to night track deer. The aroma of shit and functioning glands. But this was something else. His nose led him to the outhouse, then to the mound next to it, then to a third mound further down. Trenchmouth bent to one knee and inhaled hard. It wasn't bowel movements his nose had followed.

Out there, it was bone cold.

A boy his size could work a shovel just fine. He didn't possess much weight to bury its edge, but he jumped up and down on the thing, bruising the bare arches of his feet, enough to make headway in an hour's time. Somehow, despite the frozen crust of earth, Trenchmouth broke through. He always had been able to dig what others couldn't. He got below the petrified mess of eight-year-old human waste, deep below it after a couple more hours. It was then that he noticed something small and gray in the half light of his lantern. He bent to it, held it up to his eye. It was a man's thumb.

Trenchmouth didn't scream or throw the thing back. He bent again and unearthed the hand from which his shovel had severed the digit. It was the color of nothing, and the skin was full of holes, tunnels for unknown breeds of burrowing insects and filth bugs long since full. The clothes were intact if not brittle. And once Trenchmouth used his fingers to dig and brush away the remaining dirt, a face looked back at him, sunken and scared. Hollow and clay red. He stared at the face, and as he put his hand to his nose again, the hills around him seemed to shift at their foundations and the trees and the sky went red. Then all of it, everything, almost fell away to nothing.

The boy had an unexplainable urge to spit in the dead man's empty eyes.

He sat next to the buried man until sunrise. When Ona Dorsett walked out to the barn clutching her bearskin wrap around her chest, she did not act surprised to see him there. She went back in for his twilled wool coat and boots, handed them to the boy in silence. His fingers, nearly numb, pulled the warmth on slow and awkward. He didn't look at her.

"You know who he is?" she said.

"No ma'am."

"How he come to be buried here?"

"No ma'am."

"I kilt him."

In those times, in those parts, everybody, no matter what their upbringing or education, used the word "kilt." "He got kilt cause some folks need killin," was a phrase heard once or twice annually, and hearing the Widow speak something like it was less monstrous than a child might expect.

Trenchmouth stared at his boot laces.

"Ain't you going to ask if I had good reason?" She scanned the foothills circular, pivoting in her stance.

He waited, then spoke, "I reckon you wouldn't have done it if you didn't."

"That man there is your daddy," she said.

The boy rolled those lips over his teeth in such a way that they might break through. He sneezed, a fit of them really, for no good reason.

"He come to take you when you wasn't but a baby, a little baby," the Widow said. "He come drunk and wild and unfit to father anything breathing. Your father was a bad man." The condensation of her speech hung heavy in the air.

Trenchmouth stood. "He would have taken me from you," he said. He looked at her like a son looks at his mother when he needs more than words.

"He would have."

"He would have kilt you to do it."

"He would have." She pulled the dead man's mouth harmonica from her shirt pocket, gave it to the boy. "His," she said. "You're liable to make somethin good of it." The boy looked at the little silver and wood instrument and felt sick at the thought of putting it to his mouth. She pulled him to her so that he hugged her around the hips, his face in her belly. An eight-year-old can know a great many things, and at the same time very few. That morning, at an outhouse burying ground, Trenchmouth Taggart knew he had been raised up right by the only woman who could've done the raising. He knew he'd most likely be dead or starved were it not for her. And he knew, that since the time of his last linen diaper some six years earlier, for every day of his young life, he'd been pissing and shitting on his very own daddy. That sat just fine with him, he decided.

That evening, the Widow sat down with her children and told them things she never had before. The time was right. Due.

She told Clarissa, among other things: "Your mother was too young, and most likely had got herself where she was by way of a drunk man's forceful hand." The Widow knew things about the young mother, things like her name, Cleona Brook. Her whereabouts, Huntington by way of Charleston. Her profession, actress. The Widow even knew that Cleona was starring in a current production of *Girl of the Golden West* at the Huntington Theatre, less than a hundred miles of track away.

It wasn't coincidence that she turned to Trenchmouth that evening and spoke of similar knowledge, similar geography. While Clarissa whimpered next to the washtub in the kitchen, confused by discovery, and while the sunlight through the windows died and the room went orange and soft, the boy's practicing mother told him of his birth mother. "She is in a room alone at the Home for Incurables in Huntington," she said. "She pulls off her own fingernails. Thinks Satan is among us." Her name was spoken aloud with less sympathy than the girl's mother. "Mittie Ann Taggart."

The Norfolk & Western ran a 1:50 p.m. daily out of Williamson. Columbus and Cincinnati, all points west and northwest. But the train stopped in Kenova and Huntington, and Ona Dorsett trusted it would be good for her children, aged eight and twelve, to strike out on their own for an overnighter. Children were babied too much, that was her thinking.

Moonshine sales bankrolled the excursion of course, and the finger sandwiches in the café car were unlike anything Trenchmouth had tasted before. While he chewed, he almost let his teeth show.

All of this, the fancy train car, the fancy finger food, would take the boy's mind off Frank Dallara.

Huntington was the big city. A train conductor had taken pity on the two, drawn them up maps on paper napkins. "The Theatre and the Asylum?" he'd said. "Not your most visited sites for out-of-towners, but easy to git to anyhow."

The two split up at the corner of 3rd Avenue and 20th Street, Trenchmouth heading north to the nut bin on the hill, Clarissa east to the theatre. It was cold out, and she'd held her little brother's hand since getting off the train, something he'd never let her do at home. Walking alone and looking back at one another, it seemed like they'd always clasped hands till now.

The Huntington Theatre was of good size, all intricately carved maple, painted gold and red and blue. The red velvet curtain was stained and the hem needed repair. Clarissa asked a woman with a cigarette where she might find Cleona Brook.

"How old are you?" the woman answered. She spoke through her nose, wore a chicken feather in her silvery hair, and spat specks of cigarette tobacco between her tongue and top teeth.

"Twelve," Clarissa said.

"Too young to be told the truth, too old to lie to." The woman pointed to a door beside the stage and walked away.

Clarissa walked down a hallway lit by a single gaslight on the wall. Behind one closed door she heard moans. A woman or a man's, she couldn't tell. The next door was open, and inside, a young lady with thin wrists smacked color into her cheeks in front of a mirror. Her hair was pulled back with an elaborate assortment of pins. "Excuse me," Clarissa said.

The woman turned in her chair and looked Clarissa up and down. She sat with her legs spread, wearing nothing but a brassiere, stockings, and a pair of men's shortpants. "Do you have something for a cough?" she said to Clarissa. "I've got a terrible cough." She faked a hacking sound.

"No ma'am." Clarissa thought about moving on down the hall. "Are you Cleona Brook?"

"Cleopatra Brook. Who told you Cleona? You from the apothecary's?"

"I'm sorry, I'm Clarissa. My adoptive mother is Missus Ona Dorsett from Mingo County. She—"

"Ona Dorsett. I know that name. Was she the one that died from gonorrhea up at Detroit? The Shakespearean?" She looked around herself wildly, presumably for a production poster on the brown walls littered in newsprint and cheap fliers and dried up flowers pierced by nails.

"No ma'am, Missus Dorsett raised me after you dropped me off to her. I was just a baby, you were young yourself." Clarissa was finding it difficult to speak with her normal level of confidence.

"Puddin, I wasn't ever young," the woman said. She turned back to the mirror and snorted. Spat what came up into a trash bin next to her foot. "I was Cleona Brook, that's for certain, but I wasn't never young. I didn't have no babies in Mingo County. No, no, no babies in Mingo." She smiled then, cocked her head so that she could see her daughter in the mirror's reflection. "Got me some babies now though. One named Jack, one named Phillip, and another Bill. All of em babies even though they're grown men. Do what I tell em to, cry when I yell at em. You know, I smack those three and they call me mama, kiss my feet? It's a real dream." She opened the drawer at her chest and put in a dip of snuff. "Let me see your teeth, girl."

Clarissa pulled back her lips. She tried to make it look like a smile.

"White as white can be I guess. Hold on to that," Cleona said.

"You're my mother," Clarissa said.

"Like hell I am."

The show was in two hours. Clarissa watched her mother shut the door with her toes. She had to step back to keep it from hitting her in the face. A fat man swept the hall on his hands and knees. His broomstick had broken off to a height of eight inches, and he swept the dust side to side, breathing it in down low on the floor and coughing it right back out.

The Home for Incurables was a big stone building with over two hundred rooms. A hair-lipped nurse with calves the size of cantaloupes took to Trenchmouth, and though it was not customary to get his type of visitor, his type of story, she led him to Mittie Ann Taggart's room anyway. His obvious mouth problem reminded her of her own, and she decided to let the boy see his mother, provided she could supervise them. "She's especially active today," the nurse said. "Woke up hollerin something even louder than usual. Even took a swing at Betty." She explained to Trenchmouth that Mittie Ann would be in restraints on her bed, that it was for her own good, and that she might say some unpleasantries in his company.

"Yes ma'am," he said.

They could hear her from the end of the corridor. Speaking in tongues, no doubt. When the nurse led the boy in, Mittie Ann went silent. She stared at the ceiling, which was covered in dried up peanut butter balls. Trenchmouth looked at them, then at the nurse. "Dessert," she told him. "Mittie Ann don't believe in dessert." The window shade was drawn. His mother was sweaty and unwrinkled and green under the eyes and cheekbones.

"I knowed you was comin, so I baked you a shit cake," she said, still staring up. Despite her arm and leg restraints, she was able to turn her hips to the side, revealing a brown stain in her white gown.

"That's no way to talk or act in front of a boy," the nurse said. She pulled a towel from the bedside table and hid the woman's midsection with it. Trenchmouth covered his nose and tried not to cry.

"He's no boy," Mittie Ann said. "He's Beelzebub's offspring. Child of the one sent down to fire."

"That's just the nonsense you woke up hollerin, Missus Taggart. It's got nothin to do with him."

"It *is* him. I woke up hollerin on him cause I knowed he was comin. You figure pretty slow, don't you lips?"

The nurse looked at her shoes.

Trenchmouth started to say something, but couldn't.

"I once knew a boy like you," his mother said. Then she turned and looked at the drawn window shade. Dust floated in the crack of sunlight. "I can see through things, like this window shade." It was quiet then on the third floor of the mental hospital. "I tried not to see through a little baby boy when he was plain as day an abomination, but he spat at me and spoke to me in the English tongue, but it wasn't English, just sounded like it on the river's air. Can you imagine, a baby talkin at two months?" The nurse's hands shook, and she stuck them in her armpits to stop it.

"I got mouth disease on account of river water," Trenchmouth said. It wasn't much louder than a whisper, dry throated and cracking.

"I watched that boy die under the ice," his mother said. "That boy is dead."

They had found out what the Widow had guessed they would find out. What part of her wanted them to find. There are mothers in this world, who, for reasons of experience or malfunction, cannot care for their children. And those children need to see it for themselves before they can truly live. Clarissa and Trenchmouth had seen it.

They held hands in the empty passenger car of the night train home. Folks traveling from Cincinnati and Columbus rocked unaware in their sleepers, but the brother and sister not bound by blood couldn't sleep. The girl because she had a mind that raced, and the boy because he had no moonshine.

She did not mind his breath when he told her of the tied-down woman at the asylum. She'd grown used to its smell. And he breathed hers in as she told of the foul woman at the theatre. He'd have listened forever if she'd let him.

It was in this way that their bony shoulders banged with the train's turns. Their knees touched, and their lot in life as children without roots caused them to move closer to one another. All this ended in a kiss between them that would be their only one until the next, thirty-four years later, when Clarissa was married to a man she did not love and Trenchmouth was wanted for murder.

CHAPTER SIX

THEN CAME MORE OF

SORROW AND ANGUISH

The words split the preacher's lips asthmatic. He was small, but he preached big and airy and hoarse, like a coughing fit had ahold of him. "The sorrows of death compassed me," he shouted. "And the pains of hell gateheld upon me. I found trouble and sorrow." Frank Dallara's body went into the ground inside a rough-cut box, wet from rain. "Then called I upon the name of the Lord," the preacher went on. "Oh Lord, I beseech thee deliver my soul."

Trenchmouth stood and listened. For a time, he'd felt more anger than anguish. Folks had been talking about Anse Pilcher, the burned hotel's owner. Anse had a condition. His bones were soft. Like cartilage. His bones could be pierced just like his flesh, and because of this, most wouldn't speak poorly of "the cripple," as they called him. But he had enemies and Frank Dallara had been one of them. Those talking said Anse had told Frank a little girl was inside all that fiery construct, that he lied to see the man set ablaze. Trenchmouth thought on this at the funeral. His shoulders, broadening now, nearly split the shirt seams the Widow had sewn a night prior. When Frank Dallara's coffin hit bottom and the rough men lowering it pulled back their ropes, the boy nearly lost what little composure he had left. In a week's time, he'd lost the man closest to being a father to him and learned the vile fate of his real daddy. He'd watched his birth mother spew shit and venomous words in his direction. And he'd kissed his own sister on the mouth. It was a good deal to take in at nine years old.

The preacher preached onward. "I said in my haste, all men are liars."

That's when the boy knew that God was for the featherheaded, that religion was a salesman's game. God's man himself had said it: "liars." Trenchmouth turned then and walked away from all of them. Black-clad and bad-postured, they half-listened to the words, "deliver my soul from death, mine eyes from tears, and my feet from falling." But Trenchmouth drowned it out. He whistled while he walked away. This struck a particular funeral-goer, Frank Dallara's ugly brother-in-law Hob Tibbs, as disrespectful beyond the pale.

He followed the boy away from the mourner's circle. He pulled him by the arm behind a substantial tree, and he smacked him. "Don't you disrespect the dead," he said. He smacked again. "Don't you dare disrespect the Lord out here, you hear me?"

Folks handle anguish in a variety of ways. Somehow the nine year old knew this to be true, and it stopped him from striking the ugly man back. But Hob Tibbs had made a new enemy, had added to his list of many, and something in his face burned into Trenchmouth's brain unforgettable. Tibbs said, "You're going to be in church every Sunday, hear? I'm puttin you to work for God. You'll spit shine a cross if I tell you. Polish up stained glass for walking away from a man's burial."

Trenchmouth said what he'd said all his life. "Yessir."

CHAPTER SEVEN

FOLKS COULD FALL HARD

Church and school. These were places that didn't interest a ten-year-old boy. It wasn't that Trenchmouth abhorred scripture or couldn't learn his lessons. He could. It was the existence of those that sought to ridicule him on account of his oral ailment, to single him out and dig at him so as to break his spirit. There were boys at school who plotted little else. And in church, of course, there was Hob Tibbs.

As promised, he'd shackled Trenchmouth to the Methodist congregation. He put him to work spit shining brass and polishing glass. During Sunday services, the boy was forced to wait and clean up after communion. Shirts were to be tucked in, hems straight. And Trenchmouth was subject to the unrelenting criticisms of his mouth. "There's men called dentists these days, boy," Tibbs would say. "Might fashion you a brush outta twig and pine needle. You ever hear of a brush? Oh," he'd say, squinting close at the closed mouth, "I reckon you haven't."

Trenchmouth owned a toothbrush. He pulled it back and forth when he could stand to, but the ache it induced, along with the bleeding, would make anyone wonder at the worth of such a practice. He'd long ago tried and discounted a homeopathic mouth rinse from the Sears Roebuck, and now he used a concoction the Widow had stirred up for him, a bitter, stinging rinse for the mouth whose makeup she would not reveal.

It was a summertime Sunday, just after the Methodist Man had finished giving communion, when Trenchmouth, by this point a forced duty acolyte of sorts, was helping Tibbs in the choir room. They poured the unused grape juice back in the jug. The boy spilled it on the bitter man's shirt front.

"You little rotten shit," Tibbs said, teeth grit hard. He grabbed Trenchmouth by the collar. "You got no sense in that head, just like you got no teeth. You can't do a simple Lord's chore without foulin it all up." He was letting loose whatever it was that ate at him without rest. "Got no mama to speak of except the one in the bughouse, and even that Widow can see you got the devil in you. He's leakin out through your gums, ain't he boy?" A boil rose inside Trenchmouth then, one that had started at Frank Dallara's funeral, his first encounter with Tibbs. It was about to bust and run over. The man kept up, "And if you think Frank Dallara was any kind of daddy to you, think on it some more. That there was pity, son. No more, no less. Pity for a cripple whose real daddy was no better'n a nigger." The word was ugly, even in those times. "Some say he was half-a-one anyhow, mixed blood." Tibbs let a smile inch onto his face.

Trenchmouth, without much thought, bent at the knee and hinged back his hip. He took a full-leg backswing and let fly, trailing a black-booted shoe. This was inertia. He kicked Hob Tibbs in the stones with the force of a mule, like old Beechnut when he'd not eaten. Tibbs sucked in air with great volume. He bent double. On the dark wooden floor slats of the church's choir room, he curled into a baby's pose and whimpered like one for lack of speech at such pain.

The boy bent over him. "If anybody's kin to hell, it's you, cocksucker." He'd heard a drunk man say the word to another during a fight outside the pool hall and had been waiting to use it ever since. "And you won't see me in this here church again, ever. And you won't come calling either. Cause if you do, I'll be up in a tree behind a barrel." The words were such that a boy shouldn't possess to speak, but he did, and he wasn't finished. He leaned over Tibbs' head and spoke. "You'll fall hard as Goliath, *cocksucker.*"

Tibbs just whimpered and knotted up tighter. Trenchmouth let his saliva carry and gather in his lips, just ahead of the ravaged gums. When he'd pooled enough, he opened up in a grin not unlike the one Tibbs had given him that morning. The spit, rusty and thick, hung for a tick or two until its own weight broke and it smacked heavy into the left eye of Hob Tibbs.

Trenchmouth tore off his church-donated tie and walked out the heavy doors. He was through. For the rest of his life, he'd use the word "sir" to address any man his senior, with the exception of Hob Tibbs. He'd taken a place in the boy's brain and heart reserved only for a few. A few who'd spend their days and nights back-looking over shoulders and sniffing the air like dogs.

It was the same at the schoolhouse. Under a ceiling so low a miner would crouch instinctual, sat all ages, all grade levels, together. The teacher, Ms. Varney, switched legbacks for crimes ranging from sass talk to bad posture. She wrote on the new blackboard formulas for understanding reading, writing, arithmetic, geography, and history. But her two favorite subjects were hygiene and singing. Once, after Doc Taylor visited on head lice, Ms. Varney said this to the class: "If you care for yourself so little as to let bedbugs infest your scalp, well then you're nearly as bad as a tramp with trenchmouth in my book." Clarissa had put her head down.

When the students got to singing in unison at the end of every day, songs like "In the Shade of the Old Apple Tree," Ms. Varney inevitably told Trenchmouth, "Remember to keep yours sealed shut, young man. Humming is all this little room can stand from a stink box such as yours."

If Ms. Varney left the room, Mose Crews inevitably scampered to the blackboard to draw up little diagrams of fly infestations and cow flop inside the opened orifice of young Trenchmouth. He had favorite, scribbled phrases like *T.T. = Doo Doo* and *T.T. Stinky don't talk, he breaks wind.*

Trenchmouth never put his head down. He stared straight ahead at something no one else could see.

It was fall 1913 that a new girl came to sit beside Trenchmouth in that schoolroom, and she alone had the energy to break his stare. She even had the energy to take his thoughts off Clarissa, who'd been ignoring him since the kiss on the train.

Ewart Smith was her name. She came from Tennessee with her daddy, who was taking work in the mines. Ewart was tan. More tan than Trenchmouth even, who, after a summer of bareback climbing and digging outdarked all the kids in the segregated schoolhouse. But Ewart had yellow hair and green eyes, and her teeth were as white as Ms. Varney's chalk. The day she came in, she was introduced to the sound of laughter and confusion at such a given name. She responded by crossing her feet and bowing, one hand across her hips, the other extended to her side. Though there were a few empty seats, she picked the one next to Trenchmouth Taggart, T.T. Stinky.

By winter break, she held his hand after school, and he nearly parted his lips when he smiled at her.

CHAPTER EIGHT

WHO AMONG US HAS READ THE SIGNS

It was a simple idea really. Steel not wood. If folks would just realize that timber construction was a thing of the past, steel the future, maybe whole towns wouldn't burn. Maybe good men wouldn't die. And maybe, if the self-made railroad men laying track like match-sticks across the hill terrain of southern West Virginia, if they'd just realize that coal tipples could be fashioned heartier from the very product being mined in these hills, namely the bituminous coke, maybe the wealth would spread to the little folks. This is how Trenchmouth's brain worked. The boy climbed Sulfur Creek Mountain daily to his secret spot, a dug out, one room, underground bunker complete with homemade drawing table, ruler, drafter's compass, and school-stolen pencils. There he drew up plans. Inventions really. There he devised an outline for steel cities and suspension bridges and coal tipples. He'd never let anyone in until Ewart Smith came along. Only she knew the hideout's location, and she'd been sworn to secrecy.

Things were thawing on a particular March afternoon when Ewart knocked on the bunker's hatch door. He let her in. The hatch was on a fishing line pulley, so that when you re-closed it, a scoop net tossed ground cover across its surface.

Inside, he was trying not to stare at the harmonica he'd laid on the drawing table, the harmonica of his dead daddy. He still hadn't put it to his lips, for fear that since that particular part of him was so susceptible to disease, he might well be infected with whatever drove his father down the road to hell. He got back to business: fashioning a miniature coal tipple and a crane from scrap metal he'd collected at the mine dumps. Structure-smart, he'd used a hammer and a punch to knock out holes in the skinny tin. Slots for connecting and building upwards. Ewart stared at what would surely become a tiny city there on the table.

"Your momma's going to come after you for spending all your time away," she said.

"She ain't home." Trenchmouth didn't say where the Widow was, but ever since the Huntington woman had gone down on moonshine charges, his mother had been hard at work moving product here to there, covering tracks, fashioning cover. In the time since the train trip to Huntington, their home had been family-scarce. "Your daddy's liable to come after you, you keep comin here."

"He ain't home," Ewart said.

Trenchmouth wasn't sure she even had a home. All she'd say was that they lived up in Sprigg, a mile off the Tug. "I can't figure what shift he's workin then." He looked up at her from his growing construct.

She bit her lip. Had a look of thinking hard. "How many secrets can you keep?"

"I reckon about two hundred."

"How many you got piled right now?"

"Ninety maybe."

She wasn't laughing at his odd ways like usual. "My Daddy ain't a miner," she said.

"What is he then?"

"Preacher."

His stomach tightened. He looked back to his drawing, took up the pencil again.

"You don't care for preachers?"

He shrugged.

"Listen, T. This ain't preacher like you're thinking. My Daddy was best friends of a fella named Hensley down in Cleveland, Tennessee. They fell out cause Daddy was better and everybody knew it. Mr. Hensley though, he started up this church . . ." Ewart bit her lip again. This caused Trenchmouth to shift in his seat and lock eyes. "This promise might fill up all those hundred empty ones you got," she said. He nodded. "Mr. Hensley picked up a serpent."

"What?"

"It ain't like church you know of. Folks pick up serpents. Roll around with em sometimes even."

"Snakes?"

"Snakes." She almost laughed for having finally told someone. "Folks get bit even." Trenchmouth stared. "A couple folks died."

You could call it a box, maybe a wood cage. Copperheads and rattlesnakes knocked around inside it, their dark, translucent sides thumping at the holes.

"Who built the box?" Trenchmouth asked her.

"Daddy." They were standing inside a small backroom of Ewart's farmhouse. She'd finally let him see where she lived. The walls were stained and halfway papered, like somebody had quit on the whole place mid-job. From the second story came sounds of the adult world.

Above the two children, furniture scraped floorboards and the low tones of a man and a woman echoed untranslatable. "He's up there preaching to somebody new," Ewart said. "Convertin somebody." She bent down and put her fingers next to one of the little round holes. The snakes were quiet.

"You ever pick one up?" Trenchmouth hadn't taken his eyes off the box. Its construction could've been improved upon.

"No," she said. "I don't care for snakes."

That's when he bent down next to her and got the feeling he'd had on the train that night with Clarissa. His knee touched Ewart's, and through the thick wool fabric both sets of skin seemed to heat up. Trenchmouth put his hand out to touch her, but for reasons unknown he changed destinations. With thumb and finger he undid the little brass latch and opened the snake hatch. He reached into the slowly slithering mound and brought back a hand covered in copperhead. The snake might as well have been asleep, but Ewart hopped up anyway, pressed her back against the far wall. Brittle wallpaper fell to the floor behind her.

The snake moved up Trenchmouth's arm slow and methodical. Had it decided to bite him, the going would be tough through coat and shirt and undergarment, but it gave no indication that it meant the boy harm. He stared at its undersized head, the geometric shape of it and every perfect scale lining its being. He stared and the snake looked back at him until the gaze went blurry between them, until that snake had made it up his forearm, biceps, shoulder, and collarbone. It stopped.

Though he knew she was watching and he knew he'd never shown her his affliction, the boy opened up wide because it seemed the only thing he could do at that moment. And, as if it was an act they'd practiced together before bug-eyed kids at county fairs, the copperhead, without hesitation, slid into the open mouth like it'd found home. It rested its head on his tongue.

Ewart's hands had come up to her own mouth, holding in and keeping out simultaneously. She breathed heavy without having exercised. The breathing picked up more as she watched her friend slowly close his ragged gums and chapped lips around the serpent. He didn't bite down, just closed up slowly so that it appeared to her he was ingesting the thing.

From upstairs, the low tones got louder, the furniture scraping and floorboard creaking more imposing, as if the ceiling might come down on them. But Trenchmouth paid little mind. He held his pose, eyes on Ewart, then opened that mouth of his again, just as slow and deliberate as he'd closed it. He gave the copperhead's tail a little incentive pull and the girl watched the snake loop its head back toward her, a candy cane pose held briefly before slithering back down the arm. Then it was still.

"How bout that?" Trenchmouth said.

She let her hands fall from her face. "You've got to leave," she said.

He bent down to the open box and let the snake fall back to its brethren. "Did I scare you?"

"Daddy's done convertin. Can't you hear how quiet it's got?"

From the time he'd opened that box, his whole world had been more quiet than anytime he could remember. Quiet like it must be under the ground.

"Daddy won't like that you're here. You've got to go."

He swiveled the brass latch into place and stood up. He walked to her and kissed her on the cheek, and it was warm and dry, without the electricity of Clarissa's. Then he slid through the open door of the little back room, his coat knocking paint chips from the molding, and walked out the back. The preacher and the convert descended the stairs inside, laughing.

It was obvious to the Widow Dorsett that for her boy, school was like being put on the rack. And she didn't say a word when he announced he'd spent his last Sunday at the Methodist Church. She and Clarissa continued to go without him, and he continued to bow his head and hold their hands for the mealtime blessing. Little else was spoken in terms of Trenchmouth's exile. It was simply accepted that the boy would not be accepted. What mattered was that he learned. That he kept up, surpassed even, those that would not accept. Above all, that he did not become a miner. And it was for this reason that the Widow, on most days, left the newspaper out on the kitchen table for him to read. She'd mark the articles she thought educational with black ink advice like *Think on this one awhile* or *Ever thought of trying your hand at this?*

Trenchmouth got home from school on a Tuesday to find one of these left notes on newsprint. It was warm enough out that he didn't have to refill with coal or wood the heating stove fire, an after-school chore assigned to him during fall and winter months. He broke a piece of hard cornbread off a brick she'd left out and sat down to read. The newspaper settled him like little else could. It was almost as comforting as moonshine somehow.

The Widow had written *I hope you don't associate with these boys* above an article titled *Robbed Passenger Coach*. Some local boys had robbed a coach car containing a stock of goods for the local newsstands. They'd been caught sleeping inside a cave they'd fashioned on top of Horsepen Mountain not far from Trenchmouth's hideout. They slept between the open, stolen hampers and baskets of cigarettes, cigars, chewing gum, candy, popcorn, groceries, fruits, novels, and magazines, gorged no doubt on romance and sugar.

Trenchmouth tore off a piece of newspaper and scrawled on it *move hideout for safety?* He put it in his pocket.

A page in, she had written *Think I'll ever get me one of these?* above an ad for a cooking oven. It read *Every woman who wants a steel range will certainly buy The Peninsular if they can only get a view of it.* They could do so if they got themselves to A.H. Beal Hardware in Williamson. The power of steel. It was everywhere to behold. Trenchmouth looked at the beat up Acme cook stove against the wall. It had seen better days.

The door opened and Clarissa walked in with Fred Dallara in tow. Trenchmouth nodded and looked back to his paper.

"Hi," Clarissa said. She'd blossomed full to beautiful.

"Afternoon, little T.T.," Fred said. His voice had gone suddenly low that winter, his torso thicker. He had a mustache that looked like somebody had smudged two fingers across his lip and halfway wiped it off. Fred enjoyed pointing out their age differential.

The two lovebirds climbed the ladder to the loft and went quiet.

Trenchmouth knew that Fred and Clarissa kissed up there. The soft sounds echoed in his ears. He knew that they knew the Widow was at work on her still again, moving and hiding and covering up, and that she wouldn't be back to catch them in the act. He broke off two miniature pieces of cornbread, shoved them in each earhole, and got back to reading.

See here? she had written above another story. *Turns out you just got more brains than the rest of us, in more places, more stubborn.* It was another new finding from the scientists who were always finding. *Throat Brain Is Latest Discovery* the title read, and under that *Scientists Say Gray Matter is in Fingers and Cells are in Toes. Numerous Thinking Organs Distributed Throughout Whole Body.* According to the columnist, the fingertips of the blind contained brain tissue, and so did the throat. If a throat surgeon slipped up during his operation, the throat brain would react by refusing to cooperate.

The boy couldn't help but wonder what had been done to his mouth brain to make it so uncooperative.

He thought he heard a giggle from the loft, so he pushed the bread further into his ears and read on. Above *Railroad Progress Moving Forward*, she'd written *You could see the world if you wanted to by the time they finish this*. The big men of the N&W and the C&O were barreling through hills and valleys, blasting tunnels and building homes for workers. The word *tonnage* was used again and again to describe the coal that was bringing the railroad to West Virginia. The tonnage was here, so they were coming to secure it. To move it out to everybody else.

Trenchmouth thought of the tipples he'd seen being built from solid wood. He wondered how somebody could figure a kitchen range ought to be fashioned from steel but not a coal tipple. He ripped off another piece of paper and scrawled a new design. The power of steel. It was everywhere.

Another giggle. It made him sick. He gave the bread plugs another push and started reading out loud. Almost a holler. "Millions of dollars are being invested in coal properties, which will within a year furnish tonnage for the railroads, which are being built at a cost of more than millions of dollars." A shoe boomeranged down at him from above and caught his collarbone, hard. He didn't look up, just rubbed at his injury. Had he looked to the loft, had he pulled the bread from his ears, he would have heard Fred Dallara say, "Pipe down little boy," and he would have seen Clarissa, up on her elbows with her neck stretched to check on him, a mix of worry and sadness and defeat in her eyes.

But he didn't look up at them. He kept on reading.

He read that the druggist at the pharmacy had been confined to his bed. Like others in the county, he'd been taken hold of by Typhoid Fever.

That's when Trenchmouth saw the toy advertisement. *Mysto Erector Structural Steel Builder* the banner read.

The boy could scarcely take it in.

Under this heading was a picture nearly identical to the scrap metal tipple on his drawing table at the hideout. The picture showed skinny steel strips, holes punched and connected to other holes. It was a steel construction toy, an erector set, and some fellow by the name of A.C. Gilbert was taking credit for having invented it.

Without knowing, Trenchmouth had made a toy, and now somebody else was getting paid for it. What he'd thought was an idea toward protecting the progress of civilization was nothing more than adolescent entertainment.

He sighed and sat and stared.

His ears were plugged up while his sister broke his heart within whisper distance, and he came to understand that ideas could be stolen before they were even ideas. But no tears would smear the newsprint that day or any other, as far as Trenchmouth was concerned. He was not yet twelve and had lost nearly everything he loved. But he knew this on that day: like toys, tears were for boys, and it was time to leave all that behind. It was time to become a man.

CHAPTER NINE

WOMEN SHOOK AND SHIVERED

The hideout lay in ruin and the kitchen moonshine was running low. Trenchmouth the man-boy had laid waste to his inventions that were not his. He'd taken to kissing Ewart on the neck and cheekbones after school, whether she wanted him to or not. The girl cared for him, but his mouth frightened her just the same, and she'd not allow it near her own. He'd also taken to sipping shine morning, noon, and night, and what could the Widow say when her stock came up a little light? At twelve, Trenchmouth was somehow more man than boy. His voice had changed. He walked and talked as men do. He'd built a new shelter for her shining operations. A massive timber and twine ordeal, fashioned with his own callused hands and sweating back. So what if he stayed lit on lightning. The boy was afflicted, after all. Whatever gets us by.

Besides, the world was no place for toys or childish ideas. In Europe, folks had taken to killing each other over differences in adult ideas. At home, Woodrow Wilson's New Freedom didn't strike the Widow or any other hill dwellers as particularly new or particularly free.

There were moonshine stills to hide. Wood to chop. Fowl and game and antlered, four-legged beasts to track and lay down dead and cut open and bleed. Gods to pray before for guidance.

Trenchmouth would do all of these things between the Junes of 1914 and 1915. Had the foolish, erratic boys around him cared to listen, he'd have told them all that he could do fifty-nine push-ups. That his hunter's eye was sharp and his taste in whiskey sharper. That his pecker had sprouted hair and was often hard as a rail spike, and that like them, he was looking to dip it in some young woman's honeypot. He thought of little else.

His chance would come, of all places, among the women of the Church of God with Signs Following. Folks who professed to know no sin. No whiskey or tobacco or carnal knowledge at all. But, like it is for most of the religified, practicing and preaching are slippery handles of the hogwashed. And it would be among them that Trenchmouth's manhood was shaped.

July 4th, 1915, fell on a Sunday. Among the Methodists, confusion ran high when celebrations burned out and hangovers set in. Sabbath hangovers, the most sinful of all. But for the followers of J.B. Smith, Tennessee transplant and converter to the Church of God with Signs Following, such headaches and gut checks were not an issue. This was because, presumably, these talkers-in-tongue, these snake handlers and strychnine sippers, they did not sin in drink or smoke or fornication.

On Independence Day, leaning against their ramshackle house of worship, spitting in the dirt, Trenchmouth didn't buy it. These worshippers inside hollered nonsensically and dropped to the floor like their hearts had stopped; he could hear the thumping from outside. But it wasn't the authentic article, as far as he was concerned. And, three inches short of six feet though not yet thirteen,

Trenchmouth was almost advanced in the field of judging articles as authentic or not.

"Harla harla harla la la la da la da hardala atta," somebody shouted inside the church. Another thump.

Ewart was in there. Front row. But her daddy didn't trust Trenchmouth, didn't like boys of that age. And he certainly didn't allow converts to his church in the form of his daughter's perceived poon hounds. The boy had been held at bay a year, had never told of his natural encounter with the snakes in the box that day at the Smith house. Ewart hadn't breathed a word either. So, though he was permitted to court her a little and come by the house, the Lord's chambers were off limits.

But on that patriotic Sunday, the man-boy decided to go in. Maybe it was tongue-talking that called to him, extra loud that day, echoing like his birth mother's had echoed off nuthouse walls. Or maybe it was the flask of shine in his back pocket, from which he took frequent pulls. Whatever the reason, he stood from where he leaned, climbed the three, crumbling steps to the double doors of the church, and swung them open.

The sun's rays went funny inside. They came through the three windows lining each wall of the place, but dust hung so heavy that the light split the room like beams of translucent timber, perfectly square from the panes. It stunk in there. Sweat on top of older sweat and unwashed britches. What sex sometimes smells like to those yet to have it. Mr. J.B. Smith's eyes met Trenchmouth's from the pulpit. Smith was rocking on his heels, dressed in a plain collared shirt and brown slacks. His chest hair showed through the drenched shirt and he wiped at his forehead with a Bibled hand. He smiled.

Then he hollered "Hooo ooo hooo hay om in addeyayamana," and on into something not transcribeable with the words known to us.

It shook the boy so much so that he wasn't a man-boy at all anymore, just a boy. For a moment, he thought maybe all this *was* the authentic article. He almost moved his feet and opened his mouth. Almost fell on the floor, humping the holy spirit. But he walked forward down the aisle instead. He passed home-fashioned pews of whopperjammed chairs and benches full of folks with eyes rolling in their heads. In the front, Ewart bobbed lazily on her toes and let her head shake a little. A tall man beside her bent down and came up snake-fisted and this got everybody going. He turned to face them and held the four serpents above his head in victory. One of them got restless and struck out, bit his wrist just above the shirt cuff where the skin is most tender and white. Where the blood is closest to the air.

He flinched and kept dancing.

His hair lay flat despite his jerking, oiled up with the grease of natural neglect.

Trenchmouth studied the skinny man, his facebones like flint rock under the skin, sharp and atop hollowed shadows for cheeks. It went white fast, his face, after the serpent strike, and he bent back down to return them to their box, but only after he'd held on a while to prove it was nothing to him.

Women shook and shivered, especially the curvy one on the other side of Ewart. Even in the required plain, hanging clothes, Trenchmouth made out that behind of hers, perfectly rounded with just enough quiver, just enough solid. Her black hair hung heavy on her shoulders, shining in the dust beam from the window.

This was religion. Her shape was what he'd sacrifice for.

So he did. He continued up the aisle and past the skinny, now paler man, who sat still and tried not to die. Past Ewart who swallowed hard when she noticed him and looked to her father, who smiled and stared down Trenchmouth. He went all the way to the front, before the pulpit, brushing the sleeve of the black-haired beauty as he strode by. He bent as he had that day in the back room of Ewart's home, under the thunder of the Preacherman's conversion above. And like that day, he came up with a copperhead. It looked to be the same one. But on this day, he took up every snake in the box, nine to be precise, and it wasn't hard to do, for they slid toward his outstretched arms as if they were tree branches promising home.

They made their way to his head and wrapped around it, leaving openings here and there so that the boy could look out upon the congregation, who thump-thumped the floorboards with increasing force and timing. Some went silent as one snake entered his opened, rotten mouth, others screeched their neck chords to higher pitch and impossible syllable.

Trenchmouth didn't dance. He didn't move much at all as J.B. Smith stepped from behind his place of instruction and circled his daughter's suitor, regarded him as if a piece of art. Preacher Smith almost yelled "Hallelujah," but didn't. He waited instead. It didn't take long for Trenchmouth to tug gently on the tail of the copperhead, and all of the others followed suit. They retreated down his arms as uniformly as they had come to him. He shut them up in their box. When Trenchmouth stood again, J.B. Smith embraced him, planted upon him the Holy Kiss of the Church of God with Signs Following, a lip to lip practice between those of the same sex, signifying membership.

It was the closest another's mouth had been to his own.

Later, for some of them, would come the oil anointing, the poison drinking. The testing of the flesh with fire. But for that morning, the sight of the mouth-diseased boy and the swirling serpents had been enough. Folks in attendance felt they'd witnessed a miraculous occurrence, though they weren't sure what it was. They grew quiet as J.B. Smith took his pulpit again to read from the Book of Luke, chapter ten, verse nineteen. Trenchmouth took a seat between Ewart and the curvy one. Each took a hand and held it. One with something like love, the other with something like lechery.

To the left of them, the skinny man slumped and his hand turned blackish-gray. He hoped he would not die from his punctures, but the medical doctor did not enter his mind. Such a thought would banish him from his current house of worship, because such a thought equaled a lack of faith in God.

Trenchmouth wondered at the slow rubbing pinky of the woman with his right hand and tried to think down the slow growth in his trousers. Preacher Smith went on about treading on scorpions and the power of the enemy, and it was almost as quiet as it had been with bread-stuffed ears. Only now the quiet was a peaceful sort, maybe the one folks expect in their houses of the Lord but rarely attain for all the hot air circulating and suffocating. The man-boy sensed God, and she was a woman.

If Trenchmouth thought he'd finally had a religious experience that morning, he would re-evaluate his criteria that night. The curvy woman's name was Anne Sharples, and she had a slight penchant for bedding men of the cloth, a bigger penchant for moonshine. By outward appearances, she was a formerly devout member of the Baptist congregation in Kermit, a current devout member of the Church of God with Signs Following in Sprigg. On the sly, she was the type of young miner's widow who faked mourning when her husband was caved in, who had visions of laying down with the holy man delivering her husband's eulogy even as he spoke the casket-lowering words. Anne Sharples had few scruples.

She'd pulled Trenchmouth away from the Independence Day

picnic outside the little church that afternoon. He'd already slipped her a shot or four from his flask under cover of tablecloth. They ended up in the woods, then inside his hideout, which had recently ceased production as an inventor's asylum and awaited a new purpose. It would soon find one.

Anne lay down on the dry dirt floor like it was nothing. Above her, narrow shoots of moonlight found their way through the tree cover and then the slats of the hideout trapdoor. Such lighting made it dark enough to imagine the almost-thirteen-year-old-with-mouth-disease as a grown man. But as Trenchmouth undid his belt and felt as if his groin might explode from the pressure, she played on the few scruples she had. "I won't kiss a little boy," she said. "And I sure won't let him dip his wick in me. They're liable to throw me in the chokey for that."

"I don't see any little boys around here," Trenchmouth answered, shivering though it was night-hot.

"You old enough to fight or vote?"

"Old enough to drink," he said and pulled the flask again from his pants pocket, which was bunched around his knees. She pulled from it and coughed. He pulled and smiled. The moonlight showed her those gums again, those teeth and their ulcerated in-betweens. She'd not put that to her mouth. A different idea brewed.

"Just do like I show you and we'll both come up happy," Anne Sharples said to him. Then she brought him to her and pushed his shoulders down, away from her own. He stopped at her chest, newly aware of further curvature. But she kept pushing him down, and when he got to her waist, she arched her back, pulled up her white muslin underskirt, pushed down her undergarments, and guided that man-boy's oft-ridiculed orifice to another, hidden one of her own, one that he'd spent whole months of nights imagining. It took him aback for a moment, and he stopped short. He couldn't see much, but he felt the tickle of hair on his nose, and he smelled something unlike any scent he'd ever picked up. It was in every way opposite to what he'd followed to the outhouse burial ground all those years earlier. Unlike death, this was life's smell, like tree sap and sweat and culinary aromas undiscovered and ancient. Trenchmouth lowered himself to it.

At first, he fumbled, and she almost let her conscience tear through the moonshine haze of comfort to stop him. But then something changed. Trenchmouth, enchanted almost to nausea, began to feel something he never had in church, Methodist or Snake-handler. What had seemed false faith in the bitten skinny man that morning, what had rung untrue in all of them as they mumbled nonsense, suddenly arose in him so palpably that he could not hold it back. From his pressurized groin something seeped upward like fire through the tendons. It warmed his stomach and tickled his vocal chords. It came right up through his mouth and out the end of his tongue, which began moving itself in circles and latitudes of an unknown geometry, fast and patterned like a snake never could. As Anne Sharples began to buck and heave air, Trenchmouth let loose a string of words not unlike those of the pillars of the Church of God with Signs Following. "Harla harla la da hey hoo woo adeyanamana harla da da da," he said. The hum of it all from his tongue fibers and taste buds infected her, but not with his disease.

Trenchmouth had got religion there in the woman's nether regions, and for the woman, spent and shocked beyond words, a preacher had found his calling.

CHAPTER TEN

THE POWERFUL AND THE ONES BENEATH

They'd left him out of Mumblety Peg for as far back as he could remember. It was a young boy's game, really. As soon as he was old enough to open and close a jack-knife without bleeding to death, a boy found games of Mumblety Peg in which to compete. After school, or on summer days when the earth was soft and the blade would stick deep—these were times for bringing practice to fruition. In the fall of 1916, at nearly fourteen years old, Trenchmouth was too old to play, at least in the estimation of most boys. But the group of four littler ones had seen him walking past, and had liked his tall frame, his crack-proof, rolled sole boots, the way he spat tobacco juice out the side of his mouth. So they'd called him over to the small mountain bald, a field backdropped by trees that bled leaves of red and orange and yellow. Only one of them, a boy named Crews whose brother Trenchmouth knew well, whose mother he knew even better, expressed objection to consorting with T.T. Stinky.

But any objection was soon forgotten when Trenchmouth, in the first inning, progressed through twenty-two feats without a mistake.

He opened his Cattle King pen knife with precision. The buffalo-horn handle reflected light as he flipped it from every position: fist, fingers, cross-chested ears, nose, eyes, knees, top of the head. Each time it stuck point down, plenty deep. The boys watched wide-eyed and grunted noises of impress. Their narrow lines of sight on the abilities of orphaned, malformed youngsters such as Trenchmouth had been blown wide apart. They knew their own ignorance now to be fear, maybe even envy.

Each of them progressed through, fumbling and mumbling, until the last was beaten, and Trenchmouth, the victor, drove the peg into the ground using his knife handle. Six blows landed solid and flat as a carpenter's hammer. He'd sunk the peg, so that the loser boy, Warren Crews, was forced to do the deed. Warren was the one who had objected to calling Trenchmouth over. He was youngest brother of Mose Crews, Fred Dallara's best buddy. Mose was tailback on the ball team, and the meanest of the nastiest of the T.T. Stinky crew.

"Root, Root!" the boys hollered, shoving little, fat, Warren Crews to his knees. He couldn't even see the top of the peg, none of them could. Trenchmouth had driven it deep. Hands behind his back, the Crews boy dove in for it with his teeth, as the rules clearly dictated. Again and again he came up for air, the silty black mud covering more and more of his face. They stood around him and laughed. It was friendly teasing, even from Trenchmouth, who harbored no ill will toward the boy on account of his bad luck in sibling, but Warren Crews didn't like losing. As he came up empty again and again, and as the boys' insistence on playing out the game became ever more apparent, Warren Crews looked around in desperation. He nearly forgot his age and called out for T.T. Stinky to get down there and finish, seeing as *his* mouth was already dirty, his teeth full of muck. Warren thought his big brother would have done just that. But

Warren Crews thought wrong, and was, for a brief moment, lucky.

First, he wasn't aware that even football Mose would no longer call out Trenchmouth to his face. In private, Mose and the others still spoke of the orally-ailed one without censor. They even made up crude drawings and songs. But they'd long ago given up insulting Trenchmouth face to face, much less making eye contact. Ever since he'd attacked Fred Dallara like a mountain cat, and even more so since he'd sprouted wide shoulders and a fine mustache and won every riflery contest the county sponsored, boys only poked fun at T.T. Stinky behind his back. Had they known that in a year's time, Trenchmouth had vocalized into the unmentionable anatomies of nine women, they'd have no doubt fainted from shock. But Trenchmouth had a whole stockpile of secrets, and this one he would not spill.

So Warren was lucky, in that not knowing any of this, he didn't slander Trenchmouth and pay the price. What stopped him was the sight of Arly Scott Jr. walking by.

Good luck, bad luck. They interchange so quickly.

Arly Scott Jr. was, like Trenchmouth, nearly fourteen. And, like Trenchmouth, he was bigger than the four other boys. But Arly was black, and this meant that even a pack of puny ten-year-olds could order him around if they felt like it.

"Hey," Warren Crews shouted at the boy in the distance, who was going foot over foot along the railroad track, testing balance. "Hey nigger!"

Arly stopped and dropped his feet on either side of his balance beam. He turned and faced them.

"Why don't you come on over here?" Warren spit dirt, scraped grass off his tongue and lips using his teeth and fingernails.

Arly looked at them for a while, then began walking toward them.

Trenchmouth didn't know him, but he'd seen him around. Like every other black family in Mingo County, Arly's had come from down South for the mines. His father was in the number one at Red Jacket. And like every other black family in Mingo, he lived in Mitchell Branch and went about his business in an all-black world of school and church. Arly was almost identical to Trenchmouth in height and weight, and his sprouting muscles were just as hard and determined.

When he walked upon them, the littler ones got uncomfortable and began to fidget. They'd heard their fathers and mothers and uncles and brothers use the term Warren Crews had used, but they were still young enough to be pierced by it when shouted in the presence of one to whom it was meant to describe.

"You play Mumblety Peg down there in Texas?" Warren Crews said. Oddly, he'd stayed on his knees with his hands locked behind him throughout all this, as if to break the pose would be sin.

"Georgia," Arly said.

"Georgia then. Niggers play Mumblety Peg in Georgia?"

Arly just stared down at the boy. The other ones fidgeted more plainly. One laughed a little, tried to act tough. Another gripped his thighs against his privates, tried not to piss himself as he often did when trouble arose.

Trenchmouth studied Arly Scott's eyes, the heavy lids, the wiry brows. The small scar that said he could take a punch. He knew that Warren Crews had called on the wrong black boy.

"Well?" Warren said. "Is that all you know how to say? 'Georgia?' They just teach you one word down there? State name?" He laughed and turned back to the other boys to make sure they did the same. But he never found out they didn't. Before Warren Crews could notice the cringing expressions of impending impact the little boys uniformly wore, he'd been cold-cocked. It was a sweeping right hook, a suckerfree sucker punch delivered from high to low and with the inertia of planted feet and swiveled hips. Arly Scott Jr. was a trained fighter.

Some stood scarecrow still, some ran. Either way, they were thoroughly discombobulated by the sight of a black boy hitting a white one for insulting his race. It didn't happen in Georgia, they were pretty sure, and it didn't happen in southern West Virginia either. But it *had* happened, and Warren Crews lay asleep on the ground, thick blood, chunked by dirt, running from nose and mouth.

Eventually, they all left their ten-year-old comrade where he lay, only one of them with the wherewithal to shout a promise of revenge. Arly and Trenchmouth remained. They looked down at Warren together, the black boy rubbing his throbbing knuckles, the white boy rubbing his head. This would take some figuring.

Trenchmouth decided he didn't feel all too sorry for the littlest Crews. At eleven, he was old enough to know better than to treat somebody that way, address somebody with those kind of words. The Widow had taught Trenchmouth, along with Clarissa, from a young age, to never engage in the game of white superiority. "We are all made from God's clay," she'd said, "no matter its stain." Besides, Trenchmouth had always been less white than the whites, especially in summer, a fact the other kids falsely attributed to a stubbornly thick buildup of dirt on his skin. And had he seen more of his father than the dusty, dug up variety, he'd have known there was Indian in that bloodline, or maybe even colored. Still, by outward appearance, he was a white boy.

"I'm Trenchmouth Taggart," he said and held out his hand.

Arly turned those eyes on him. He didn't speak back or change the stare, which had the kind of calm to it that can precede a snot-knocker as easily as a handshake.

It was nice to see it in another, that "something else" look of the eye. He'd been embarrassed for revealing his own after Fred Dallara kissed Clarissa. It came from someplace less knowable than a steady diet of moonshine and ridicule. This particular something was there before all that.

Trenchmouth almost told the other boy how he once bit someone for kissing his sister, but it seemed anxious, foolish. Instead, he said, "I reckon your daddy'll have your hide for this here." He pointed at Warren Crews, who whimpered and tried to get up on his elbows.

Arly's hands re-fisted, and he turned his stare back to the boy on the ground then, as if he might have another go. But the whimper turned to a cry and Arly's whole being eased up. He answered Trenchmouth without looking at him. "You'd reckon wrong then. My Daddy told me, when they look down at you, start em to lookin up." His voice was a pitch deeper than Trenchmouth's, his accent big and round.

Before Arly Scott walked away, he snorted twice, gathered up what he could in his throat, and spat on the ground before Warren Crews, who was, by that point, all-out crying the kind of cry reserved for mamas, the kind he'd have to be rid of in a year or two if he hoped to get anywhere in life.

Trenchmouth didn't forget about Arly Scott Jr. He knew somehow that the handshake he'd offered would someday be returned. And the fallout he'd worried over, the revenge on the Scott family for one of their own having struck down a white boy, never came to pass. This was on account of various abnormalities brewing in the hills. First, Arly Scott Sr., little Arly's father, was a quiet yet commanding miner who everyone knew had been a prizefighter in his youth, and they all respected that. Arly Sr. had single-handedly integrated the late night meetings that were slowly building toward a certified coal miner's union, and though some hated him for this integration, most recognized their enemy not as one with black skin, but one with green hands.

Second reason no one came looking for the Scotts was that George Crews, fat Warren's father, was rising among the ranks of the local coal operators, and a new sense of public image and city manners discouraged him from vigilante justice. Besides, George's bulge-pocketed buddies told him, the little Scotts among us will be crushed soon enough for their attempts at rebellion.

And third, a reason not known to most, was the fact that the Crews family patriarch needed desperately to avoid attention upon his clan if he hoped to get truly rich. It was only recently that he'd found out about his wife's betrayal of their Methodist traditions. Only in the last few months that George had unearthed the lies. It was these lies that sent her off early on Sunday mornings to care for her unstable sister in Williamson, while in reality, as he would come to hear through the ever-burgeoning rumor mill surrounding the place, she attended the Church of God with Signs Following. She'd been sucked in by a snake handler from Tennessee, and George had only pulled her back out with threats of beatings and separation and financial ruin. Had he known that she was also one of nine women paying top dollar every Sunday evening to visit the mountain hideout of a teenager, who knows what he'd have done. Had he known that she was, like the other women, handing over increasing sums of her husband's currency in that hideout to secure the sweet burn of expert moonshine and the heavenly exhaustion of a tongue-talking, ventriloquist-cunnilinguist, George Crews may have killed his wife. That, or maybe he'd have been reduced to nothing. To crying the pitiful, mama's boy cry his son had cried when he made the mistake of believing what so many in power believed. That things were to stay as they were. That the powerful would stay there, in power, and that the ones beneath would stay beneath, all dark-skinned and coal-blacked and rotten-toothed. And maybe things would stay this way for a while, but change was coming as fast and reckless as the N&W lines, and if triggered, it just might fell trees and men alike.

CHAPTER ELEVEN

FOLKS WILL DUST YOU QUICK
AS LOOK AT YOU

Winter came premature that year. The long walk to and from the Church of God with Signs Following each Sunday cracked Trenchmouth's lips, anesthetized his toes and fingers. But he got there on time, heeded the same instructions J.B. Smith gave him every week: Be sure to take up all the snakes at once. Don't open your mouth and let any in, folks didn't know what to make of that one. Don't stand so stock still. Move your feet a little. Move your tongue too. If you don't feel the Lord speaking through you, make something up.

The boy's act had brought more sheep to the flock, and his gig became a regular Sunday ritual. J.B. Smith knew the boy's tongue-talking to be fraudulent, but it added flair to his natural magnetism for snakes, and flair put asses in chairs, and asses in chairs put coins in hats, and coins in hats put food on the table, liquor under the basement stairs. Coins converted whores to the Lord.

Trenchmouth had even started to forge his tongue-talking while in a woman's nether-regions. The genuine article, the God he'd found down there on Independence Day, had ceased to draw out holy babble. He'd had to fake it after the six or seventh time. All part of the act. What had been, at least that first time with Anne Sharples, an awakening, had transformed into a job. They never let him kiss their mouths or dip his wick. Some had even worried so heavily on the contagiousness of his disease that he'd procured a medical almanac to show them it wasn't contagious. Ewart wouldn't set foot in his hideout anymore, much less speak to him on account of his newfound tendency to avoid her, ignore her even. But, between the women and the small fee he charged J.B. Smith for his services in church every Sunday, Trenchmouth's coin sack was getting heavy. He was saving up for something, he just didn't know what.

On a particularly cold Sunday afternoon, Trenchmouth sat at the kitchen table in silence with Clarissa and the Widow. They hardly spoke in these days of awkward adolescence. Brother and sister went so far as to avert contact of the eye. But all hands touched when the Widow said the blessing.

"We give thanks O Lord for the food before us and the family beside us." They all said Amen. They all ate. Wet wood cracked and hissed at them from the heating stove, alongside small chips of coal and coke stolen from slag heaps and found on railroad tracks. The sheet steel pipe hadn't stayed air tight. The Widow coughed. The windows fogged over thick and milky.

Clarissa knew that her mother knew that Fred Dallara was after her cherry. Trenchmouth knew that his mother knew he was taking up serpents and making a fool of himself at a temple of blaspheme. But, she believed that adolescents would make their mistakes, with or without her warnings against them, so she kept quiet.

On that Sunday, the quiet got to be too much. "In this life," the Widow said to them, "there's folks that will force your hand." She picked at the chicken back on her plate, fingers shiny with grease. She did not look up at them. "What you need to ask yourself is why you let em. What's your cut? There's bamboozlers among us, and if you get dusted enough times by one of em, you forget how it is to be alive, to be free and easy." She was deliberate with the words then. "You get used to the notion that life isn't but two things: gettin bamboozled or bamboozlin somebody yourself. And there isn't no *real* living in either." She brought her food to her mouth with both hands, rolled the chicken back circular like a corn cob, toothing every bit of meat from the bone.

Clarissa excused herself and went up the ladder to the loft where she'd pen another letter she never planned on delivering. She'd hide it where she hid all the others.

Trenchmouth sat with the Widow and ate and looked occasionally at his pocketwatch.

"You got somewhere to be?" she asked him.

"No ma'am," he said. A woman more than twice his age would be waiting at the meeting spot for him in an hour. It would be her second time, so she'd know to expect him early, to not worry when he blindfolded her and led her to his hideout somewhere on Sulfur Creek Mountain. This was how it was done, the other women had told her, "so we don't know where it is exactly." The second-timer would wait and shiver and know that soon her shivers would be of a different variety, and that warmth would rise, toes to head, like a fire flood, all because a poor, malformed boy who took up serpents could do something no grown man ever could or would. But on this day, she'd wait forever. Her shivers would be of one variety only. Trenchmouth was not coming.

Instead he sat in silence with his mother, then helped her with the dishes. And he looked out the fogged window glass at the woods, the tree limbs angular and black and without leaf. The branches against the sky, thin and searching, like the blood vessels he'd looked at in the medical almanac. The Widow's words had gotten to him. He'd heard when most folks only listened. His cut in this game he'd created wasn't worth it. He'd thought himself the bamboozler, but he'd become the bamboozled, and it was time to end it.

Frank Dallara's death had brought him to the dry rituals of the Methodists, and there he was used, and he'd only gotten out by chopping down Hob Tibbs. The want of Ewart Smith had brought him to the Church of God with Signs Following, brought him to the snake-handlers and the tongue-talkers and the holiest parts of a woman. But again, he was used, and he'd only get out by heeding the Widow's words.

He stood and stared out the window, out beyond where the tomato garden had flared in spring. At the edge of the woods stood a figure. A boy, or maybe a small man. He was gone as quick as he'd appeared.

After a while, when the dishes were washed and dried and put away, the boy and the Widow sat again at the table, and she poured them a little kitchen whiskey. Then she pulled a newspaper from her apron pocket and slid it toward him, a particular passage marked with a star. *Bruin are Plentiful* it read. The story was out of Huntington. *With the big game season open, the lovers of the sport are flocking to the mountain region to hunt bear, which are reported very plentiful this season.* The article described how folks ran bears to their caves with packs of hounds and killed them. The theory was that the mother bears returned to their caves to protect their cubs, that this accounted for the hard fight the bruin put up. It concluded, *While the sport is dangerous, it is very thrilling.* Trenchmouth looked up at her.

She almost smiled, then spoke. "I reckon between the two of us, we don't need no hound dogs."

"I reckon not," he said.

His fourteenth birthday was a week off. She'd already been to Williamson for his present. It was under her mattress, wrapped in butcher's paper. A Winchester Model 1907 she'd procured from a police officer turned pawnbroker, a man who'd give up a testicle for a drop of white lightning. It was a .351 caliber, self-loading. Five round magazine, pistol-grip walnut stock. Until that Sunday, she'd not decided whether to keep it for herself or to give it to the boy. Not until that moment at the table over moonshine and the written word and the shared love of tracking and facing down the most beastly of beasts. Boys his age could take righteous paths or wicked ones, and the Widow had steered her boy back from wander.

A week later, the boy and the Widow found themselves subjects of the newspaper. When word spread of the slain black bear, the photographer for the *Williamson Daily News* had arranged to meet them in town. Outside the bank, he set up his folding Eastman Kodak and depressed the small button. The result was published the next day: *Local Fourteen Year Old, His Caretaker Bag Prize Bruin*. The scales had weighed the black bear in at 460 pounds, and he'd measured over three feet tall. These were both local records as far back as anyone could remember. In the photograph, new Winchester in one hand, the bear's mighty claw in the other, Trenchmouth had actually smiled. Had actually opened up for all who wanted news to see.

One of those who saw was a fellow from Washington, D.C. by the name of Arthur H. Estabrook. He and his partner, Ivan E. McDougle, had been traveling through the area on their way home from the Blue Ridge foothills of Virginia. There, they were conducting ongoing experiments on the region's people, poking and prodding them in hopes of explaining why such downtrodden folks continued to exist and threaten the quickwitted, racially-pure American well-bred. They had labeled these mixed-ancestry hill people "The WIN Tribe." This stood for White, Indian, and Negro. The head circumferences of the WINs, the foot and Achilles lengths, the slope of brows and propensity to dysentery and bad grammar and poor diet and interbreeding and mixed breeding especially, all these would help them figure out how such hill people came to be, and how we might all avoid becoming like them.

Eugenics was the movement of these men, and Mr. Estabrook, over his morning coffee, had trained his magnifying lens on the newsprint mouth of the dark white boy who'd slain a prize-winning bear. "We've got to find this boy and analyze him," he told his partner.

The goddess Liberty on the Two Dollar Silver Certificate spread her arms wide in protection. The bill was old, wrinkled, and it was not more money than Trenchmouth had seen in a sitting. Before quitting, he'd accumulated a treasury from the women who needed his touch. But this currency caught his eye for three reasons. First, it was held out to him in offering as soon as he answered a knock at the door. Second, the man doing the holding was dressed more proper than anyone Trenchmouth had encountered, and so was his sidekick. Their cashmere Mackintoshes and tailored trousers commanded respect. The third reason the boy accepted the money and invited them in was that behind them, uncomfortable and bespectacled, stood a young woman who you simply didn't turn away if she came calling. She was a city girl. Black velvetta hat, double-breasted jacket with fancy buttons. Under her satin-folded skirt she surely wore a winter corset, but her shape, with or without it, was something that would raise any country boy's pup tent.

He was home alone.

They took a minute to acclimate, but had seen much worse. They chose to stand, turned down Trenchmouth's offer of coffee. "As I said before, we're in the employ of Dr. Charles B. Davenport of the Eugenics Record Office," Mr. Estabrook said, wiping at his nose with a handkerchief.

"You want to measure my head?" Trenchmouth said.

Mr. McDougle stopped gawking at the patchwork walls, wondering about the contents of the loft. "You know what eugenics is?"

"I read the papers." Trenchmouth winked at the young woman. She looked away, wrote in her opened book.

"I must say I'm impressed," Mr. McDougle said.

"Tell me, were you born in this area?" Mr. Estabrook asked.

"I didn't hear the lady's name."

"This is our senior student assistant, Miss Margie Avon. She's the first young lady to study sociology at William and Mary." Estabrook didn't motion to her or look her direction when he spoke her name. Neither did McDougle. She wrote in her book some more.

Trenchmouth got the impression they ignored the girl in public, did the opposite in private. "William and who?"

"William and Mary, the oldest—"

"Tell me," Trenchmouth said, employing the introductory statements of his guests, "does Miss Avon bed up in a separate room at the hotel, or do you all share a real big one?"

"I beg your pardon?" McDougle pretended to be insulted.

Trenchmouth kept his eyes on her. She didn't look up from the book, but her face went red as ripe crabapple. "I said, do you camp out on your study trips when there ain't room at the inn?"

They were baffled. Estabrook lowered his voice and stepped

forward. "We've just come from Grundy, Virginia. Are you familiar with it?" His moustache carried too much wax.

"I reckon I'd better be," Trenchmouth answered, looking the man of equal height in the eyes. "I spent a month in their pokey." He'd never heard of Grundy.

"For what crime may I ask?" McDougal was, for all his sociological book smarts, short on real sociology. He knew not when his leg was being pulled.

"For makin love to the Fire Station mule," Trenchmouth said.

Bestiality, Miss Avon wrote in her book.

Estabrook let it go. "Are your ancestors from Grundy?"

"Nossir."

There was a pause. Trenchmouth used a rag to take the dented coffeepot from the stovetop.

"May I ask where your ancestors are from?"

He poured coffee into a straight-seam cup, took it with him to sit at the table. They watched him sip one-handed while leaning back on two chair legs. Through thick steam, he watched them write in their books. "Where are my ancestors from? Paris France London England," Trenchmouth said. "Are you going to measure my head?"

They asked if they might watch him eat, suggested it was close to suppertime. He opened a can of sardines and, with his pocketknife and fork, cut the little, greasy lengths into five pieces each, equal in size. Then he inhaled them off the plate, his pursed lips a slurping vacuum, an assembly line of sorts, one piece, then another, then another. He began pouring sips of coffee into his cupped palm, drinking it in the same slurping fashion. They wrote furiously.

He said his blessing when the meal was finished rather than before. Half tongue-talking, half a list of surrounding counties, whispered. They tried to take dictation, tried to write his nonsense words on pages next to the words describing others encountered in their studies. *Freed Negroes. Mixed Half Breeds. Low Down Yellows.*

They measured his head after he asked again. The girl, at his insistence. They agreed only if she was gloved. He almost fell asleep from the sheer pleasure of her touch.

He made up and spoke on special customs for them to write about. Drinking squirrel blood to clear up foot fungus, hot poker in the ear for a stomach ache. When asked about the Widow, her source of income and earning capacities, he lied convincingly. Tobacco farmer, he said. Outhouse builder. About to strike it rich. When asked why he hadn't taken her last name as his own, he lied again. His surname, he said, had to be kept that way to continue the family name, as his father had run off to Paris France London England.

They wrote it all down.

The time came when McDougal asked, "And your mouth ailment? I'd say persistent gingivitis? Have you seen a physician?"

"Beelzebub," Trenchmouth said.

"Beg your pardon?"

"The one sent down to fire. He give me this mouth." He took another slurp of his coffee, cold now, swashed it around inside his mouth, spat it on the floor in front of Miss Avon's pointed boots of fine leather. "Dust flakes on the river air," Trenchmouth said, "just like those there." He pointed to the whirling specks caught in the fast-fading sunlight through the kitchen window. "They can infect a body, through the gums, the mouth and the throat brain. Beelzebub's cells, don't make em mad." He smiled full on. They quickly cut off their stupefied stares, looked down, wrote more.

"I can see through things," Trenchmouth said.

The door opened and the Widow came in with her finger on the trigger of a Derringer inside her coat pocket. She'd heard them talking from twenty feet off, got prepared for those that would sabotage her shining. "Who are you?" she said. Trenchmouth sat still, looked past his mother's silhouette to his sister, holding a sack of something. She was miniature through the opened door. He'd stopped smiling.

"I'm Arthur H. Estabrook of the Carnegie Institution, ma'am." He'd planned on continuing, but she cut him off.

"Out," she said. Miss Avon had already slipped through the doorway.

"We were hoping to speak with you as well."

"Out," she said louder, and the men listened, spoke no more save a few parting courtesies.

Clarissa came in and began unloading goods from the grocers. The Widow stared at the boy until he started doing the same.

In all the awkward comings and goings, the door had been left open too long. It would take a day or more to push out the chill.

For as much as the Widow didn't like strangers in her home, she held off punishing the boy for a good little while. The next day in town, she went to the hotel housing the three city sophisticates. They'd stayed at the Urias, rebuilt after the fire that killed Frank Dallara. Anse Pilcher, the proprietor, wasn't in a hurry to talk to the Widow, nor she to engage him, for like Trenchmouth, she despised the man. Witnesses had said he'd allowed Frank Dallara to burn, could've pulled him out but didn't.

The eugenicists had checked out. She asked around. Traveling through, folks said. Professor-types. Nation's capital.

She waited another day to say anything to the boy. Then, after dinner, when Clarissa had gone up to hide from the only people in this world who loved her enough to die for her, the Widow stopped drying clothes at the iron-and-rubber wringer, wheeled around, and smacked Trenchmouth hard across the forehead. He'd been waiting for her to say if his chores were done.

"It isn't even that you let them people in here," she said. Their home, like everybody's in those mountains, had always been open to strange travelers. "It's that you sat with them and let them pick at you like a monkey in the jungle. I know what they do, *how* they do to people like us. And you gave em more of the same."

He wanted to tell her he hadn't. That he'd thrown a purposeful wrench into their scientific machinery, one-upped their high-minded talk with talk of his own. Talk so crazy it would cause them to second guess their eugenic gibberish. But he didn't say any of it because he knew it was time to listen, and because he didn't know anymore if what he'd done was so revolutionary after all. In retrospect, it may have been plain stupid.

"Men like those want to brand you and hang you out to dry." Her hands were on her hips then, and Trenchmouth, shamed, couldn't look up much higher anyway. "They got to trace you back like a hound dog's blood line, call you part Powhatan or Negro, explain to the folks riding cable cars why anybody'd want to stay in a hole between two hills like this one." The Widow worried that she was losing him again to bamboozlers, that just after rescuing him from wicked wander, he was back to being used. She let go her hip grip and slicked back her hair. He looked up momentarily and noticed the grey in her roots, something that hadn't been there last time he looked. "They had their way," she said, quieter, more tired, "we'd all be the same."

"As them?" he asked, genuine.

"Just the same." She looked at the redness where she'd smacked him, wished she could rub it away. "Or maybe, they'd have us just not *be* at all."

CHAPTER TWELVE

HERE CAME A WAR OR TWO

The reason folks like Mr. Estabrook found fascination in the dispossessed always had roots in something like envy. Envy for upward bootstraps. Envy for those they didn't focus on: those among hill folk who, despite the world against them, had an intangible drive for mastery of one thing or another. And Trenchmouth was one of those. Beyond his skills of digging and climbing and inventing and pleasing women, which only a handful of folks were aware of, lay his obvious aptitude for lining up and taking a shot. That is, he could sight and drop most any target with most any weapon. What Frank Dallara had seen all those years earlier had come to full fruition with practice. The dead-eye boy had fallen a prize bear. The crack-shot had collected trophies. And such riflery merits did not go unnoticed in trigger-happy times of impending World War. Even in the hills of southern West Virginia, folks had been itchy since the day a Sarajevo boy not much older than Trenchmouth had stuck his revolver inside the car of the Archduke and squeezed the trigger. The Black Hand had spoken and the world had to listen to its fallout. Within a year, the papers told of the Germans, their use of poison gas.

Four short months after Trenchmouth's fourteenth birthday, his president declared war on those gassy Germans. The man-boy wished himself older by a few calendar lengths. He wanted to knock down something other than big game.

But June 5th, 1917, came and went. Conscription they called it. The *Williamson Daily News* declared *No Slackers Will Be Found In Mingo*, and it held true. Every man of fighting age joined up. This excluded coal miners whose duty it was to keep producing in time of war. But in Mingo, even the miners couldn't help but go to war, and scores of them came home asleep forever. *Nowhere on top of earth can be found a more fighting bunch of brave young men and every one seems ready to go when the bugle call is sounded in this county*, the newspaperman went on. Twenty-one to thirty was the rule, but younger got in. Still, despite his older size and look, Trenchmouth was just too short in the tooth. So while the district attorney called on all county sheriffs to report the names of slackers—those eligible but not enlisted—Trenchmouth sat and fidgeted and twice watched *The Narrow Trail*, showing at the Hippodrome. On the screen, background orchestra roaring, the good Outlaw Ice Harding broke a wild horse and called it King. Together, they held up stagecoaches. Then the Outlaw rode out of town. For a boy of sixteen, there was nothing more beautiful than an Outlaw riding away free.

While the older boys fought and died, Trenchmouth practiced his marksmanship and his Outlaw stare. Now and again, he sparred with Arly Scott Jr., who was a promising young amateur.

By the age of seventeen, Trenchmouth had given up on school.

When Ewart Smith's father, J.B., died from a snakebite, he used her vulnerable state to finally dip his pecker into that honeypot he'd so often been denied. For her, it was outright painful. For him, disappointing. Over in no time and plain awkward. So, he took to avoiding Ewart at all costs.

He also avoided Clarissa and Hob Tibbs and Ann Sharples, the latter of whom had started up a makeshift whorehouse in the Urias Hotel on Main Street. One of her earliest working-girl recruits was the sad, abandoned Ewart Smith.

If any of these folks from the past got in Trenchmouth's line of sight, he changed direction. He drank alone in his hideout. The teenage years had made him morose, and as the paper told of the war's end, another one, closer to home, began to brew. It was an odd time, and the paper told of that too. Its pages were marked by public notices of application for pistol license. Trenchmouth wasn't the only one itchy.

The *Daily Mail* told of the winner of the Nobel Prize for Chemistry, a German who'd invented the gas of the dead, an asphyxiating yellow-green nightmare. Ethics, it seemed, were out the window. The power of invention mattered most. And in the face of power, good working people found themselves capable of enlisting the basest of their instincts.

The men were already mumbling and organizing, already listening to Mr. John L. Lewis and his thundering pronouncements, when the headquarters of Superior-Thacker blew up. The coal company's main building exploded to ring in the new year of 1920, and for a two mile stretch, folks' windowpanes and storefronts paid the price in shatter. As usual, the company took no onus.

Coal trucks rumbled everywhere, rough shot across crooked streets, cracking them up like iced-over streams, and still no culpability was claimed. North of Matewan, in Kermit, Gray Eagle

Coal Company labeled those public roads private and lined them with gun-strapped, shadowy men to back their claim.

All of this was talked over between miners. All of it silently ingested and turned to burning rage. The rage was powerful enough that it made unlikely comrades out of otherwise separate and supposedly unequal men. Black and white men who would normally never set foot in one another's homes. Men like Arly Scott Sr. and Bill Blizzard spoke on the situation over coffee and sometimes whiskey, early in the morning and late at night. And, increasingly so, they talked about it in front of the wife, the kids. They had more time to do so, having been fired on the spot for wearing their District 17 Union credentials after an organizing drive moved through the hills like salvation.

This was how Trenchmouth came to know firsthand that the union, like the railroad before it, had come fast and hard. And with it came his day to make a name for himself.

It came on a Sunday afternoon. At the Scotts', Trenchmouth and Arly were sparring with a couple pairs of Arly Sr.'s beat up old gloves. Arly Sr. encouraged daily sparring, along with jumping jacks, push-ups and sit-ups. Such a regimen had paid off for Arly Jr., who was undefeated in four amateur fights. Quiet and wise for his years, he looked to be going places.

In the kitchen, the boys heard Bill Blizzard stand up and say, "It's high time we did something other than talk, by God." Trenchmouth stopped slipping punches to look in that direction and caught a straight right from his friend. He ended up on his tailbone, a little sore in the nose but listening. Arly did the same. Arly Sr. looked over at them briefly. The two boys read in his eyes the command to go on about their business. They started in on their push-ups, to be followed by sit-ups.

"Sid will back us," a friendly man named Ed Chambers said. The

Sid they spoke on was Sid Hatfield, Matewan's pistol-packing chief of police, newly appointed by Mayor Testerman and friend to miner's troubles. Hatfield was a rough man, young and with eyes that cut like a shiv. He had ridden those cars into their deep holes at one time, right alongside the others, and he knew how the company regarded their laborers, how they dealt bad hands. He could toss up a spud and air it out with his sidearm, and he'd used that same weapon to kill a mine foreman five years prior during a scuffle. Self-defense is what he'd called it. So had the courts.

"These Baldwin-Felts boys has gotten too big for their britches," Blizzard said, and he set his glass on the table hard, so that it nearly shattered. The Baldwin-Felts men were detectives hired by mine operators as little more than glorified thugs, a foreman's armed big brother. They stood behind and in front of company whims, and like the companies, they had little care that four-hundred men had died in the past year down those holes, unlucky inheritors of explosion and cave-in.

"What we've got to do is get to these scab trains before they reach town," Arly Sr. said. The mine operators had taken to bringing in hordes of men to work for those who no longer would or could. The week before, Little Arly and Trenchmouth had thrown rocks at one such load of men, and Trenchmouth, for the fun of it, had even lined up a shot on one scab, his Winchester empty of ammo, his finger off the trigger.

Walking toward the men in the kitchen that day, having just been hit in the face and wearing his outlaw scowl, Trenchmouth chose to reveal this. "I had one of em in my sights last week," he said. "I wasn't going to shoot him, a'course. But I sure could nick him if I wanted."

They all went quiet, and both Arlys shook their heads, as they often did when the strange white boy spoke. But everybody knew Trenchmouth's skills as a marksman, and a skinny miner said, "That ain't a bad idea now. Shootin to hobble but not to kill." The men looked confused. The skinny miner clarified. "Not the scabs, mind you, but them thugs who pistol-whipped little Jerry last week. They could have a leg shot comin."

They almost laughed at the idea then. Almost brushed it away and moved on. But the memory of that unlucky miner's face emerged in all their minds simultaneously. The purple, cracked impressions the gun butt had left. And the loss of their livelihoods was omnipresent, along with loss of scrip at the company store, and the threat of losing their homes, also company-owned. All this stirred into the base instincts that had risen to the surface, and the result was the inclusion of the two seventeen-year-olds to the circle. One of them suspected he was about to get used yet again, but he didn't care, because this time he'd have a gun in his hand. All he had to do was shut one eye and bend a finger.

The boy who had once fashioned miniature coal tipples from scrapmetal now found himself toppling giant ones with dynamite. He and Arly Sr. and Arly Jr. and the others laid the explosives down by night, and by day there was nothing left but black holes where coal was to be loaded. They dynamited the tipple at Red Jacket and the one at Tomahawk too.

Scab workers were run off from reopened mines by way of rifle fire. It was just scare tactics, never more, until the day somebody fired back.

Trenchmouth was on strikebreaker duty in McDowell County, along with Arly Jr. and a young miner named Kump. Kump was only there because he'd inherited an automobile and could provide transport. They laid on their stomachs behind a downed maple tree and ate bologna sandwiches. When the time came, they lit up the slow, single-file line of scabs with the unmistakable echo of the high-powered rifle report. They strafed the mine's entrance, careful not to hit anyone. But the mine operators had sent along some Baldwin-Felts boys that day, and they located the source of echoes, raised their own small arms up to return what they were getting.

The first round to come close caught the young men's attention. It kicked tree bark into the open mouth of Arly Jr., who promptly hit the deck. The next one caught the young miner Kump in the jaw and tore open his face. His blood had been tapped, and it issued down his pale white neck in wide red lengths, gathering in his shirt collar until the fabric could hold no more. Kump went broadside crimson then, and he fell forward, alive but silent as the dead.

Trenchmouth had not seen such ugliness envelop a man before, only deer and bear. Even then, there was never such contrast of skin and blood, such streaming horror to behold. But he quickly turned away from the sight of it, and lined his true sights on the Baldwin-Felts detectives. Two of them. Three rounds left in the magazine. First, the tall one in the bowler hat. One shot, shin bone. No doubt shattered. The man was one moment upright and aiming, the next crippled, in the time it took Trenchmouth to close that eye and squeeze that finger he'd closed and squeezed so many thousands of times before. Without thought, he shifted his position leftward, and the squat detective sat in the notch of his barrel. This time it was the thigh, a meaty target, and the man buckled as his friend had before him. They'd both dropped their guns and lost their hats. There was something pathetic in the way a man moved when he'd taken a bullet.

One round left in the magazine. Trenchmouth back-and-forthed the detectives, sighted one hobbled man then the other as they attempted to pull themselves to cover. Trenchmouth lined up their heads, so perfectly round and slicked, sunlight striping the hair tonic and the sweat beads gathered in mustaches. It was always like this when he hunted. Magnified. Microscopic.

He sighted their breast pockets, shoulder seams, hearts, gut, and kneecaps. Then the lifeblood of all men—the recess between their legs. But he did not fire. Trenchmouth may have been many things, but murderer was not one of them.

The "Oh Lords" emanating from Arly forced a change in focus. Trenchmouth dropped behind the log and looked. "Oh Lord Jesus," Arly said again and again with the raw desperation of a funeral goer. His hands hovered over the downed man, but they knew not what to do.

Trenchmouth shouldered his rifle and crouched beside his friend. Together, they stripped themselves of their coats, cut lengths of wool using Arly's pocketknife. They wrapped and re-wrapped the lower face of the young man they knew by last name only. Steam came off his wound and disappeared in the chill March air, indistinguishable from their own breath.

When the blood slowed, they hoisted him and ran. Arly clutched wrists, Trenchmouth ankles. They footed through the woods to Kump's awaiting automobile, a semi-reliable 1914 Model T Touring Type.

Arly at the wheel, they picked up downhill speed just about the time the mine guards reached the road on foot, out of range as soon as they raised their rifles. But, as was always the case in southern West Virginia, when one hill ended, another began. The mine guards stood winded with their hands on their knees and watched the automobile move out of sight. But before it did, the Model T sputtered as it climbed. Kump quickly spoke through the blood threatening to choke him. "Gas tank," he said. "Gravity feed."

"What?" Arly hollered.

Trenchmouth had heard something about it. The tank was under the seat, and on a steep enough incline, no gas could get to the motor unless the vehicle faced downhill. As he spoke on this to Arly and they got the car turned around, one of the mine guards noticed the trouble, and, along with the others, got to moving again. By the time the car was in position and climbing in reverse, with great difficulty, up the incline, the men were within range again. Bullets zipped past the windshield every three or four seconds. One lodged in the grill with a heavy sound. Arly got the trap moving enough so that at the top of the hill, turned around yet again, they were able to put distance between themselves and their pursuers.

They'd cheated death, gotten free, then cheated it again when automotive invention nearly failed them. They'd almost perished in a hail of bullets inside the contraption, rolling backwards up a hill. It was comical. When it seemed okay to do so, Trenchmouth started to laugh. He open-mouthed whooped it up there in the fast-moving Model T, and so did Arly Jr., who'd only ever piloted a car once, on flat land. The wind carried their calls to the spaces they left behind, so that they almost forgot a man lay in the backseat, bleeding near to death.

Knocks at the hideout door had always and only come from two folks. In the old days, it was Ewart. More recent, Arly Jr. But on a mid-March morning, sunlight streaming through the groundcover and the cracks in the trapdoor, an unfamiliar rap sounded. Trenchmouth had been on edge since the shooting in McDowell, and though he wasn't sure whether or not the Widow had officially kicked him out, he'd taken to sleeping most nights at the hideout, winter having died off. He'd spent a small portion of his savings on a revolver, a beat up Colt Cop & Thug .38, and he trained it on the trap door from where he lay under the heavy hide of his prized bear.

Above him, a voice said, "I heard you pull back that hammer, son. Why don't you ease it down now. I got my hands on two of em, and I reckon you know as well as any that two is better'n one." He'd left little doubt to his identity, and Trenchmouth did as he was told. "Your weapon put up?" the voice said.

"Yessir."

"Good boy. Now open sesame."

Again, he did as he was told, pulling the chain and squinting up at the thin silhouette above. Two Gun Sid lived up to his name even before he'd acquired the moniker, which would come later. On that morning, he holstered his sidearms and slid down inside the five by seven foot room. He pulled the door shut. "Whew," he said. "Stinks in here. Like assholes and oregano."

Trenchmouth had met Sid Hatfield before, in passing. But in his close-quartered presence, he'd lost the ability to talk, much less laugh at the unique phrasings of a lawman.

Hatfield wore a three piece suit. His shirt collar was high and wide like his cheekbones, and those eyelids weighted down way past his years. He sensed the younger man's hesitation and got down to it. "I hear you had some troubles in McDowell," he said.

For a moment, Trenchmouth considered that the sheriff was there to uphold the law, that the stories of Sid's involvement with the miners were exaggerated, that maybe he should pick up his Colt from where it lay beside him before he was handcuffed and led to a cage. But he sat stone still.

"What you got to understand is two words," Hatfield went on. "Two words that I've said over and over and will keep on sayin over and over until my bones is roadway for moles and beetles." He looked at Trenchmouth with something like respect, something like savagery. "Self-defense," he said. "Two words. As long as another man has picked up a gun and used it to try and end your life, you got no cause for worry in ending his. End of story." Trenchmouth hadn't ended anyone's life, but Sid had come to reassure the boy just the same. Ease his mind. Still, he'd come for more than that. "I want to show you something," he said, standing from his crouch to re-open the hatch. "I'll let you put on your britches. And if I was you, I'd think on where to move this here hideout while you do." He lifted himself into the light and shuffled to a nearby tree. He leaned on it and looked up, directly into the sun.

Sid Hatfield had known that morning that the sun wasn't long to stay, and he was right. By ten a.m., the sky spoke somehow of dusk, and a cold front was coming, quick. The wind and the purple-gray character of the air would have warned other folks of a tornado, but not here. Here, there were hills to knock down such foolishness from mother nature.

They'd driven through it, Trenchmouth and Sid, hoping the rain wouldn't hit. Neither spoke as they rode. After a while, Sid pulled Mayor Testerman's Ford Phaeton right into the Lick Creek tent colony. Trenchmouth had seen it before, at the start of winter, but now it was crowded, overflowing with evicted miners and their families. The price of striking was coming in higher, and this was more evident at Lick Creek than anywhere else. It took him a minute to even get out of the car. "Well. C'mon boy," Hatfield said, already walking into it all.

Trenchmouth followed. The makeshift streets of the place were mostly quiet. Everybody huddled around small fires in front of their tents, or slept against each other inside them. He had to step around a dog laid out on its side. It was bug-bitten all over, pus and skin and little hair from ears to tail and back. It could have been dead. It could have been sleeping.

A child ran from a tent on the eastern side of the camp. He couldn't have been older than three. His mother hollered after him in Italian, no doubt decrying the fact that he wore no shoes. Everywhere was coughing, the kind that hurts just to hear, and everywhere was wretchedness, wet dirt trampled rotten and paper tumbling on end.

Sid Hatfield walked over to a black family, whose matriarch cooked pinto beans over cinders kept hot by rocks the size of baseballs. "Mrs. Belcher," he said to her and nodded.

"Benjamin," she hollered at the heavy canvas tent behind her. A black man came out followed by another one. The first was unfamiliar to Trenchmouth, but the second was Arly Scott Sr. He either didn't notice or didn't care that Trenchmouth was standing behind the chief of police.

"Sid," Arly Sr. said, and he held out his hand. They shook. The man named Benjamin looked at his boots, knocked off dried mud.

"You seen the New York fella around?" Sid asked.

"Spoke with him this morning. He's around," Arly Sr. said.

"Good." The lawman looked all about, as if for enemies. "Arly, you know young T.," he said. It was strange to hear the single initial used this way. No affectation, no meanness.

Arly Sr. nodded at Trenchmouth and frowned. "You supposed to be out of eyeshot for a little while, isn't that right?"

"He's broken no law," Sid said.

"This here's Benjamin Belcher, my nephew from Chicopee, Georgia. He come up October last year for the mines."

Benjamin Belcher had already made Hatfield's acquaintance, but he stepped forward and shook Trenchmouth's hand, still looking at his boots or the ground around them. Under his breath, he said, "October and already I got no work to speak of."

Arly Sr. spoke sharply to his nephew then, "Union takes care of you, don't it? That ain't paper money you was counting in there? Ten bills a week, doctor for your boy's condition." There was some anger there, between kin. Living like dogs will do it to you.

Anger. It was in the eyes of Benjamin Belcher and his wife and the boy poking his misshapen head from the tent's folds. They resented Arly Sr., that he'd built his own house, had known never to live on company-owned property. That he'd risen in the ranks of the union and begun fraternizing with white folks. To them, there was nothing but trouble in this, and the strange hill people around them made it all harder to bear.

Sid eyed the men, then spat on the ground beside him. "Well," he said, "I'd better find this newspaperman and set him straight."

"I already got him together with Bill Blizzard," Arly Sr. said. "He got an earful on the type of people we got livin here." The type was hard. Proud. Stubborn.

Sid and Trenchmouth walked away from the Georgia family's tent. As they did, Benjamin sat down on a log and played his harmonica. Trenchmouth turned to watch. It was the most beautiful sound he could remember hearing. He thought of his own, unused mouth harp. The instrument his Daddy had played. He studied the way Benjamin the southerner cupped the little thing with his hand, opening and closing it to let that sorrow out. It was the blues, the sound of a people bent but not broken, and Trenchmouth memorized it.

They found the reporter from the *New York Times* crouched by a makeshift trash pile. He was talking to a girl no older than six or seven. "Oil cloth," she was saying, in response to his question as to what she slept on inside the tent. "But Daddy don't have nothing but the ground, and it's real hard."

The newspaperman wrote with furious speed. Trenchmouth and Sid stood behind him, waiting for the interview to cease. The man was unaware of their presence. "Brothers and sisters?" the man inquired.

"Two," she said and stopped short for a moment. "Three almost. Stillborn in February." She spoke those three words like she'd heard the older folks around her speak them so many times in the days since. Like name and rank, crops and weather. Her lips were cracked on top and bottom both. The cold had gotten in. She licked them and pulled at the dried-up skin with her teeth, dead-eyed to the man in the gray suit and spit-shined shoes.

Sid Hatfield cleared his throat. The reporter turned and stood up. In his eyes was the look of someone unfinished, someone wanting more misery to make into type so people with heat could sigh and shake their heads. Men like Hatfield and Arly Sr. welcomed men like Mr. Bern, the esteemed journalist. They even set up interviews and meeting times and gave advice on transportation to such city types. All of it brought attention to their people, and attention brought change, hopefully for the better. But, while they extended courtesies, they did so with a quiet air of shame and mistrust. A knowledge that Mr. Bern and his colleagues would never get it right because they *could* never get it right.

Trenchmouth watched the girl walk away. She stopped and turned back to them again and again, waiting on something to happen. Then she made her way to the tent where her mother lay prone on a thrown out piece of rug, infected with a disease unnameable to a doctor of medicine.

Sid motioned to Trenchmouth. "Mr. Bern, I'd like you to meet Ben Chicopee, local newspaperman." He'd made up the name on the spot from a combination of another man and the place he came from. Trenchmouth was confused, but he trusted the skinny lawman who'd found his hideout. He shook Mr. Bern's hand.

"Who do you write for?" Mr. Bern asked. His eyebrows had been recently trimmed, a grooming practice reserved for women, Trenchmouth thought.

"Why didn't you give that girl a nickel for her trouble?" Trenchmouth said.

"I beg your pardon?" Mr. Bern angled his eyes for a closer look at the gums and teeth.

"The girl. She looked back at you five times, waiting on a little something without wantin to outright ask for it. Why didn't you slip her two bits at least?"

"I'm not in the habit of tipping young girls for their—"

"And I'm not in the habit of trimming hair what don't need it, but I know a hungry child when I see one."

Sid Hatfield laughed out loud. He sidestepped so that he could clap both men on their backs. "Alright," he said. "That's just alright how you word types have at it, but let's get to it, what say?" He smiled again at Trenchmouth before he handed Mr. Bern a list of infractions upon the rights of good working people by those that sought to control them.

Later, he smiled as they ate supper together at Charles Lively's little restaurant on Main Street, passing white lightning under the table in plain view of Mr. Lively, who hovered.

Sid smiled yet again that evening when he drove away from the young man he'd re-named and professioned in order to hide his newfound vigilantism. Trenchmouth watched him disappear down the hill. He said to himself, out loud, "Chicopee, newspaperman."

The sheriff had liked Trenchmouth. And what he'd shown him that day at the Lick Creek tent colony, without having to say a word, was that to keep on shooting was not a sin against any God anybody had heard of in southern West Virginia. To keep on shooting was the just and righteous thing to do.

CHAPTER THIRTEEN

THEY HAD GRIPS ON THEM

By May of 1920, Trenchmouth had shot to injure three more mine guards. All three had dared to trade bullets with a dead-eye. His nights remained relatively sleepless. But he rested some on account of a new, more remote hideout on Sulfur Creek Mountain and a habit of sharing whiskey and tobacco with Sid Hatfield at the Blue Goose Saloon.

He'd met Mother Jones and hugged her. He'd listened to Bill Blizzard's driving speeches on the rights of men, gathered past dark at the Baptist church with so many miners the pews spilled over to wall space. The union was said to be three thousand strong.

On the 19th, the noon train carried in thirteen men in fine suits. They were Baldwin-Felts, there to do more evicting for the company, and their leaders were two of Sid's sworn enemies, Albert and Lee Felts. It rained on and off.

Mayor Testerman ordered up warrants for the arrest of the agents. Sid had taken offense to their illegal carrying of guns and the way they threw furniture from the home of a woman whose husband wasn't there to stop it. By three o'clock, folks were arming up.

Trenchmouth, along with some others, had been alerted. He stood inside Chambers Hardware, Main Street Matewan, with his Colt .38 tucked into his belt, his rifle in grabbing distance on a shelf next to a package of wood shims. He stared blank at the little, rough-cut things and thought of Frank Dallara all those years back, calmly laying his fresh-carved sling-shots onto store shelves just like these. For a moment, he wished weaponry had never moved past that ancient invention. That David and Goliath might still meet with nothing but tree branch and stone. But it was long past.

The Baldwin-Felts men had suppered early at the Urias Hotel, where it was known that smacking whores around, whores like Ewart Smith, was overlooked by the hotel's owner, who smacked the girls himself. Now the detectives walked with little care past the opened back doors of the hardware store, past glaring, angry men on all sides. They had grips on them, and it wasn't only a change of clothes inside. The men were going back to the depot to catch the five o'clock to Bluefield. Trenchmouth watched the No. 16. from inside as Sid and Al Felts exchanged words about warrants, about who had the right to arrest who. Young Kump, whose voice had been permanently altered from the jaw wound suffered in McDowell, stood from where he had been rocking in a chair next to Trenchmouth. "A warrant for Sid?" he said of Al Felts's purported document. "Liable to have been written on gingerbread." His voice was no more than a confused whisper, but since being shot, he was more determined than ever to be in the thick of things. He went to fetch Mayor Testerman from his jewelry store.

The mayor agreed that the warrant Felts produced was no good. Trenchmouth watched through the doorway as Felts, Hatfield, and Testerman talked. They were all men of law and legislation in some form, but they were as opposite in their hearts as men could be. A stubby man to Trenchmouth's left lit a cigarette. He spit tobacco flecks and laughed a little. "Nothin but more talk," he said. It almost seemed true. But then the look on Sid's face changed. Those eyes told it. Those hooded eyes. They went smaller, nearly disappeared to nothing.

Most had thought it was just talk, earlier in the day, when the hardened police chief had said he'd kill every goddamned one of em without any goddamned warrants, but Trenchmouth knew the weight of words. And now, square in Albert Felts's face, Hatfield spoke another word. It was the same one that had spurred the first real fight Trenchmouth ever saw, outside the pool hall seven years before. The same word he'd used to bury Hob Tibbs in shame inside his own church. Sid Hatfield said it soft, but he said it nonetheless: "You cocksucker."

Trenchmouth plucked his rifle from the shelf and sighted the detective's head. He kept his off eye open long enough to see Felts pull his sidearm. The two shots were almost simultaneous, Trenchmouth's first, sunk deep into the brain folds of Albert Felts, who must've willed his finger to squeeze after his stance had been altered, for his bullet, no doubt meant for Sid, instead hit Mayor Testerman in the stomach.

Then Sid had both guns out, firing as he pleased at the others, who fired back and were fired upon by others still from inside the hardware store, across the tracks, and from open windows a story up. It was deafening. But with the eardrum damage came calm for Trenchmouth, and he moved forward as a trained soldier might have, out the open doors, his rifle still in the crook of his shoulder, his cheek still pressed to the stock.

The detectives had turned and run, shooting over their shoulders like desperate men do when they know they've misjudged their place among things. Their locomotion set them apart from those with planted feet. They were the hunted, whether they knew it or not. And the crack shot had stepped into the middle, swiveling at the hips with four shots left in the magazine.

He was the Widow's boy, and as it had been for her, a scurrying animal was the easiest somehow to hit.

One man ran faster than the others and made a foolish attempt to return fire. He was sighted first and promptly dropped. Three rounds left.

Everywhere men used short guns without result. The revolvers emptied themselves, hip originated and wobbly, bullets cutting through sky until they lost inertia somewhere. Albert Felts's brother Lee had emptied his as soon as it started, and had himself been the target of another man's .32 pistol from ten yards off, but neither fell. Out of ammunition in one gun, pulling out his other, the younger Felts ran. This only set him apart in the scanning eyes of the young riflery champion. He exhaled and squeezed and Lee Felts crumpled just as his brother before him.

Two rounds.

The next found its way into the chest of a detective who'd just shot an unarmed miner. Somehow, the detective kept breathing. In fact, he ran, tried to open the front door of the bank. He never got inside. The man fell, then struggled to pull himself up. Art Williams, a miner who'd taken the second, still-loaded pistol from Lee Felts's dead hand, walked up behind the struggling man and used his own comrade's weapon to end his life. The shot was taken so close that Lee Felts's gun, and William's hand that gripped it, were blood spattered.

One round in the magazine.

But it was nearly over already. What detectives still breathed were either on their way to safety or shot nearly in half by small packs of miners quick to pull a trigger. Trenchmouth lowered his weapon and sat down in the street. The warring had moved away to the edges by then. A man whose left hand had been shot off tried to climb an alley fence one-handed. They back shot him before he reached the top. Another lay with half his head gone right outside Chambers Hardware, no one sure who'd killed him because so many had fired.

On all sides of him, close-quartered, Trenchmouth felt the palpable smack of life's end. It was in the hummingbird whir of passing bullets, the clumsy footfalls of those trying to scrape and claw their way out of it all. It was in the high-pitched shrieks of more than one of the Baldwin-Felts men, able-bodied former police officers who had known not what they walked into that day. They found themselves praying to God to be anywhere else but here.

One of them made it to the river where he waded, then swam across to Kentucky. Two others, one shoulder-shot, made it to a passing train and rode off gripping the steel caboose ladder. Another, who was off buying cigarettes when the shots started, hid and tore up his detective's papers and waited it all out, escaping, like his buddies, on the next train through.

A couple of them managed to drop a miner each before meeting their ugly end. Lee Felts had somehow killed an unarmed miner with one shot to the forehead, and another unarmed miner was dropped mid-run. "Oh Lord, I'm shot," were his ending words.

The quiet afterwards was unholy. Men didn't know what to speak to one another having seen what they had. Some joked, but none really laughed. Most smoked, and one or two, off by themselves, tried not to cry. Trenchmouth stood and watched as the dead were lined up in the street. Dragged by the armpits, their boots cut ridges in the mud. Rain came in the form that taps your hat brim every few seconds, then not at all.

Mayor Testerman was dying slowly, his wife at his side. Others were tended to as they sat in storefronts stopping blood with rags.

The No. 16 train arrived after all, and the passengers aboard craned their necks and stared at the row of dead men laid out for them to behold. The engineer nearly lost his handle on things as he gawked. Trenchmouth watched their faces, clicking past one after another. A mother and her three little ones. A man with an eye patch. A frail girl whose eyes couldn't understand what they saw. He watched her watching them as the train slowed near to a stop. What ugliness for a child to see, he thought, and then he had to check himself so as not to cry. He kept his eyes on the girl until he no longer could, then looked back at the dead by his feet. One of the killed miners was closest to him, and a single drop of blood had dried on his earlobe, pale and clean otherwise. Trenchmouth stared at the red marking. It was perfectly round. Dark. It began to widen in his gaze, until it filled up and covered over the young man's head, his body, everything around him. Dark, glowing red, like the sun had landed on the earth.

Someone kicked a dead detective beside the miner and Trenchmouth jumped. He looked back to the train but couldn't find the girl. A hand brushed against his back, and he turned to see ugly-scar Kump holding the Colt .38 he'd had tucked in his belt. Kump had disappeared during all the shooting. "I'll give it back," he said, smiling the way no man should in front of so many dead. Then he walked down the line of them, seven dead Baldwin-Felts, and put a bullet in each until the hammer hit hollow. No one cared to pay much mind, and Trenchmouth hoped the little girl had passed on the train. He couldn't look up to see.

Sid Hatfield walked over and stood above the lifeless body of Al

Felts. He took the warrant he'd had issued that day from his shirt pocket, opened it and spread its creases. He slapped it on the dead man's chest, stood up again and spat. "Now, you son of a bitch," he said, "now I'll serve it on you."

CHAPTER FOURTEEN

STRANGE DAYS AND MORE OF THE SAME

Mr. Bern of the *New York Times* wrote about the "shootout," as folks had taken to calling it in the days following. It made the front page for a while. In the eyes of people everywhere who toiled with their hands, the Baldwin-Felts men had gotten what was coming to them. They'd burned and bulleted and evicted their way through towns and families for too long, and they'd come upon one town, one sheriff, who'd had enough. At least this is how it was spoken on by most in the days following. Trenchmouth didn't do talking of any sort. Mostly he drank. Drank to sleep. But his slumber was ravaged with the kind of nightmares reserved for men who kill other men, and when he sat up alone in his new hideout, he thought his heart might explode from the force of blood coursing through it. More than once, he put his revolver to his head.

At midnight on June 1st, the same day Sid was arrested in Huntington for sharing a hotel room with Mayor Testerman's widow, Trenchmouth ran out of moonshine. It was time to leave the hideout, something he'd not done in ten days. There was only one place that called to him. Home.

He kept to the dark insides of the ridges skirting Warm Hollow. He moved as a tracker moves, without rustling ground, without any sound, as the Widow had trained him to. When he'd circled the house twice and convinced himself no one was there that shouldn't be, he walked through the front door.

Both women were seated at the kitchen table. Both had nothing but their undergarments on, and they fanned themselves alternately with the Sears Roebuck. They looked at him there in the doorway like they'd expected him at that very moment. "I reckon we can say he's alive then," the Widow said to Clarissa, who laughed so that she hog-snorted in between. It was the laugh of someone desperate not to cry. Trenchmouth took off his muddied boots and closed the door behind him. He watched Clarissa cackle. Then the Widow started in.

The women were sweaty, and they were drunk.

On the table between them was a lantern, and next to it, a jar of the house pull. The best blend. Trenchmouth felt his stomach lurch, his tongue swell at the sight of it. He walked to the table clumsily and reached out for the jar. When he got there, the Widow kicked him in the shin and smacked his face hard. She pulled the moonshine to her breast and held it there as if it was a child. The laughter was over with. "You ain't earned the right," she told him. "Ain't even truthfully lived here since you was a boy, not in your mind. Not in your body for damn near six months."

Clarissa got up and hugged him. She felt his shoulders, his back, his arms. Gripped at him to make sure he was real. For Trenchmouth, it was like the time with her on the train all over again. Electric. He rested his head on her shoulder and they stayed like this.

The Widow paid the display no mind. "I believe those detectives reaped what they sewn. But if you had the kind of hand in it they say you did, well . . ." She looked at the top of her boy's head there on her girl's shoulder, the two of them swaying, Clarissa because she was drunk and heard music that wasn't there, Trenchmouth because he'd fall if he didn't follow. "I'm your mother," the Widow said. "I'll help you. But you got to get out of Mingo altogether now. That's all there is to it."

Clarissa began to hum in his ear. "Down by the O-H-I-O" she hummed, fast and joyful. She'd heard it on Fred Dallara's new gramophone. They were set to be married in August.

But at Fred's place, on Fred's shoulder, she'd never felt like this. This was happiness in the face of death and impending warrants for arrest. This was child's glee in the shadows of a shitstorm waiting to break loose. Her brother was alive, she thought, and then, just as quick, she thought of Fred Dallara again. The fancy word *fiancée*. But Clarissa kept smiling because she was drunk and because it seemed funny to her in that little, crumbling house that her fiancée didn't drink moonshine. That he thought those who did were mountain trash. Fred Dallara thought the union was foolish at best, dangerous and worthy of breaking at worst. So to keep her laugh from turning to a cry, she stopped thinking of the man she was to marry then. She hummed louder in Trenchmouth's ear. Led him in a made-up procession of steps across the creaking floorboards. She hummed and sang what few words she knew: "put my arms around her and kiss her again, down by the Ohio, she's just a simple little country girl I know." Clarissa sang loud enough so that she no longer heard the Widow, and neither did Trenchmouth, as she said to him, her boy, "tomorrow you'll eat what I've got to fix, say what goodbyes you need to say, and be gone."

The next morning, Trenchmouth walked creekbeds forty pounds heavier. The Widow had pulled an infantryman's pack from a trunk

in the loft and filled it. Her uncle Homer had worn it in defense of
the Confederacy during the Civil War. Her father had fought against
Homer, his own brother-in-law, wearing a similar Union pack, but
somebody had taken it off him while he lay holding his breath,
pretending to be dead, at Kessler's Cross Lanes. Somehow, her father
had managed to hand down the enemy's backpack to his daughter.
It was a dusty monstrosity, but it had held up. Black canvas, brass
mounts, it rode high up on a man's back. The compartments were
plentiful. While her boy had slept inside exhaustion's relief, she'd
filled each one with what she knew he'd need. Moonshine. Dried
beet and water canteen. A jar of the mouthwash concoction she'd
made for his condition. Anything that held long and packed little. In
one compartment she'd packed just before he walked out the door
was something he'd never seen. "It was my husband's," she'd said,
"Richard's. Your Daddy had he lived to be." It was a big silver flask
with an intricate etch. She showed him how it worked. The bottom
left section released with the press of a thumbnail-sized catch at the
cap. Inside the released section, completely encased, was a Double
Derringer, silver like its housing. "Like he did before you, use what's
here with temperance," she told him. She meant both the shine and
the pistol.

Even with four boxes of fifty rimfire cartridges, .22 longs at that,
there was room in the pack for a few of his own things. His real
daddy's harmonica. Map and compass. A pen, pocket knife, and
hunting knife. Paper and pencil.

He was almost to Arly Scott's house when the pack grew heavy
on his shoulders. He switched his rifle's strap from his left to right
shoulder and back, but it never rode comfortable next to the pack.

They were sitting on a wide chopblock in the dirt patch behind
the house, Sr. and Jr., praying in song. Mrs. Scott stood above them,

her eyes shut and her fists half-clenched. She sang, "Whoa, Satan's like a snake in the grass," and the two men answered, "That's what Satan's grumbling bout." Mrs. Scott went up a pitch, "He going bite and conjure you," and again they answered her, "That's what Satan's grumbling bout." Then, together, they intoned, "And I won't stop prayin, I won't stop prayin, I won't stop prayin, that's what Satan's grumbling bout." Trenchmouth stood behind a rhododendron bush and waited until they'd finished. Had they kept on, he could have listened all day. He'd lost God somewhere along the way, but in that sound, in their voices, he could almost feel him again. When he'd wiped the wet from his eyes, he approached.

"Every time I see you, I shouldn't be seein you," Arly Sr. said without standing up. He acted as if it was no surprise that the boy would appear out of the woods nearly two weeks after the shootout, a shootout Arly Sr. had not been a part of. His nephew Benjamin Belcher had decided to move back to Georgia and had picked the morning of May 19th to leave. Arlys Sr. and Jr. had heard about the bloodshed in the tent colony as they shoved bedding into a trunk. By the time they arrived, the dead were lined up, their blood had soured black, and Trenchmouth was off and running.

"I'm on my way to disappear," Trenchmouth said. Mrs. Scott turned from him without acknowledgment when he nodded to her. She went inside shaking her head.

"You want some coffee?" Arly Jr. asked. Trenchmouth nodded that he would and Arly Jr. followed his mother through the screen door.

Arly Sr. struck a kitchen match against his thumbnail and lit a skinny cigar slow and even. "I ain't going to ask you about how many you shot," he said. Both looked down and neither spoke for a full minute. There was a bullfrog calling from the grass within spitting distance. "I see you got you a backpack. Going to be gone for a while."

It was the kind of small talk that meant something. "Don't forget your push-ups. Sit-ups and jumping-jacks too now." Arly Sr. turned his head quickly toward the front of the house. He extinguished the cigar on his boot heel and stood up. Automobile engine. "Our guns is hid," he said to Trenchmouth. "You got another one?" The Colt Cop & Thug was where it always was, where it had worn two small sores next to his spine. He pulled it from his waist and handed it to Arly Sr.

"It's Sid and Kump," Arly Jr. hollered from inside.

Everybody eased up.

The five men met in front of the house. Sid Hatfield had taken to stopping by the Scott's more and more. Some thought it was because he knew Trenchmouth would turn up there. Other folks said he wanted to enlist the Arlys for dirty work, as they'd stayed clean on the 19th. As they were colored and therefore more expendable somehow. Either way, they all stood together that early summer morning, Sid lazily leaning against Kump's Model T, Kump fidgeting and looking generally malformed about the face and neck. The other three were guarded, uncomfortable even. Trenchmouth couldn't look at Kump since he'd seen him shoot men who were already dead.

"More trouble comin down," Sid said. He looked Trenchmouth in the eyes like he was mad the young man had taken his advice and found a hideout he couldn't locate.

"Anse Pilcher going to testify against Sid," Kump said. He was too excited for anybody's taste, and he was only there because he had an automobile. "Anse been runnin his mouth, claims he seed Sid blow up the tipple at Tomahawk way back." But they all knew that had been Trenchmouth's doing. He'd lit that fuse.

The message was there: Do away with Anse Pilcher, proprietor of the Urias Hotel, friend to the Baldwin-Felts men, quick-handed smiter of the women he employed to please them, Ewart included. Anse Pilcher, the soft-boned cripple who'd let Frank Dallara burn. Trenchmouth's neckhairs stood up at the mention of his name.

Sid said nothing, just kept staring at Trenchmouth. Then, without unlocking his stare, he said to Arly Sr., "You reckon I might get at one of them cigars you roll?"

"Come on in the house," Arly Sr. said. They went up the porch steps. Below them, Kump climbed into the driver's seat and shifted two rifles to make room in the backseat. Halfway inside the door to his house, Arly Sr. turned and watched his boy climb into the beat-up Model T, Trenchmouth following him. The look on Sr.'s face was unfamiliar to those who knew him, for rarely did he display fear or uncertainty. Inside, Sid Hatfield spoke to Mrs. Scott, who held her hands tight against one another to stop them from shaking. She did not return the sheriff's greeting, for had she parted the lips set against a worry with no end, she surely could not stifle the cry caught in her throat.

At one a.m., from the roof of the dead Testerman's jewelry store, Kump, Arly Jr., and Trenchmouth lay prone and alert as they had done on strikebreaker duty in McDowell so long before. Kump and Arly were getting anxious. They knew Trenchmouth had long since lined up a clean shot through the second story window of the Urias Café. It was just across the street, an easy distance for the crack shot. Kump, always oblivious, kept saying, "Blow his brains out, T.T." Arly bit his tongue, assuming that his friend, having had to kill just days before, might now find killing an undoable act. And, on any other night, with any other target, he may have been right. Trenchmouth had thought long and hard in his hideout on never again taking another man's life. But what he saw through the frosted glass of the

Urias Hotel ended such thoughts of reform in a hurry.

Through the notch and groove on his rifle, everything, as usual, was magnified. But his target had grown more complicated. For most in the throes of the mine wars, Trenchmouth didn't need much more reason to shoot Anse Pilcher than he already had. But the hotel owner had made killing even easier. As Anse sipped from a bottle hidden under the serving counter, he pretended not to notice one of his customers, the only man in the place at that late, closed-for-business hour. The man groped at one of the young ladies who worked the hotel. The lady was Ewart Smith. The customer giving the unwanted attention was Hob Tibbs.

Trenchmouth wondered if one more squeeze of his trigger would end his service to the union. And if the recipient of that squeeze was Anse Pilcher, friend of the enemy, murderer of Frank Dallara, and abuser of his one-time girl, then he could surely bring himself to do it. Now two targets had given themselves over to him, but he'd already decided he only owed one shot. He could reconcile this problem.

Most folks would never believe he planned what happened next, but most folks never truly knew Trenchmouth Taggart. In the end, the reason he was stalling on taking the shot had nothing to do with his conscience or nerves. It had everything to do with compass points, geometry lines. Trenchmouth was waiting for a pattern to take shape, and when it did, he squeezed his one allotted squeeze.

He had aimed the shot so that it hit Anse Pilcher in the chest, where soft bone and cartilage could not slow it down as it passed in and out of a chamber of his heart, between two flaccid ribs in his back, across the small room and into the left cheek of Hob Tibbs, where it lodged and burned like hell's blue tips and caused him to release his grip on Ewart Smith's bosom, fall from his wobbly parlor chair, and scramble for the coat closet where he prayed to his

God and pissed his cotton drawers.

Arly Jr. and Kump looked at one another with open mouths as Trenchmouth stood from his position and jumped off the roof onto the lower one next door. From there, he dropped himself to the street and ran to the Urias. He scrambled upstairs, grabbed Ewart by the forearm, and ran back down again. When he shoved her into the car in front of him, Kump already had the engine idling, and the three of them, Kump, Arly Jr., and Ewart, were incapable of speech. Throttle was all that was managed. And it was almost enough. They'd made it a quarter mile out of town and onto an unnamed road when the grade became too steep. The Model T quit again. "Son of a bitch," Arly Jr. said, finally breaking the silence. Ewart tried to dab Hob Tibbs's blood off her summer corset. "You didn't fill the tank again?" Arly hollered.

The veins on Kump's neck swelled. "Don't no nigger talk to me like that," he said.

Ewart and Trenchmouth watched the two men from the back seat. Kump looked straight ahead and put the vehicle in neutral. Arly looked hard at Kump. "What did you say?" They were drifting back down the hill now, fast. Ewart kept at the stains and tried not to cry. Arly said again, "What did you say?"

Kump managed to get the thing turned around, same as Arly had done the first time in McDowell. But now *his* hands were on the wheel, and he ignored the repeated question from the comrade to his right. They started to climb the hill backwards. But it was too steep a grade, steeper than the one in McDowell, and they kept stalling out in reverse.

Halfway up, another Model T turned onto the unnamed hill. This one was a 1920, a coupe, and its gas tank was lower to the ground. It came up the incline quick, and before Kump could manage another go in reverse, the smaller, faster automobile was within any man's range. It stopped.

"Get out," Trenchmouth said to the two up front, as he slowly opened his door and took hold of Ewart's forearm again.

A man stepped from either side of the coupe. Neither spoke a word and each raised a pistol.

Trenchmouth reached back for the Colt tucked into his pants and found nothing. He'd given it to Arly Sr. that morning. He grabbed his backpack from between his feet. "Get out now," Trenchmouth said, and he did so himself, pulling Ewart to the ground next to the car.

"No. I damn near got it. Let me just—" Kump's mouth exploded before he finished. The same place he'd been shot before, only worse, and they kept coming. One split the middle of his nosebridge. His feet ceased to work as the rest of him did too, and the vehicle careened forward, down the hill toward the men unloading all they could. Arly Jr. bailed out of the moving mess with a bullet in his left shoulder. He hit the ground fifteen yards down from Trenchmouth and Ewart. Trenchmouth pulled Ewart across the ground into the brush beside the road. When they got there, the shooting ceased as the two men had to crouch and shield themselves with their hands as a car piloted by a dead man smashed into their own, grill against grill. Glass broke up and spread out everywhere, but the coupe had stopped the heavier touring car, and Kump had come through the windshield to rest face down on the hood, dead as the car below him.

Arly Jr. tried to get up from the road, but he'd hit the ground hard, and he had a bullet in him. The men stood back upright, their pistols reloaded. Trenchmouth, with no weapon other than the flask derringer tucked deep in his pack, did not go to his friend. A voice ordered Arly to raise his hands up and he did so. Convinced they weren't going to shoot Arly, Trenchmouth whispered to Ewart to stay quiet and they began crawling into the woods.

The voice called out, "You remember me, nigger?" Then, "Mose, get after the one that run off up there." Trenchmouth and Ewart crawled faster, then stood up and ran. But Trenchmouth could still hear the voice as they went, and though it was faint, he recognized it somehow. "You think you can whoop me again for callin you what you are? I growed a little, ain't I?" They were just out of earshot, all-out clambering up the hillside thick with trees when he knew for certain: Warren Crews.

CHAPTER FIFTEEN

WHO HAS WORN AND WHO HAS BROKEN?

There was a battalion of the 19th infantry regiment deployed to Mingo County, after pleas from the governor for help to stop the killing. Coal operators were pleased. Martial law had been declared, meetings and demonstrations banned, the carrying of firearms outlawed. The green fisted could stop looking over their shoulders. Mr. Bern reported all of it in the *New York Times,* and people all over, just like people in Matewan and Red Jacket and Williamson, split on who was right and who was wrong. Newly appointed mine guards like Warren and Mose Crews walked a little taller with the army backing them. Behind closed doors, they pistol-whipped Arly Scott Jr. and asked him again and again, "Who else was in the vehicle?" He never spoke a word.

Ann Sharples saw the butt end of a gun herself. Anse Pilcher had been a friend to those with influence, and when Ann Sharples answered their whereabouts questions with words like, "Ewart's gone back to Tennessee," and "I never heard of no Trenchmouth," they hit her, hard, because it was easy for them to do it. Whores were used to catching beatings.

It was George Crews's men who did most of it. Warren and Mose's father had risen to the rank of president of the White Star Mining Company in Merrimack. His wife, a former customer of Trenchmouth's, had died of typhoid fever, though some folks claimed syphilis, and George was less concerned with his public image. He was set on breaking those that defied him.

Arly Sr., angry that his boy was being held on murder charges without any proof he'd pulled the trigger, organized men in secret and consoled his wife who wished they'd left for Georgia with the Belchers on May 19th. She didn't get out of bed much.

Sid Hatfield beat his murder rap. He and twenty-two other defendants were acquitted of all murder charges stemming from the May 19th shootout. It was a circus of smiles and back-patting for all except those kin and friend to Al and Lee Felts. They just stood and swore revenge to themselves. Some Felts sympathizers grumbled that one defendant wasn't even present in order to get acquitted. "The tooth boy," one man said to a reporter. "He done shot up most of the law men that day, all on his own." Some said the tooth boy had shot Anse Pilcher and skipped town back in summer. Others said that was wrong, that the killer in that incident was already in custody. It was the colored boy they said. The one with too much pride for a colored boy.

So Sid walked free unlike young Arly, and folks just accepted this as proper. Sid was a man of the law. In this manner it became clear that to most folks, Arly Jr. was nothing more than what Warren Crews had said he was, a nigger.

But men will fight together though their reasons be different. So it was that after martial law was gone, on a May Thursday, almost a year to the day since the shootout, the steady flow of scabs returning to the coalfields would think twice yet again. George Crews's town of Merrimack was laid bare. Striking miners hacked away the telephone and telegraph lines strung across tree-covered hills. A cow horn signaled the start of the shooting, which lasted three days. Homes and businesses, mine property and scabs, officers of the law, all felt the destruction of 10,000 bullets.

After the Three Days' Battle, folks were used to sleeping in their cellars for fear of stray shells. Strikebreakers quit scabbing, lucky to draw breath, as their buddies had been carried from the woods without any left. The governor pleaded with the new president, Warren Harding, for more troops. He was not heard.

Sid Hatfield continued to walk his streets, now as an elected constable, with men at his back and pistols on his side. But a new charge arose, one which linked him and Ed Chambers to the dynamiting of a coal tipple at Red Jacket. Trenchmouth had been the one to blow up that tipple, his knowledge of its construction a handy skill in knocking down such a beast. But Sid was arrested and would be tried alongside Ed in Welch, McDowell County. The site was four miles down the mountain from where Trenchmouth now hid with Ewart, under cover of the steepest terrain the Southern Appalachians offered. Surviving on what most never could.

He'd built them a little shelter, camouflaged of course. There was trip wire and a noisemaker to warn of potential intruders. They ate okay. The Widow's provisions lasted a while, and Trenchmouth laid traps for squirrels and rabbits, even fished some in a nearby stream. Winter had been tough, but they managed. They lived like a young couple might have in the pioneer days. They laid down together and the awkwardness of their first attempt faded. Kisses on the mouth accompanied such routines, but Trenchmouth never opened his lips.

The moonshine was rationed into nightly portions, with Ewart permitted to sample only on Saturday. The Widow's mouthrinse concoction also threatened to run out, and when it did, his condition would start to require more moonshine. This was a problem. He scratched at his thin, forming beard and read again and again the note he'd found from the Widow inside the pack. *Get to Dr. Warble in Welch when you can. He's a fine dentist, and one of my best customers. I reckon he's one of the few who truly knows the source of his supply, as he and Richard were good friends. Warble knows how to put in the gold crowns, and if you plan to be gone from here for a while, those teeth will need to be fixed for fear of more infection and pain.* It was nearing time to visit the good doctor who had given him his name.

Trenchmouth knew things. Current events, folks called them. He even knew of the impending August 1st trial of his two-gun buddy. This was all because Ewart walked into Welch now and again for the paper, careful to keep her face down, to not draw attention. It was on one of these visits that she met Dr. Warble at his office and told him of Trenchmouth's oral situation. She made an appointment for her man on August 1st at four a.m., as he'd asked her to. She also told the good doctor what she hadn't told Trenchmouth yet. She was fairly certain that she carried a child.

She left Welch that morning feeling good for having told someone. Now, she supposed, she could tell her man. She didn't even keep her head tucked as she walked back toward the hills, didn't keep to the alleys. By this point, more than a year had passed since the shootout, and no one much cared what had become of the crazy, dead preacher's whore of a daughter. Trenchmouth, on the other hand, was a man, who, as a juvenile, could be linked to more than one murder, though some would call it self-defense.

Ewart told him of her pregnancy and he was happy. But he didn't say much on it. In those days, he didn't say much of anything. Mostly, he thought. He thought about giving up the gun. There were nights when he pledged to himself to never raise a firearm to another man again, and there were nights when this seemed impossible. He thought about how he couldn't remember things. Things from childhood and things from yesterday. Things from moments when he supposedly took men's lives or handled snakes or dug up a dead man who was his father. The quiet of the woods made memories turn to dreams. He wondered if he could not remember things because of all the moonshine he'd drunk over the years. While he wondered, he sipped moonshine. It was, and had always been, the only way to get to sleep.

Ewart lost the baby in late July. There was so much blood that Trenchmouth thought about picking her up and running to town, giving up on hiding altogether. But she told him it would stop soon enough. That it happened some. That it was early enough along where she'd be fine. Coming from her line of work, Ewart had experience with such realities.

He rubbed her back and stomach where she ached. He blew on her hot forehead while she slept.

When he left at two-thirty on the dark morning of August 1st, he carried his derringer flask. He wore plain clothes, a set the Widow had packed him. On his head, a found golfer's hat, something he'd not be caught dead in were he a free man. His beard was patchy, but it was enough to cover his youth.

The plan was to be in and out of Dr. Warble's chair by ten a.m., gold-toothed and swollen and costumed. Moonshine and mouthrinse replenished. He'd be able to watch Sid Hatfield go into court from the cover of the inevitable crowds. Watching wouldn't do much for Sid, Trenchmouth reckoned, but he felt it was right somehow. Not that he owed Sid or anybody else, but he'd feel better being there. It wasn't right to let it all go just yet.

Dr. Warble was standing in the dark street at four. The two of them went in the back door to his office without a word. They only nodded. Inside, Trenchmouth took a seat in the chair. He took out a small wad of all that money he'd saved from the hideout ladies, but Dr. Warble shook his head. "It's not necessary," he said. "Your mother has been good to me. I owe her right plenty. But I do have something for you." He pulled four jars of moonshine and one of mouthrinse from the top shelf of a locked cabinet. He did not say another word about the Widow, just smiled as he set them down next to Trenchmouth's pack.

It was dark in there save one glaring light in the center of the room, just above the chair. It stunk of medicinals, burned the nostrils to breathe. Dr. Warble was readying things. "I'm going to give you some nitrous oxide through this mask," he said. Then, pointing to another one, he said, "and through this one, I'll drop something called diethyl ether." It was a gauze contraption that would fit over Trenchmouth's face. "I can drop as much or as little as I need to keep you asleep and not feeling a thing. Understand?"

"Yessir," Trenchmouth said.

"Good."

Sid Hatfield had two gold teeth. Trenchmouth would be getting eight. Four top, four bottom. The molars would stay as is, but folks couldn't see those. No one would ever have to look at his old teeth again.

The gas came, and Trenchmouth went.

In his dream, everything was tomato red. He stood in the hollow by his boyhood home, by the outhouse. By Beechnut the mule and the well. All of it was clear but hazed over somehow, smeared the color of iodine. He looked around him at the mountains. They shook at the tops almost unnoticeably. Quick shivers, like a man in a seizure that passes fast. But the quiver in these mountains wasn't passing. It kept up, became accompanied by a howl. It was high-pitched and wobbly, like a woman wailing, a whistle electrified. Then, as he watched through the red glow, the mountains came down. They crumbled as nothing he'd ever seen, as if someone had pulled the ground out from under them and they had no other recourse but to fold in on themselves. It was horrifying. The mountains were no more. And then it was over.

When he woke up, his cheeks were stuffed with bloody gauze and Dr. Warble was nowhere to be found. He felt for his pocket watch. His head was hard to lift and his face felt like it was no longer there. It was past noon.

Trenchmouth stood and fell back down against the chair. It was quiet and the window blinds told him it was overcast outside. He picked up his moonshine-loaded backpack, breathed in deep and stood again, stumbled to the door.

Coming out of the alley, he saw the police, state and otherwise, congregating around the courthouse steps. He stepped back into the alley and heard the footfalls of a man approaching. Trenchmouth put his hand on the derringer flask tucked into his belt and turned to face the man. It was Mr. Bern, the *New York Times* reporter. He was dressed in a gray suit and fedora hat. His pants were cut too long.

"Hey fella," he said. "You don't look so good." Bern did not recognize the man he knew as reporter Ben Chicopee.

Trenchmouth managed to say, "What happened?" through the gauze and swelling.

"You mean at the courthouse? What'd you just walk out the forest, friend?"

Mr. Bern got a stare that seemed familiar to him, frightened him, and impelled him to answer all at once. He frowned and said, "Sid

Hatfield and Ed Chambers were shot down going up the steps to trial. Five, maybe eight bullets apiece by all counts. Right in front of the Mrs. Missuses? How do you write that plural?" For him, the world was words. He took a pencil from behind his ear and a pad from his jacket pocket. He never got to writing. Trenchmouth knocked both from his grip and kicked the man in the groin. He didn't wait to see him drop and moan, just peered around the brick building again to look at the courthouse. At what he couldn't approach, what he'd missed altogether.

He wondered for a moment if this was real or if he was still in Warble's chair. Inside his dream where everything buckled and howled and rocked to the ground. But the only thing buckled here was Mr. Bern, and Trenchmouth walked slowly over to him, knelt down and lifted the man's wallet, complete with press credentials. He wasn't sure why, it just seemed right.

Then he moved on past Bern toward the edge of town, his face beginning to throb, the four fresh jars of mountain magic beginning to call to him like they hadn't since the dark days of the previous May. He stopped. In his ether stupor, he'd not asked Mr. Bern the question now echoing in his mind: who pulled the trigger? But he stood there only a moment or so before walking on. It was a question whose answer required more shooting. More killing and running and hiding, without end. He'd not ask it. He'd not do anything but walk away.

Sid Hatfield was dead and gone, and the Trenchmouth who came back from Welch that day was not the one who left. He drank. Hard. He was unable to speak to or look at the woman who'd lost his unborn child. He considered the last two years of his life, let himself think too much on what he'd done. They were thoughts so powerful that even the moonshine couldn't keep them at bay. When a man has killed another, one way or the other, he has to think on what he's done. And when he does, when he really thinks about taking away a life that could have been lived, he'll break. And that's what Trenchmouth did.

He left Ewart in the middle of the night. There was a note that said he was sorry. Some money. Enough food to hold her a little while.

This time he went deep enough that no one would find him. He walked straight into the hills of Mercer County, bordering the Blue Ridge. These were big hills. Big enough so that when a man let himself be swallowed by them, he couldn't walk a few miles for a newspaper or some dried goods. He couldn't know what would come to be in his absence down below.

He couldn't know that his woman, on her way to her grandmother's in Tennessee, only made it as far as Keystone, McDowell County. Keystone was a street of taverns. Whorehouse row. Come one, come all, they said, and men listened. A writer from neighboring Virginia wrote of the place. *The Sodom and Gomorrah of Today* he called it. Ewart said she'd stay a couple nights. Then a week. Then six months.

Trenchmouth couldn't know that Arly Jr. had his day in court. That he received a sentence of life imprisonment in the West Virginia State Penitentiary at Moundsville. Guilty, they called the young boxer who'd hoped to be a middleweight contender. Guilty of the murder of Anse Pilcher. Trenchmouth's last trigger squeeze through the Urias Hotel window had ruined the life of his only friend.

He couldn't know that Charles Lively, the Baldwin-Felts spy who'd posed as a union-friendly Matewan restaurant owner, had been the one who pulled the trigger in Welch and then planted guns on Sid Hatfield and Ed Chambers. Self-defense is what Lively had called it.

So had the courts.

Trenchmouth couldn't know that two thousand people lined the streets of Matewan for Sid Hatfield's funeral procession. They walked, some shouting sorrow, across the Tug on a bridge that swayed under their masses. Workers put down their shovels and picks and hammers for an hour of the working day, state-wide. The *New York Times* gave the funeral front page.

It all added up to more striking and more bloodshed. And, finally, it built to the amassing of ten thousand armed men, miners and otherwise, from all over the state. They rode in on outlaw trains and walked ridges on foot. They would meet their enemy at Blair Mountain, in Logan County, and it would be a war to end all wars. Bill Blizzard fired them up, and few failed to march. The infantry was brought in to hold them back, as was a squadron of army planes, dispatched from Langley. Men were to be rained upon by the airborne machine guns and gas bombs of their own nation's military. But it did not come to pass. Instead, President Harding dropped from his planes an order to lay down arms. The order was followed by the miners, but only after they'd seen more die, covered and carried to the awaiting train cars.

There were those who wished the rotten-toothed teenager with the dead-eye aim had been among them in the Battle of Blair Mountain. Or that he'd been at Sid Hatfield's side on the Welch Courthouse steps. "He'd have dropped em all," some said. But mostly that boy was forgotten in the sorrows of those years. His mother, the Widow Dorsett, did not forget. She thought of him while she tended her still, dreamed of him when she slept. Clarissa did not forget. She thought of him as she bore Fred Dallara a second child and cooked and cleaned and changed diapers and stopped talking a streak like she used to. Nor did her husband forget the boy who had once attacked him like an animal. Fred Dallara was a suit, an executive with the White Star Coal Company. Two of his fellow suits, Mose and Warren Crews, spoke daily to him on their belief that Trenchmouth Taggart was somewhere close-by, maybe on high with his cheek to a rifle. They called him a murderer. They said he'd show himself someday, that they'd get him if it took five years, and they asked folks questions, watched them close. Like Hob Tibbs, these men came to spend their days and nights back-looking over shoulders and sniffing the air like dogs. It was the only way to be ready for Trenchmouth Taggart.

They didn't know that the wilderness had taken him.

BOOK TWO 1946–1961

The blues is our antidote,
and Long Tongue, The Blues Merchant,
is our doctor.

—Jerome Washington

CHAPTER SIXTEEN

IT WAS REGIMENTED LIVING

The jack-in-the-pulpit had yet to fully flower. Its middle, a straight column through a leafy tunnel, gave the small plant the look of a butter churn. A gnat landed on the leaf's hooded arc and went still. The wind swayed the flower, and the gnat stayed put, until, for reasons unknown, it flew down into the striped column and waited there, trapped and dying slowly.

The canopy above was thick, not unusual for May. Fifty foot trees gave shade and relief from the sun. Below, a box turtle with a reddish head stepped deliberate past the jack-in-the-pulpit, paying the flower's capture no mind. The turtle's shell was smooth as a bowling ball, evidencing its antiquity. Behind the turtle, the ridge fell off into a short but steep slope, and at the bottom of the slope lay a grass bald. It was small, the size of a football field, halved. At the far end of it, a man hung a door on his newly constructed outhouse. He held nails in his teeth and his hands said he'd wielded a hammer plenty.

The man's name was Clarence Dickason, originally from Big

Stone Gap, Virginia. He was a fifty-two year old with skin as black as his grandmother's, a woman born into Virginia slavery. Like her, he sang while he worked. He'd been doing a good deal of it in recent weeks, raising a small house before he framed the two-seater latrine quarters. On this May evening, he was expecting his wife and children to join him from down the mountain, in Bluefield, after some time of living apart. He put his hammer in a toolbox sitting atop a rough-cut sawhorse. Through the nails still in his teeth, he sang, "Well, lovers is you right? Oh, yes we right. Bluefield women read and write, Keystone women bite and fight, carry to the mountain boys, carry to the mountain."

Clarence Dickason was sharp-eyed still, despite his years of hard-living. But he did not detect the man above him, flat-bellied on the ridge's edge. The figure was thin and long. He wore nothing on his callused feet. The man's beard mixed with ground cover as if he had grown into it. Had he been standing upright, the beard would reach his belly. His hair was to his shoulders. Matted. The wrinkles surrounding his eyes were many and deep. Like those on his forehead, they recessed and housed the kind of dirt that cannot be washed away.

As the sun dropped behind the poplar trees circling the bald, it shone on the mountain man's face. Lit him up. He squinted, the only movement he'd made in an hour's time, and as he breathed in the evening air through his mouth, the sunlight reflected momentarily off the gold inside.

The thatched hut was on a mountain stairstep. It was the lee side of a steep ridge, three-thousand feet in the air. Weather tended to move west to east, and this kept the whole place relatively free from the worst storms could offer. The hut's doorway faced southeast to let in morning sun. It didn't take long to heat. There was enough room to stand or lie down inside, little else. Insulation was thick, half a foot of leaves, ferns, and mosses packed and mortar-solid. A bedding of cattail and grass took up most of the floor, while the pointed ceiling housed a storage space. In it was a rolled-up thatched blanket for winter, alongside a rotting backpack full of a man's tools for sustenance. A door plug constructed of bark slabs leaned against a wall.

The fire pit was six paces from the door, the mountain stream fifty.

Between them, feet braced under a thick, hillside root, the mountain man counted out his sit-ups. "Sixty-four, sixty-five, sixty-six, sixty-seven." He'd taken to inclined sit-ups when flat became too easy. Each morning he completed a hundred. Then the same for push-ups. Then jumping jacks. Best he could figure, he averaged seven miles daily of running in temperate months, all on incline, all barefoot until the cold came.

His clothes were sewn together pieces of former clothes. He'd strung belts of vine and leather. On the belts were loops for carrying knives of both the steel-forged and bone variety. Pouches held greenbrier berries and ginseng tubers and ramps, the latter of which he ate five a day, most times raw, for he was convinced of their power to keep him young. His pores sweated their stink. The man ate grasshoppers and slugs and katydids.

When he hit one hundred, he sat, his feet still wedged under tree root. "Please don't be fearful," he said aloud. "I make my home in these parts. My name is Chicopee." He'd forgotten some things and remembered others, like the fake name he'd once heard. "My name is Chicopee," he said again. He was rehearsing speech for a time when he might introduce himself to the new neighbors down the mountain, the first human beings he'd set eyes on in twenty-four years.

"Chicopee," he said again. Then he pulled his feet from under the root, somersaulted backwards down the hill twice, sprung himself upright and began to run. His skin was tough, a tanned hide with muscles rolling and clenching underneath, hard as the bones they rode. While he ran, he sang, "Bluefield women read and write, Keystone women bite and fight, carry to the mountain boys, carry to the mountain."

The dug-up dead man's harmonica had not touched lips since 1902. Chicopee had stared at the small instrument by firelight for the first two years on the mountain. But he'd never put it to his mouth in those early days. He'd read its intricate engraving aloud. *Marine Band. M. Hohner. No. 1896.* Tarnished brass on pearwood, a beautiful little mouth harp. It was only when he'd started having conversations aloud with himself that he played it. "You got gold teeth now, Chicopee," he'd said on a cold October night in 1925. "Can't no infections bust through solid gold." And so he'd started playing. In a year, he cupped that harmonica to his face as if it was another extension of his hand. As if, like his teeth, it was made from the earth's most valued currency. His tongue hit those ten holes serpent-quick. He blew hard and soft and medium, shook twenty reeds side to side until they howled and moaned almost to breaking. It became his four inch path to salvation, to avoiding hysteria nightly.

Now he only played on occasion. When something threatened the peace he'd finally come to. A brewing storm. Two or more days of rain. Neighbors.

He played every song he'd ever heard, in one version or another. Most oft-played were two songs. "Down by the Ohio," was one. Though he couldn't know it through the confusion that stirred his brain, he played this song because a woman walked the earth, one who'd kissed him and sang in his ear. One named Clarissa. The other tune was "I Won't Stop Praying," and again, though he couldn't place its origin any longer, it somehow told him that a friend might still live and breathe. A friend with a mama who sang for the sins of all men. A friend named Arly Jr.

As May turned to June, Chicopee blew a new tune. He'd heard his new neighbor sing it, a song about women and places he'd not thought of in years. Places like Bluefield and Keystone, Mercer and McDowell. Coalfield towns like the one he came from. Railroad towns. He'd heard a human voice other than his own down in that grass bald, and it got him to thinking. Out there all those years, until he'd heard the song of Clarence Dickason, until he'd seen the man building an outhouse, he'd almost come to accept that he'd made all of it up. That all those blurry memories of a rotten-toothed childhood were the mind tricks of a man who'd lived always and only among trees and turtles and deer and mud, a man touched in the head. None of that other had ever existed, save in dreams. People and coal tipples and trains and sling-shots and rifle sights and mules and outhouses and the nether-regions of women and snakes and tongue-talkers and Model T Fords. These were made up things.

But here was a harmonica. And here was a flask with a gun inside. And here was a memory of a woman named Widow, saying, "Keep this here flask on you. It's a magical flask. A never-ending flask. As much as you sip its shine, it will refill and keep you in peace." And he had sipped. And it *had* refilled, like magic. Its contents kept him going. And on its silver surface, and on the bark-stripped sides of a shagbark hickory tree when flask space was used up, he'd notched the days and weeks and months and years since coming here to the mountaintop. Those notches totaled 9,069 days. 1,295 weeks. 298 months. After a while, he forgot what they stood for, those little etches. His pen knife dulled and the tip broke off from etching time's passage. So, he began to sharpen the little pecker bones he cut from raccoons he'd tracked and trapped. Their hides made winter hats, their ribs wind-chimes. And their rock-sharpened peckers, the etchers of time.

Tonight, he etched another line on the tree next to his fire. It was June 1st, 1946. He looked up at all the little notches. The fire made the time-marks wobble and dance. "Please don't be fearful," the mountain man said aloud to the tree. "My name is Chicopee."

Then, as he sometimes did, he got out the derringer flask. He practiced, again and again, the fluid, complicated motions of retrieving the gun inside. The trip latch was greased with milkweed oil. He could draw the hidden weapon in four seconds.

That night, he checked his supply of .22 shells. Still two boxes. He loaded the gun and did what he needed to stay sharp-eyed.

The acorn didn't have a chance. Even at night, even thrown twenty feet into the air, he could line up his shot and put a hole through it. Magnified. Microscopic.

CHAPTER SEVENTEEN

THEY WOULD STARE

By mid-June, it was hot enough to wash in the mountain stream. Chicopee stripped naked, shoved an acorn up each nosehole, and laid down in the clear, moving water. He held a tree root in his fist to keep himself steady against the current. His feet pointed upstream, his head down, so that his beard washed back over his face. He raked through it with the fingers of his free hand. When he stood up afterwards, he wrung out his hair and beard. Then he did a little drip-dry dance, still naked, to help along the sun streaks hitting him through tree cover.

In the storage space of the upper hut, he dug out a pair of slacks and a shirt that had remained intact. The shirt was a yellowed white and the slacks were black. Tucked in, bearded, and barefoot, he looked like an actor in a stage play, a caricature of the Hatfields and McCoys.

He put the harmonica in his shirtfront pocket, the derringer flask in his pants.

He started down the mountain with the aid of a walking stick, one he'd cut and carved himself. It was twisted sassafras, stripped and dried. Head high, the staff allowed him to maneuver on the most drastic of inclines. Over the years, he'd speared fourteen copperheads with its sharpened end.

Chicopee approached the ridge drop-off where he'd first watched Clarence Dickason a month prior. This time, for fear of messing his clothes, he did not lie down on his belly. He raised and lowered his bare feet methodically, careful not to stir sound. From behind a hickory tree, he watched the bald below. There was movement inside the little clapboard house. It reminded him of one he'd once known.

A white woman walked out the front door to shake a rug. She was younger than the black man who'd built the outhouse. Maybe by ten or twenty years. Her hair was yellow in streaks, brown in others, pulled back and held by a lash so that her neck showed thin and curved. The sun held above. Half the homestead caught its light, half lay in shadow. It was approaching six o'clock. Suppertime. Chicopee could smell beans, fatback. Cornbread.

A child ran from the opened doorway to the pretty woman shaking the rug. She paid the little boy no mind. He was waist-high on her, maybe four or five years old, and he was a handsome, sturdy boy. His hair was thick and black. His skin was darker than his mama's. To Chicopee, he looked colored and white at the same time. And so he was, and so it became evident what was going on in the little house with the little outhouse next to it. He'd heard of it before, but never seen it up close. The words flooded his head. Other folks' words: race mixing. Mongrel Virginians. The WIN tribe. Such words shook him and he looked down at his feet, the toenails he'd cut that afternoon with his Bowie knife. WIN tribe. It was another of the suddenly recalled confusions he'd been facing with more frequency since seeing Clarence Dickason and hearing his song. They were confusions of the dream world and the waking. Memory and past.

He looked up again to see the woman and the boy returning to the house. Clarence Dickason brushed past them on his way out. He kissed the pretty woman and stepped out into the yard holding a sleeping baby in his arms.

Chicopee looked at the small blanket, the small thing it held. He smiled. Then he took his first step from behind the tree, not so careful against rustling. He stepped foot over foot down the hillside toward the family who'd come here to get away from onlookers and those who would judge them and threaten their lives and stare. Always they would stare.

When Clarence Dickason saw the bearded mountain figure stairstepping the hillside with a staff in hand, he took the baby back inside to his woman. He picked up his Winchester and walked out again to meet the man. When he got back to the yard, Chicopee was twenty yards off.

"How can I help you?" Dickason hollered. His rifle was at his side, pointed at the dirt.

The mountain man stopped fifteen yards away. He laid down his walking stick so as not to appear threatening. He raised his left hand in a sort of hello gesture. Then he raised his right so that he appeared to be putting his hands over his head. A surrender. A target. A man up against the firing squad.

Inside, the woman and the boy watched.

"No need for all that," Dickason said. He stood his ground and watched Chicopee through squinted eyes that had seen what white men were capable of. He had faith and he had experience, and the two together left him with waiting, just waiting. Finally, Chicopee lowered his hands. Still ten feet off and stepping slow, he reached one of them outward, toward Dickason. It was a handshake offering, something he remembered offering thirty years earlier to another whose skin color made such gestures mean more. This time, as he reached and inched closer, he aimed to say the words he'd been rehearsing for a month. But all he could think of was his name, and even that clenched up and came out wrong when he opened his mouth. As he got within five feet, he managed, in a near whisper, to say, "Chicky."

"Well," Dickason answered. "Well, I suppose that's your name? Chicky?" He still hadn't moved from his stance. Carefully, he swung the rifle behind his back into his left hand and reached out his right in greeting. They shook, then stepped back from one another a half pace. "Clarence Dickason," the older man said. He up-and-downed the beard and the matted hair, the skin like an animal's somehow. The clothes so oddly hung on the man's scrappy frame. He surmised things. He said, "I reckon you live out this way?"

A nod to the affirmative.

"Well, Mr. Chicky, I've got me some small children here, a woman just done with carryin one of em, so I thank you very kindly for stoppin, but I can't offer you supper just now." He knew a man such as this one might have more like himself waiting to come down the hill, waiting for a signal to come get whatever it was they were after. He knew that for some, just the sight of a black man and a white woman, their children somewhere in between . . . for some, this was enough to shed blood. "So, I'm pleased to meet you sir, and I thank you kindly for stoppin," Dickason said.

Another nod, this time an exaggerated one to signal he got the picture. He opened his mouth to bid Mr. Dickason goodbye, but again, the words choked off. So, Chicopee, or Mr. Chicky, as the man had called him, turned and scurried back to the ridgeline. He picked up his walking stick on the move, used his leg and feet and toe muscles to scamper back up to where he'd come from.

Dickason marveled at his movements, his speed. Then his woman came up behind him. "Clarence," she said, "don't run him off on account of the way he looks." She yelled out, "Hey. Mr. Chicky." He turned, crouched in mid-climb, nearly on all fours against the slope. His beard reached the uneven ground below. Seeing him like this, Rose Kozma reconsidered. But she was a born-again Christian, the daughter of Catholic Hungarian immigrants who had, in recent years, embraced the Pentecostal. She looked at the mountain man and waved him back to the house to join them for supper.

They ate. The baby, a girl named Zizi, Hungarian for "dedicated to God," cried from the blessing to the clearing of plates. This was good and bad. It agitated the nerves, but it helped cover the fact that Chicopee, for the duration, did not speak a single word.

Clarence stood in the makeshift kitchen, sinking plates into a washtub of water heated on the cook stove. He made sure not to keep his back turned on their guest. Rose stood from the table. She was tired and the baby was hungry. "Doctor calls it colic, all this here fussin," she said over the child's screams. "I'm going to nurse her in the bedroom, Clare," she hollered. Clarence nodded and scrubbed. Chicopee was left seated and alone with Albert, the boy. As he'd done all through supper, Albert stared at the mountain man's mouth.

"You got gold teeth?" he asked.

A nod yes.

"How many?"

With one hand Chicopee held up five fingers, the other, three. He watched the boy count them up.

"Eight," he said.

Another nod. Smart boy for four years. Behind him, on the wall, hung pictures Rose had painted. Ocean surfs crashing down on sand and seagulls flying high. Big, exaggerated flowers, so heavy they bent almost double. Yellow and red oil paints mixed into orange. These were thick, caked paintings. Chunky, some might call them. To a man who called wilderness home, they were beautiful.

"Rose is the artist of the family," Clarence said. He'd walked back to the table, drying his hands on his trousers. He sat down and rolled a cigarette. Then another. "I was born with music in my bones, but Rose? She got that paint."

"How bout you open wide, show me all eight at once?" Albert said.

Clarence put the cigarette in his lips. "Hush Al," he said. Al sat on his knees and rocked, looked at his daddy and then back at their guest. Clarence handed Chicopee the second cigarette, struck a match and lit both. For the two men, the one who'd not had tobacco in twenty years most especially, that smoke went down like hot heaven. Chicopee coughed. "I lined track most my life," Clarence said. "Coal strike laid me off the N&W five years back. I been tryin to make a go with the music ever since. Got a band, but they ain't no real money in it." Albert jumped off the bench and ran out the front door. His father paid no mind. There was still light out, the kind that fades imperceptibly, orange and calm like sleep. "Come up here on account of all that, and the other thing." He looked to the back bedroom, where Zizi had finished nursing and begun crying again. "Where you from?"

Chicopee pulled hard on the cigarette. He breathed it out and looked down at the table, cut from oak. The Hohner sat heavy in his shirt pocket. "I brung this with me," he said, and pulled the harmonica out.

Clarence almost smiled. "Alright," he said. "Alright now." He stood and struck another match, lit the two kerosene lamps mounted on wall brackets. Then he leaned his head toward the front door and whistled high and loud, a signal for Albert, whose footfalls soon sounded, followed by his panting. He remained out front, riding a rocking chair across the grass like a horse.

The harmonica caught the flickering light of the lamps. Chicopee put it to his lips as Clarence sat back down, humming. Rose came out from the back with Zizi, who was all-out wailing again. Rose looked as if she might cry then, and the men, set to make noise resembling song, sat upright and looked at the mother and daughter. All were helpless to end the roaring. Chicopee listened and watched. His insides ached to help that little thing quiet. He stood and held out his arms. Rose looked at Clarence, who nodded no halfheartedly. Then Rose gave their guest her youngest child.

Zizi nuzzled against all that hanging hair. Her screams became grunts. Her grunts became sighs.

She slept.

"Well I'll be," Rose said.

Chicopee looked down at the creases in the baby's wrists, the way her fine hair grew outward from her temple into the eyebrow. He smiled full-on then, exposed his teeth in a way he never would have before.

"Well I'll be," Rose said again. "Chicky Gold. Chicky Gold the baby man."

Later that evening, when they did get to music making, the guest from the mountains held the baby with one hand, the harmonica with the other. As was usual, he'd worked out a tune after hearing it only once. He blew high and low, shook short reeds and long. Clarence recognized the tune as one he'd sung so long ago. One he still sang. It was a song for laying steel and a song for building shelter. He sang along with his strange new acquaintance that night, though he did so softly, as Rose, asleep in the back, did not approve of secular music.

He sang, "Well, lovers is you right? Oh, yes we right. Newborn baby born last night, walkin talkin fore daylight, carry to the mountain boys, carry to the mountain." Then he smiled at the man draped in hair, who smiled back a mouthful of mineral that men kill for and pan faraway creeks to get.

Zizi the baby slept like she never had. Clarence Dickason shook his head. "I'll be damned," he said. "Chicky Gold the harmonica man."

He came back the following Saturday. Hands were shaken and bellies were filled. Then, Rose was afforded evening-time sleep. Zizi went quiet the moment she was put in the arm crook of Chicky Gold the baby man. She slept under a beard blanket and did not stir. Not even when the little front yard on a mountain bald became a two-man show. Clarence Dickason and Chicky Gold the harmonica man, an impromptu mess of harmonica and beat-up guitar. Vocals in the style of gospel and blues and shouting mountain jug bands. Holy hell blues, folks would later call it.

On a break, Chicky Gold looked down at the baby girl in his arms and then up at the stars in the sky. He didn't say much in the company of his new neighbors. Clarence pulled the slag glass cover off of the small lantern in the grass between them and lit two cigarettes. After they were smoked, Chicky leaned to one side and pulled the derringer flask from his backpocket. The time was right.

"Uh-oh," Clarence said.

Chicky would not tell his new neighbor about the magical quality of the flask, that it refilled itself endlessly. He simply handed it over. Clarence looked to the house, his tee-totaling saint of a commonlaw wife inside. Then he spun the cap off the strangely heavy thing and put it to his lips. He tilted. Then he tilted back some more. Nothing came. Clarence shut one eye and peered down the hole with the other.

"It'll fix you up just right," Chicky told him.

Clarence looked at him and nodded, confused. He decided not to say anything about the flask being empty. But it was. It was dry as cremated bone and smelled like it had been for twenty years. Clarence wondered about the faculties of the man who held his youngest then. For a short time, as he had been before and would be again, he was scared as hell of the man.

Chicky took it back when offered. He swigged its non-existing contents and said, "Ahhh." Re-screwed the cap. Then Clarence sang and fingerpicked a version of John Henry called "Gonna Die with a Hammer in My Hand." His sidekick picked it up halfway through. He accompanied with a mouth harp wail so high and so lonesome that if anyone had been in earshot, they'd swear the player held that Hohner with two hands, not one. They'd swear it was a hillbilly Sonny Boy Williamson blowing that air.

It was in August that Clarence's band was coming, and he'd told Chicky all about it. Told him he should come. It was to be a week-long event, one for which Rose and the children were departing. Her father was meeting her halfway down the mountain. He had friends lined up to carry supplies back a week later. Such friends were hard to come by, for they had to be willing to trek a steep incline with a heavy pack. And they had to be willing to deliver a white woman and her groceries back to a black man living in exile. But the plan came off, and on the day Rose, Albert, and Zizi left, Nelson, Willie, and Johnnie showed up.

For two nights and two days, Chicky Gold hid on the ridge. He watched the all-black band play, off and on, in the front yard. They slept on the grass after playing past four a.m. They smoked and drank whiskey. Nelson Bird was the oldest of them at sixty-two. A gray-headed restaurant owner from Princeton who always wore a white flower in his lapel. He played a five string banjo clawhammer style. Willie Carpenter was a Bluefield baseball star turned coal miner turned railroad grader. He slapped a stand-up bass like he meant it. And then there was Willie's nephew, Johnnie. Johnnie Johnston was only twenty-one years old. He played the hell out of a piano, had started when he was four. When no piano was available, as up on the mountain, he blew a little harp. Cupped his hands on it like he'd been raised up in the Mississippi Delta, though he'd never left Fairmont, West Virginia, until he joined the Marine Corps. The War had hardened the young man, got him to drinking heavy. He came home wild, and after short-timing jail back in Fairmont for stabbing a man in the thigh, Johnnie had moved to his Uncle Willie's in Bluefield for work. Lifting and laying down track for the Norfolk & Western had outlined his muscles in shadow, and, much like a younger Chicky Gold, he was never without a hip flask, knife, and pistol in his pants.

The older men found themselves wishing Johnnie hadn't come. God-fearing and church-going, they found themselves scared, guilty by association. But when they got to playing, all that rode off. For the young man brought to the music a feeling that this could be something. This could go somewhere.

Chicky came down on a Tuesday morning while the men slept off the night prior. The firepit in the yard still smoldered. They laid next to their instruments on burlap and bedrolls, the morning air just right for sleeping. Chicky cleared his throat to awaken them, and when he did, Johnnie Johnston pulled his piece before he opened his lids. From his back, one hand still behind his head, he trained the pistol on Chicky.

Willie got to his knees and said, "Whoa, whoa, whoa. Hold it now Johnnie."

Chicky smiled his golden smile and said, "Been a while since I looked down the hole of a pea-shooter. Tickles a little."

Johnnie recognized whatever it is that lets a man know he should think before he acts. "I can make that stop for you," he said.

"Hold it Johnnie," Clarence said. "This here's Chicky Gold I was tellin you all about. The harmonica man." He'd mentioned on the first night that a mountain man might stop in, a crazy one to be sure, but harmless. A baby soother. And he could play that harp.

Old man Nelson sat up and rubbed at his eyesockets.

"This woodhick?" Johnnie said.

"Yes."

Johnnie took in the man before him. Tall, thin. More hair than a sheep dog. A picture of the worst the world imagined when they heard the words "West Virginia." He lowered his weapon.

By noon, they were all full on eggs over easy and bacon and coffee black as coal sludge. With the passing of hours, they talked to the white man with less hesitation. Except Johnnie. He mostly sipped from his flask and rolled cigarettes. He smoked without the use of his hands. He also rolled up reefer. Willie would have none of it, but old Nelson partook, and so did Clarence. When it came his way, Chicky did as they had, inhaling and coughing. He began to stare at Johnnie Johnston. On Johnnie's left shoulder, visible when he stripped to his no-sleeve undershirt, was a snake tattoo. Chicky's skin started to crawl from the reefer, like he'd taken up serpents again himself. He thought that any minute, he'd stand up, tear his clothes off, and scream bloody hell. Somehow, he managed to sit tight and ride it out.

He didn't sip their drink at first, even when the sun went down and music got made. The joint had brought some feeling on him he couldn't place. A feeling like the other men were watching him close, like he'd known them from somewhere else.

Once, after it had grown dark out, Johnnie Johnston stood up to relieve his bladder, and Chicky saw in his gait a young Arly Jr.

He didn't talk much, didn't laugh much at their jokes and memories, mostly of their time lifting and lining track to song. This was how they'd met. They laughed on how they used to introduce themselves to folks at saloons and parties. Willie would say of Nelson, "This is N." Nelson of Willie: "And this is W." N&W. A man named Otis would introduce Clarence: "This is C." Then Clarence on Otis: "And this is O." C&O. The railroad and the jobs it brought were as ingrained in these Mercer County men as the mines were in Mingo men. They'd taken to naming themselves after company initials, like they owned it. Most days, the company owned them.

Old Nelson smiled while he ate and while he talked. And in between sips of his coffee. He fingered the frets on his banjo and told stories from his childhood. "Used to be they wasn't no frets on a banjer," he said. "Used to be you'd make one from a groundhog."

Johnnie laughed, the scoffing kind. Nobody else said a word.

The old man continued. "Trap him, take his hide, put that hide down in the ashes and leave it set there awhile. Couple days, get you a knife, slice away the hair. Carpet tack that hide on a cheese hoop, fix a oak wood neck on there, and you got a fretless banjo."

"What'd you use for strings?" Willie asked. He turned foil-wrapped potatoes down in the red cinders with his bare hands.

"Horse hair. Stretched."

"Sheee-it," Johnnie said. "Alright, country."

Nelson looked over at Chicky, whose beard and hair and sunken eyes were exaggerated by the fire's dance. "Where you from, Chicky?" Nelson asked.

Chicky sat still on his stone seat. He turned to the mountain behind them and pointed up. Nobody said a word. Then, as if on cue, they laughed together. Chicky joined them.

Johnnie stopped laughing first. "Yeah, you a funny woodhick," he said. He turned to the old man. "Mr. Bird, let me ask you. Why you keep puttin your eyes to the white man here? Keep askin him the questions, like he the one with answers. You ain't noticed he don't take your whiskey when you offer?" He turned to Chicky. The whites of Johnnie's eyes had gone rusty. "You fraid to sip what a colored man done sipped on?"

Chicky stared back at him. The other men swallowed, shifted. In their time, in their places, black men didn't speak to white men this way. The fire's pops got louder. "I brung my own whiskey," Chicky said. He shifted against the log he sat on, pulled the derringer flask from his pocket.

"Yeah, we done heard about your whiskey," Johnnie said. "Invisible whiskey."

"Come again?"

"That flask right there is dry as desert sand, woodhick."

Chicky looked down at the flask. Issued a challenge, his paranoia had given way to a calm confidence. It was a sureness of hand and a disregard for danger reserved for movie outlaws. Slowly, imperceptibly, he moved his left thumb to the small catch near the rim. "Well," he said, "I wonder why it's so heavy then." In a fluid, single motion, he tripped the catch, caught the falling piece with his right hand, turned it so that the gun dropped out into his now empty left, and trained the weapon on Johnnie Johnston's head, the flask now in two pieces between Chicky's bare feet. He remained seated on the rock all the while.

At first, no one spoke. None of the men were strangers to guns, but this was something else, at least for the older three. A bullfrog called.

Johnnie Johnston never moved. He lay on his side by the fire, rolling a blade of grass between his thumb and finger. He spit in the dirt. "You got to know who you point a gun to," he said. "I done some things so cold . . ." He'd visibly lost a little of his edge. The face staring back at him had seen colder, and he knew it. But he couldn't stop the words that had come up his throat and onto his tongue. "Motherfucker," he said. "I'll hang a rope and drown a glass a water."

Nelson Bird sighed then.

Chicky kept his gun on Johnnie. "Willie," Chicky said. "I notice you got tough hands with them taters. Why don't you toss one off yonder, high as you can." Willie hesitated, and while he did, Chicky addressed Johnnie again. "Cocksucker," he said, "I'll dynamite your house and put a third eye 'tween the two you got from three hundred yards." Then, to Willie, who'd frozen at the sound of these last words spoken: "How bout them spuds? You going to toss one up?" Willie finally obliged, slinging the thing high above his head before it could burn his fingerprints off. Chicky spun on the rock and fired, twice. In three seconds time, the little over-under was spent, the silver-wrapped potato hit the dirt, and Johnnie had his own gun drawn. He kept it on Chicky as the mountain man got up and walked to the potato, several feet off but still within the fire's light. "Hot potato," Chicky hollered, tossing it back to Willie. Willie caught it and dropped it on the ground next to the fire. They all looked down except Johnnie and Chicky, who knew already what was there. Two holes, perfect and clean, an inch apart. Chicky smiled at the man who could end him any second. The gold was distracting, exaggerated like the rest of him in the firelight. "Hang a rope and drown a glass a water," Chicky said. Then, sitting back down on the rock, he said it again. He took his harmonica from the shirt's front pocket and blew into it. Talked into it really. The harmonica sang the words, low down dirty like: "I'll hang a rope, and I'll drown a glass a water." Chicky stopped playing and turned to Clarence, who sat stupefied, holding the bottle of whiskey they'd been passing all evening. "Clarence," Chicky said. "I believe I'll sip off that stuff you been offerin now." He smiled again, looked down at the aired-out spud. He thought of a name he hadn't in years: Sid Hatfield.

Nelson Bird cleared his throat.

Chicky took the bottle Clarence held out for him. He swallowed whiskey hard. It burned, and it instantly changed everything inside him and all around him, and he knew that from then on, he'd stay lit on the stuff for as much of the day, every day, as he possibly could. He looked to Old man Nelson. "To answer your question? Mingo. I come from Mingo."

Johnnie lowered his pistol, stuck it back into his belt.

CHAPTER EIGHTEEN

RADIO SATURDAY NIGHT

For Chicky, the word "radio" spurred thoughts and memories of electric telegraphs, tickers, and big companies with names like Westinghouse who had operations in places like Pittsburgh and Chicago. Radio was something the navy could take over if they wanted to. But the way Johnnie and Willie spoke on it, radio was entertainment for regular folks. They said there was a station called WHIS in Bluefield that had the strongest signal for a hundred miles. Such talk baffled a mountain man, but confusion ran high all around in the four days following the potato shoot. This was on account of the sheer volume of whiskey consumed. With consumption came music, and with music, friendship. Or at least the mirage of friendship. And the two who were tightest were those who'd nearly killed one another. Chicky and Johnnie had made a song to end all songs up there on the mountain bald. The piano in back of Nelson Bird's restaurant was calling to Johnnie Johnston. He knew that if he put it to use with the bearded man's harmonica, and if they could get on the radio, they would have something as gold as the teeth Chicky wore.

So it was that the mountain man forgot everything he'd learned in twenty-four years time. All he knew was that he had a taste for drink again and he'd follow whoever he had to, to quench it. He returned to his thatched hut on the lee side of the mountain just long enough to camouflage it and barricade its opening. Before he did, he gathered his old Confederate pack, its contents surprisingly still useful. There were shells to replace the spent ones in the derringer. He reassembled its secrecy. There was the old tin water canteen, the compass and map, the brittle paper upon which he'd written things that made no sense until the day he sharpened his last pencil to nothing. There was money, the kind that folds and the kind that clinks, still useable after all that time. He covered up every trace of his habitation, though it was remote enough that a body would be unlikely to find it.

Before he walked away, Chicky Gold stared at the place where he'd lived for better than two decades. The cheap booze in his bloodstream didn't sharpen the eye like the Widow's shine. Instead, it deadened men to their surroundings. Slow and easy, it made every place the same. Looking at his home on the hill, he felt nothing, and the turtles walked on by, and the flowers swallowed the gnats, and the mountain stream ran, and the man who had come to live among all of them put in a dip of snuff Clarence had given him, and spat on the ground.

So it was that the mountain man came down from the mountain.

On the way, they crossed paths with Rose and Albert and Zizi, who laid in a bundle sling across her mother's back, crying. Three men carried supplies and sweated and spoke nothing. They nodded to Chicky because some of their people still lived like him. Chicky held the baby. She went quiet and slept. He put her back in the sling and Rose kissed his cheek. "You watch out down in there," she told him. Clarence shook his hand before returning up the mountain with his family. He turned four times to see his band disappear, minus its founding member.

Within two weeks, Chicky had almost acclimated to the little mattress he slept on in Willie's toolshed. Most nights, it got too soft under him, and he found himself sleeping outside, beside a dogwood tree. Willie's wife looked at the man from the kitchen window each morning. She shook her head. "He's like a animal," she told her husband.

Soon, he'd nearly acclimated to the telephone poles and fat round cars. The indoor plumbing mysteries and the plywood boxes housing tiny moving pictures. Two different Bluefield saloons kept these boxes behind the bar. Television, folks called it. Big, drunk men roared as they watched a tiny, grainy black man knock out a white one inside the little box.

"Did you see Joe Louis on the television?" railroad men asked Johnnie. Then they up-and-downed the long-bearded hillbilly at his side, frowned.

"This here's Chicky Gold the harmonica man," Johnnie told them all. "We going to cut a record together, me and him. Get famous." They stayed good and drunk and Johnnie said the same things over and over to everyone they met. Chicky just flashed his gold teeth, which either frightened, confused, or tickled folks enough to smile back and walk away.

Within three weeks, through Nelson Bird's connection with the local rich he served food to, Johnnie and Chicky had landed a spot on WHIS's Saturday night program. It was a live broadcast of local talent. Country music mostly. White country. But gospel had opened the door for black talent as well, and since the station manager was in Charleston on business, the young disc jockey nervously welcomed them in.

The control room was dark, a single light hanging above a giant, cherrywood table covered in gadgetry. Chicky had never seen anything like it. The phonograph machine next to the table was slick and black and compact, just like the record that rode it. A tower rose on the opposite side, and stuck to it were knobs and needles, the latter dancing back and forth as the quartet of clean-cut singers on the other side of the glass sang into the microphone. It was a giant silver microphone, and it hung down in the center of the studio like a lifeline for the desperate. The disc jockey faded to himself, and into his own shining, hinged microphone said, "And once again folks, that was the War Eagle Four with 'Wildwood Roses.' Back after this." He flipped through papers clipped in front of him, beside him, behind him. He flipped switches.

It was dizzying.

He spun on his office chair and faced them. "I'm a little overwhelmed this evenin," he said. His hair held too much pomade and his skin was pimpled. "And frankly, you all wouldn't be here if that old colored restauranter didn't kiss Mr. Schott's behind blue." He'd only glanced at them. "I have you all down here as Chicky and Johnnie?"

"Yessir," Johnnie said. He snubbed a cigarette on his shoe heel and stuck it in his pocket.

"Looks like there's three of you."

Willie had come with his bass. Old Nelson and his banjo had been slowly pushed out of the sound that was emerging. It was just a matter of time before the same went for Willie.

"He's bass accompaniment," Johnnie said.

"Uh-huh. And how come you do all the talkin? What accompaniment is barefoot Outlaw here bringin to the table?"

Nobody said a word. The young disc jockey stared for a moment at Chicky's dirty feet. "Never mind," he said. "You all need to get in there and set up on the piano and whatever else. You know the drill. We come back live in two minutes." The starched shirt-and-tie white boys emerged from the studio, laughing. They stared at the upcoming act with a mix of condescension and disbelief. The disc jockey tried to mediate. "Takes all types fellas," he said.

"I reckon it does, Jimmy," one of them answered. "If by all types you mean two niggers and a woodsman." They laughed a little louder as they walked out the control room door.

Willie was ready to go home. Johnnie laughed a little himself and memorized their faces in his mind. Chicky was flat drunk.

They walked into the small, bright studio the other men had vacated. Jimmy the disc jockey came through on the two-way to finalize things. This confused the hell out of Chicky, who was starting to wonder about the whole deal. "How you want me to introduce you? Chicky and Johnnie just don't ring right." the booming voice said. Chicky ducked like it might land on them somehow.

Johnnie answered. "How bout 'Two Niggers and a Woodsman?'"

"How bout something else?"

"We're the West Virginia Shine Guzzlers," Chicky said. He pulled out his harmonica and blew it a little. He and Willie took their spots under the central microphone, Johnnie took his at the beat-up baby grand.

"If you say so," Jimmy came back. "And I have you all down as country, gospel, *and* blues? I don't know what that means, but . . ." Willie slapped his bass, turned the pegs. "Bout thirty seconds now. Song title?"

"That's just how it goes," Johnnie said. He let his fingers hover over the chipped keys, eyes shut tight. He lit another cigarette.

When greasy Jimmy introduced them and gave the signal a few seconds later, Willie dropped in a slow, low, catchy bass line. Johnnie came in second, smooth and easy. Chicky waited, then let rip a reed-splitter. They had it down. Johnnie kept his eyes shut as he started to sing:

Well, I'll drown a glass a water
And I'll hang a rope
The devil he done come to me
Took away my hope
Well, I'll put that stick a dynamite
Right on under your nose
Cause I done seen the worst a man can see
That's just how it goes

The voice, the whole sound, was smoke-shot vocal chords and sticky-floor toe-tapping, holes in the soles. Chicky played part of the song with his nose. It was holy hell blues all right, and the only country or gospel to be heard was not a brand greasy Jimmy the disc jockey had ever encountered. This was sin music if he'd ever heard it, and though he let them play it out, his palms sweated through their grip against his rayon slacks. He mumbled a nervous outro to commercial, flipped the switch and strung together a sadly ineffective string of curse words, ending with, "Now get the hell out of here."

This all took place in front of the on-deck act, a country group from Mingo County. They had liked what they heard and said so as they crossed paths with The West Virginia Shine Guzzlers, who smiled a smile only possible when real music gets made. Only Willie was hesitant. After all, the music they'd made over the airwaves was outlaw music, and Willie was a family man.

"That was real good. Real different," the young lady said to them. She wore a daisy flower behind each ear. She had her eye on Chicky, who saw something in the brunette beauty that set his core to rumbling. Her band called themselves The Mingo Four. She was vocals, with fiddle, dulcimer, and banjo backup. All men, all older.

In the hallway outside the control room, Willie, Johnnie, and Chicky laughed and patted each other's backs and smoked their Chesterfields. They could hear Jimmy, frustrated, giving his instructions to The Mingo Four, but they couldn't make out the song title or the specifics. Soon, the band struck up and out there in the sparse-lit hallway, the acoustics were just right. The muffled fiddle squeal, the quiet dulcimer, the old five-string, they were just discernable enough to calm the excitement. And when the young woman's voice broke through, it was beautiful. Church solo beautiful. They could make out her words.

Well, boys, you've heard that tale
About a Mingo dead-eye shot
Who on that 1920 day couldn't fail
To give Al Felts what he got

The boy was full of rotten teeth
But his eye was keen and sure
He held the miners' deep belief
That their lives were surely pure

Out on the hallway stairwell, Chicky's sight went red. Everything blurred. The howling in his ears commenced and his knees gave. He dropped like a man in the midst of a stroke.

Johnnie and Willie kneeled to him, slapped his face a little. They listened for his breath, found it, and carried him out, just as greasy Jimmy said to the radio-listening public, "And that was The Mingo Four with 'The Ballad of Trenchmouth Taggart.'"

CHAPTER NINETEEN

A PIKER HAD NO HOME

The lead singer of The Mingo Four was Miss Louise Dallara, daughter of Fred and Clarissa Dallara. She was born to the couple, a quiet housewife and her Mingo County sherriff husband, in 1928, before the Depression hit and the union's fire burnt out completely and the coal companies reigned again. Fred Dallara had risen almost to the top of one of those companies, White Star Mining, before stepping out of the way of the Crews brothers to take a position in law enforcement. Such a post would allow him a different kind of power, one that included the right to protect his citizens and his family from any who might ever shake foundations again. Fred was cold if not civil to his wife and children. He'd remained close with Mose and Warren Crews, men who'd seen to it that Arly Scott Jr. stayed locked up in Moundsville for the rest of his days, an example to those who might question the strength of their dead daddy's business.

Fred didn't speak to his youngest daughter Louise any longer, not since she'd graduated high school and moved out on her own to be a musician. Her interest in music, in his estimation, was nearly as ill-advised as her admiration for unions and socialists and forgotten local heroes in the struggle.

Folks spoke little on that long past fight. The Scotts, Arly Sr. and his wife, had moved back home to Georgia. Bill Blizzard went less fiery. And in the schools, no one taught a stitch on the Matewan shootout or the Battle of Blair Mountain.

The Urias Hotel stayed in business, as did Chambers Hardware. Matewan, Logan, and Welch had remained fairly quiet, while in Keystone, whores continued to service men from all walks. Ewart Smith did so, until she became pregnant with her third child and finally left for Tennessee. No one knew if she made it.

In Bluefield, the man who'd shot Sid Hatfield dead, Charles Lively, lived and prospered in various business ventures. His children bore children and he was a proud grandfather, semi-retired and comfortable.

Up Warm Hollow, the tilted pioneer house of cat-and-clay and clapboard construction still stood. And inside, the Widow Dorsett still lived. But only barely. She was seventy-seven years old. Clarissa had begged her to come live in town with herself and Fred. There was plenty of room with the kids grown. But the Widow refused. "I'll be just fine," she said.

Laying flat on the ridge above her house, the house he'd grown up in, Chicky Gold knew none of this. He didn't know who'd killed Sid Hatfield, or what had become of his friends Arly or Ewart or his enemies the Crews brothers. He didn't know if his mother was alive or dead. In Bluefield, folks weren't concerned with their small-town Mingo neighbors. Before he'd left Bluefield to find things out for himself, he'd not asked enough questions to get people wondering about him.

After his brain had shut down in the halls of WHIS, he'd come to in Willie's shed with The Mingo Four's lyrics still in his mind. He'd said to Willie's wife, "Ma'am, I'll leave here and not bother you again if you'll allow me the use of your kitchen shears and your washtub." She obliged, and Chicky emerged from the steam-filled bathroom with a respectable, three-inch beard and short hair. He almost looked handsome.

Willie didn't think much about his departure, but Johnnie nearly shot him again. Johnnie was set on traveling to Philadelphia and Detroit and New York City, putting together some gigs and building their song catalog. "You ain't nothin but a woodhick anyhow," he told Chicky, his back turned, as the gold-toothed smile closed up and the shakes of whiskey withdrawal set in. Standing in his newly purchased Bostonian shoes and gray felt Fedora, Chicky Gold said to his piano man, "Be good, Johnnie."

On his way out of Bluefield, he'd stopped in at WHIS and learned from greasy Jimmy the name of the young singer, Louise Dallara. When it was spoken aloud, he'd nearly dropped to the floor again.

He'd been on the ridge above the cabin of unhewn logs for two days since. He slept in short intervals. He'd not seen any movement inside. The outhouse still stood, though it looked to be unused. The tomato garden was gone. The little barn in shambles.

Up there looking down, Chicky Gold cried and sipped just enough whiskey to hold off the worst of the shakes.

Clarissa came on a Thursday morning. As soon as she'd stepped inside the door, Chicky came down the hill.

He opened the door without knocking.

Clarissa was leaning over the Widow, who lay on her side in a double bed where the kitchen table used to be. Clarissa straightened and looked at him. Time had been kind to her; skin, eyes, hair and all. She met his gaze with her own and frowned.

"Clarissa," Chicky said, taking off his hat and nodding.

The Widow had not yet looked up. "Fred come along to dance on my grave?" she said. Her voice had gone higher and a little shaky.

No one answered her. She raised her head up and looked at her boy. Then she laid it back down again. "Well," she said. "I know I done lost my mind now."

Clarissa sat down on the bed and brushed through her mother's hair with her fingers. Something the size of a plum had caught in her throat and she thought she might pass out for lack of air or throw it up, one or the other. Speaking was beyond her.

"Those straps I see across your arms? That old Civil War pack still hangin on?" The Widow's eyes were still sharp.

"Yes ma'am," Chicky managed.

"What do you call yourself?"

"Chicky Gold."

"Let me see you smile," the old woman said, and she lifted her head again.

He did what she told him to. Clarissa began to cry. The Widow laughed and said, "Old Dr. Warble can fix up a set a teeth, can't he?" She put her head back down on the pillow and sighed like she might be as overcome as Clarissa had been. Instead, she patted her girl's hands with her own, thin-skinned and rippling with veins that were night-crawler thick and purple. "I knew God was hangin me on for this," she said. "Knew it was for somethin like this." She waved him over and he put the backpack on the floor, sat down on the bed opposite Clarissa, the Widow in between. "You know I'll be goin right quick now that you're here."

"Yes ma'am," Chicky said. Clarissa swallowed the plum and straightened up and wiped at her eyes. Her stomach burned but she smiled at her mother and went back to stroking her hair. She could not look at the man, his shining teeth. He studied her only for a moment, then looked down at the Widow. She had fallen asleep. She wore a nightgown sewn by her own hands, white cotton. A sheet covered most of her, but he watched the blood beat through the veins on her neck, followed the deep wrinkles from there to her chin and on up past the mouth and nose to the closed eyes, the forehead. The hair was white as the unwashed gown. While the rest of her had shrunk, her ears looked to have grown somehow. He put his fingers to her cheek and left them there, moving them up and down a little, so that they touched the fingers of Clarissa. Again, the electricity came immediately. But they did not look at one another.

Before she died the following evening, the Widow told her boy to open up the chest in the loft, bring down the locked box inside. He did so. She told him where to find the key, a flour container on the cook stove. She'd never gotten a steel range.

Inside the box were newspaper clippings she'd saved for him since he'd left home, each marked with her penned notes. There were stories of families dried up in the depression, gnawing on the chicken bones of the rich folks' wastebaskets. Another World War, described in high-toned, vulgar terms. In the margins, she'd written, *And men just go on, back to the ways they did each other before they knew to talk.*

There were stories from a newly formed newspaper out of Richwood called the *News-Leader*. Under these and a mess of others, at the bottom of the box and wrapped in twine, were faded clippings, near to tearing. They were from the *Williamson Daily News* and they told of the aftermath of the mine wars. Sid Hatfield's funeral merited photographs, grayed now from age. There were a few stories speculating as to the whereabouts of the *rotten-toothed Taggart boy,* alleged to have shot more than a few in those days.

"If they hadn't used you up in the union," the Widow said, "you'd have made a right fine newspaperman." Her breathing had slowed to almost nothing.

Clarissa stood next to them in the kitchen, ricing potatoes for their guest. Then she was outside the house, waiting.

"Under them newspaper clippins is all the proof in this world that you was ever here," his mother told him then. A birth certificate, the only one, since fire had swept downtown Matewan. Some informal adoption documents, the sole copies. She cocked her head against the pillow to look at him straight on. "You take that lockbox. And you keep on doin what you got to do. You understand, Chicky?" She'd forced the name out. Unnatural but necessary. For a moment when she asked him if he understood, her eyes were alive again, like they'd been when he was a boy. Beast eyes. All-knowing, all-seeing, fair, learned eyes. They dimmed just as quick as they'd come on.

He said he understood.

Her every muscle and tissue and tendon eased then, and she sunk into the bed. She said to her only boy, "Don't get bamboozled."

These were the last words of the Widow.

Though she'd not attended services since 1920, the Widow would have her send-off in the Methodist Church. She'd not wanted to fight arrangement-making in her last days, so Clarissa and Fred were allowed to have at it as they saw fit. This would mean proper ritual. Church-goers and business owners and a preacher talking from memorization. It was fine with the Widow. She'd not be there for it.

It turned out that her boy *would* be there. After she was gone in the little kitchen bed, he'd kissed her forehead and stepped outside to smoke a Chesterfield, speak to Clarissa. She told him of the funeral plans. He scraped little tobacco pieces from between his gold teeth with his thumbnail and listened as she made small talk, talk of things to be done. A list of death's ugly chores to make sure nothing real got spoken between them. "I reckon you won't be able to come to the service?" she'd said.

"I'm able," he'd replied. Then he thought about telling her of the last twenty-four years of his life on the mountain. How he hadn't even known if she was real or a dream a month prior, how he'd forgotten who he was himself just as he'd forgotten everything. Instead, he reached out and brought her to his chest and held her there. He kissed her on the cheek and walked away. There was something damming up her chest and throat then. She almost ceased to breathe.

And so it was that he walked through the congregational doors he'd last stepped out of after kicking Hob Tibbs in the testicles so hard the man couldn't twitch a toe. He was under the cover of his fedora and his beard and all the age that he'd acquired from living hard in the hills. Clarissa had spoken to no one of his return.

He sat two rows back from the front pew, where Clarissa was elbow to elbow with Fred, who still wore a scar from the first time he'd dared to kiss her in sight of her brother. Next to him were two grown boys, both home from Morgantown where they were getting the education their Italian ancestors hadn't. Next to them was Louise Dallara, songbird and revolutionary. As he sat and stared at the back of her head, Chicky began to think of Louise as his own daughter.

They stood and sat and kneeled and listened and spoke in unison. The preacher spoke the same words he'd spoken when Frank Dallara had been put to rest: "The sorrows of death compassed me." Hob Tibbs, wearing a facial scar himself, sat in the tall-back cherrywood chair next to the preacher. He wore highwater slacks and tried not to doze off. The sun through the stained glass showed him to be an old man, weak in his up and down movements.

When it was time to view the open casket, folks filed past. There were more present than anyone had anticipated, for a moonshine aficionado will stay sober long enough on a Sunday morning to pay tribute to his savior the distiller.

Chicky stood with his row, and filed past her as they did. He'd taken his hat off inside the Lord's house, of course, and he ignored the feelings of exposure. He looked down at the Widow, who looked ashen and ridiculous in a dress that was not hers. In the makeup of an embalmer. He smiled and touched her cold hand. Then he looked up and locked eyes with Hob Tibbs, who nearly shit himself to see the boy who'd once vowed to kill him.

Chicky Gold winked at him and moved on down the line.

He walked out the double doors into the hazy light of a day threatened by thunder clouds. While he strode to the bridge, Hob Tibbs scurried inside the church to inform Sheriff Fred Dallara that a fugitive was among them. A murderer. The sheriff looked at his wife, who ignored him. Then he got up and walked out, Tibbs in tow.

They'd not catch him that day. They didn't know he'd picked up his stashed backpack and walked across the Tug into Kentucky to see the hole his adopted mother was to be buried in. They couldn't keep him from saying goodbye, from seeing her final place. The hole was square cut and even, unlike the one he'd dug up to reveal his daddy. He felt he should put something down in it, something to keep her company, but she'd not want that. For a moment, he thought of pouring out the jar of shine she'd given him before she died, pouring it right into the dirt. But that time hadn't quite yet come for Chicky. So he stared at the hole and thought how fitting it was that we all end up in the ground, covered. Swallowed. Mixing with all the other dead and the little, unnamed bugs that eat through us and move on down the line. The Widow's hole was twenty yards from Sid Hatfield's tombstone, a giant black rock with the likeness of his face carved in it. Under this were the words *We Will Never Forget.*

In the newspaper clippings she'd saved for him, he'd read and re-read the printed name of the man who'd killed Sid. A man who lived in Bluefield. Charles E. Lively. Chicky had plans to visit the man, but he wasn't first on the list. That spot was reserved for another.

The train ride to Moundsville had been uneventful. There was a bar car where Chicky had almost fallen asleep, full-stomached on bologna sandwiches and beer, rocking that perfect rock of a locomotive. He'd long ago decided never to ride in an automobile again. Not after the business with the Model T and the blood that seemed to run every time he stepped inside it. No mind that they were bigger and safer and faster now, he'd ride rails or walk. The car was a fool's invention. A death trap.

The day before the funeral, he'd made two phone calls from the saloon in Matewan and secured a prisoner visitation pass under an assumed name. It was truly magnificent what the telephone could do for a man.

The depot wasn't far from the State Penitentiary at Moundsville. When he approached it, he nearly turned around for fear he'd set his own trap. The main building was four stories, cut stone like the rest of the sprawling place. A castle of sorts. Towers were everywhere, iron latticework slicing up the sky. Chicky could see the prison wall. It was thick and he estimated its height to be forty feet. Two guards stood atop it in turrets shouldering Winchesters.

Chicky's press badge, no doubt an antique, got him through security. "Alright, Mr. Bern, I've got you on the register here," one prison worker said to him. Another remarked on the merits of the

New York Times, then laughed to show how he truly felt. "I'm just pullin your leg, Mr. Bern," he said. "We got a subscription to your rag here at the prison, truth be told. Warden likes to wipe his backside with it."

The square of glass they called a visitation window was roughly the size of a dictionary book or a Bible. It had an elbow rest, a wooden chair pulled up to it, and vent slats so you could hear who you looked at. When Arly Jr. walked up and sat down, he had his hands stuffed in the pockets of his cadet grays. His face said he knew the man staring back at him, had maybe even expected him.

"You Mr. Bern?" he said. His hair was cropped short and gray at the temples. He wore thick black spectacles.

"I am."

"Newspaperman?"

"That's right." Chicky became afflicted, as had happened in recent days, with a powerful and sudden instinct to cry. He'd not anticipated it here, inside a cage for men, and he quickly swallowed it away.

Arly breathed deep and looked down. The top of his head revealed an unusual balding pattern. When he looked up again, he was shaking his head and wore a smile that was hard to read. "You must be crazy comin into this place," he said.

Chicky thought on the words. "I reckon I am a little crazy. Been livin on a mountain for a good little while."

"It shows."

They spoke on the intricacies of living off the land, then on Mingo. Who was still there and who wasn't. Who was dead and who was still breathing.

They spoke on Joe Louis, television. Cars. Arly never once looked the other man in the eyes.

Chicky caused a break in the flow they'd established when he asked, not in so many words, what it was like to live at Moundsville. He'd made the mistake of bringing up Arly's place of residence— he'd mentioned the obvious: that they were inside a penitentiary. Arly looked down again. "You got to go on and do that?"

"Do what?"

"Ask me a question like that? 'How you holdin up in here, Arly?' Like we friends?"

"I'm sorry Arly. I—"

"You know what they opened up a mile from this place the year before I come in?"

"What?"

"Coal mine." He was still looking down, down at those tucked away hands. "You know what the warden's name was back then, in '22?"

"Huh-uh."

"Pilcher. Otto Pilcher. That name mean anything to you?"

Chicky sat back in his chair. He went dizzy.

"Ol Otto was Anse Pilcher's first cousin, come up through the lawman ranks and married a little girl from up thisaway. Everybody loved Otto. 'He's a reformer,' is what they always said. Otto cleaned up the mess left to him. No more *inhumane* treatments put on those convicts, not up at Moundsville. But he had a special spot for a nigger that done kilt his cousin. Nigger got found guilty by a jury for it, so he got some payback comin." Arly was rocking back and forth a little now, trying to keep himself from busting wide open.

Chicky's face went white.

"So I noticed first thing he did was take out the heavy bag in the exercise yard. Took away the gloves for sparrin, the striking bag. Man's got but one choice and that's baseball, and I ain't never seen the point in no baseball." Both men thought back to the days when they'd laced up the gloves together. Arly went on. "Then, they sunk me down in that prison mine, contracted out from Sewickley, eighty feet deep, but I wasn't no trustie like the rest of the boys. They slept in the mine camp, a mile outside the wall. I come back every night on foot, followin the guard on horseback. Get to sleep in my five by seven, only cell in the block without a ray a sunshine during daylight. Call it the 'bad angle cell.' Saturday nights, Warden Pilcher come past the bad angle, ask me how do I like it up in Marshall County. I say I like it just fine and stare at him, cold. And he knows that I'm the kind a man to whup a cracker quick as look at him, and he waits on me to break, reach through and bust his mouth open so he can really put it on me, but I don't. I keep goin underground for the Pittsburgh Vein, keep footing it back and watchin them lifers go on to Camp Two at Martinsburg for the Public Road. Road campers was on the honor system, guards don't even carry no rifles. They slept in cabins, slip whiskey in, women I heard too. I didn't slip nothin but punches from an invisible sparrin partner, bang out sit-ups and push-ups on my knuckles." Arly spoke the words as if he'd done so many times before, but he never had. Not out loud. Never to his mother and father, who'd quit coming years before at his request. Never to the few friends he'd made inside.

Chicky wondered why he'd come there. He watched the slightly bowed head of his boyhood friend, stared at that balding pattern. It occurred to him that as a boy, Arly Jr. had been known as quiet. As one who spoke as little as possible. Not on this day. Chicky tried in vain not to hear what he heard.

"So by the time ol Otto retires, I got me a couple of close-as-you-can to friends in here. Stretch and Nat, both from McDowell. They say the new warden goin cut out this ridin me down. Say I got road camp comin. Farm work instead of mineshaft. Beets and cabbage, horseradish and kale and tomatoes and rutabaga. Cons keep what they can't can, eat it fresh in they cells. But then, all at once, that T.B. hits hard. Stretch and Nat sunnin themselves at the tubercular, that's the prison hospital back in '31. Boom, Stretch dies on a Friday the thirteenth, Nat six days later. Back to no friends. That same Thursday, new warden assumes his post, comes by my cell. Warden Jones. 'Your fat friend croaked,' he says. 'And my wife is Anna Elizabeth Pilcher, niece of Anse. And you can damn sure bet you goin down that mine shaft and you'll keep pickin that bone if that's what the boss wants, Saturdays and Sundays too. Cause that's what little boys get for striking against the mines, takin up arms,' he says to me. Then he says, 'You done bit the hand that fed you, and you goin pay for it till you thought parole was just a word in a dictionary.'" Arly bent his neck down deeper, and it was hard to tell if he laughed a little or just sniffed. "Well, I came up off my bunk and got that son of a bitch by the throat with my left, brought my right back and let it sail. I don't know how I came back and forth through the bars clean, but I did, eight or nine times until he was out on his feet, got so heavy that I had to let him drop. He was face down snortin his own bloody teeth fore the guard knew what happened."

For a moment, Chicky let himself believe that Arly's story might end right there.

"That's when Warden Jones opened up the little room in North Wagon Gate. It's where they used to hang men before they built the death house, where they hang em now. Anyway, they quit usin the weighing machine over there back in 1900 or so, but he hired out a engineer buddy to fix it back up. Just for me. Longest a man lasted in the machine was thirty seconds, that's what I heard." He looked at Chicky, really looked, for the first time. "You know what a weighing machine is?"

Chicky shook his head no.

"That gold I see on your teeth?"

Chicky nodded yes.

"Watch out on that. Somebody's liable to pry em out of your head for pawn." Arly laughed and looked back at his lap, his hands in his pockets. "Weighing machine is nothin but a plank, solid oak, set inside a groove on a frame. This makes it so you can raise it or lower it to any height you want. Hook came down from the plank, chain on that, handcuffs on the chain. Warden put the handcuffs to me hisself. He raised up that cross piece till I had to tiptoe to keep from screamin. They didn't hardly touch the floor. Then he raised it just a hair, set it for me by pluggin in those two iron pins, in the holes up there, held it steady. I watched it all. I said to myself, shit. No wonder ain't nobody gone past a half minute." He laughed again then. Looked Chicky in the eyes. "My fingertips popped open like firecrackers. Blood ran all over, fingernails just flew, like they was on a hinge. I reckon I almost made forty seconds, but my Lord, I heard myself scream like a little ol child, like Warren Crews that day, you remember how he sissy-wailed, 'T.?" Arly smiled at Chicky. He was reminiscing through thick glass and thirty years of anguish.

Chicky cringed at the initial that had once signified his name. T. He tried not to cry, not to sissy-wail from all of it right there in front of him. All that madness he'd thought he'd known the pinnacle of until then.

"Anyway," Arly went on, "they don't tell you that the worst of it comes later. You think weeks, months. But it don't work that way. That swelling just goes and goes, and you don't say nothin, and they don't come put you in the mines anymore, or put you anywhere, and you just hope them sores and bubbled-up splits don't turn to blood poisoning. Cause then you die. But then you think, hold on now. There wouldn't be nothin better than blood poisoning, just like you thought one time that there wouldn't be nothin better than tuberculosis. But none of death's ways ever come to you, and you stop takin visits from your people outside, and the warden don't come by no more, and you can't do no push-ups or hang yourself with your bedsheet cause your hands ain't nothin but bricks." He pulled them from his pockets and held them to the glass.

Chicky's stomach clenched and his breathing went funny so that he had to wipe at what had come from his nose. He saw something behind that glass that he'd never speak of again. Something he'd spend days and nights trying to forget. As much as he knew he shouldn't, he looked away.

Arly put his hands back in his pockets and went on. "And then you get to thinkin crazy, real crazy. You hear a visitor's comin for you, and you decide you'll see that newspaperman name of Bern who gets on the docket after fifteen years of nobody, cause you know damn well who it is. You wondered if he'd come, what he'd say. Ol Stinky T. If maybe he'd get shackled up since he's the one who done pulled the trigger. But he sits down and wants to know how you're doing, what it's like in here. So you tell him what it's like. See how he takes it." Arly watched him for a moment, how he was taking it. "And you tell him, right fore he leaves, that you and him wasn't never friends. Cause even a white boy with a messed up mouthful of teeth's got more worth than a colored boy. Wasn't *never* friends, just somebodies who ain't enemies cause you both lookin down a barrel at some other white man who is. Ain't no friends when it comes to black and white."

Arly stood and knocked his chair down with the backs of his knees. He turned from the glass and the man on the other side, whose own head was now bowed.

Arly Scott Jr. walked back to the cell block without ever breaking stride.

* * *

Then came the nightmare of the piker. He could not go home and he could not sleep. He belonged in a cage and he had to roam free. A would-be-brother-in-law was a man *of* the law, and he sniffed the wind for a chance to be hero of a time long since gone.

Marshall County wasn't dry like so many others. Chicky had stepped from the prison doors into the liquor store. He still had money from all those women, all those years past, and he aimed to spend it. Two pints of Old Cobb Whisky put him on the road to shaking loose the sight of Arly's hands. It almost put him to sleep on the train back to Bluefield.

Old Cobb was dark as maple syrup. It was the opposite of his dead mother's shine, the single remaining jar of which he still had not sipped. Old Cobb was rotgut stuff, 90 Proof, and it made a man mean. From his seat inside the passenger car, Chicky shook his head side to side to wipe away visions of the weighing machine. He thought he could smell the blood that had run.

At the station in Charleston, he stepped off the platform to get some air. But he was drunk and fell to his knees. A man offered to help, and Chicky hissed at him, got back on the train.

Outside Beckley, when the porter asked if he might be more discreet with his pint-sipping, Chicky stood up and faced him. Had the train not swayed and sat him down again, he would have hit the man square on.

He stared at the empty seat next to him. He thought of Clarissa, their overnighter back from Huntington when he was a boy. The nut house and his birth mother. But still, visions of Arly's hands interrupted, screeching their way into his mind's eye without warning. He sipped hard and winced, finally fell asleep.

He slept through the stop at Matewan, avoided the eyes of Mose and Warren Crews, sent to the depot by Fred Dallara to watch folks boarding and getting off.

When the porter woke him up, they'd made it to Bluefield. He took a scrap of paper from his backpack and read the address written there. *12 Magnolia Way.* By one a.m., he was at the address, lying on his stomach under the porch. He passed out again.

At six, Chicky awoke, slid out from the crawl space and took the derringer flask from his pack. He looked at the thing and marveled on how he could have believed, for twenty-four years, that it could magically refill itself. He wondered how men could get how they got.

He popped the latch and checked that the gun was loaded, both barrels.

When he stepped through the back door to the kitchen, its squeal did not rouse the old man asleep at the table. His oatmeal had gone cold, and the newspaper had fallen to the floor. Hair grew from his earholes, gray wisps given up by scissors.

Chicky stepped to where the man snored in his hardback chair. He pressed the little pistol to the base of the neck, raising up the old man's head. "Charles E. Lively," Chicky said. "Murderer in cold blood of Sid Hatfield, I come to carry out your sentence of death."

Lively did not speak at first. He did not even move, save straightening his neck. Then, as Chicky's finger tensed before the nickel plated trigger, Lively spoke. "There are two words in the English language you should familiarize yourself with, son." He paused, then uttered them: "Self-defense."

Chicky thought back to a time he'd heard this same utterance from another man. It occurred to him that folks could define damn near any word in damn near any fashion they pleased to fit their aims.

The mean edge provided by the Old Cobb Whisky was about to wear off, and it was time to squeeze or walk away. Chicky had decided on the former when a little girl walked from the hallway through the swinging kitchen door.

"Granddaddy," she said. Her nightgown had little stitched roses across the chest, yellow and pink and red. Somebody had taken time in making it. She looked at Chicky, then her grandfather, who spoke to her.

"Go on back to bed, Alice," he said.

She stood her ground, eyeballing them both. In her eyes, Chicky saw what he'd seen in the little girl on the train back in May 1920. The little girl who'd had the bad luck to see seven dead men, knocked down like dominoes on wet dirt. That time, still a boy himself, he'd looked away from the girl. Everything had gone red and wrong. This time, he'd not look away.

None of the three in the little kitchen spoke.

Something occurred to Chicky, as he stood there, gun pressed to another man's head in front of his own granddaughter. Swollen and gauze-mouthed in Welch that day so long ago, he'd refrained from asking Mr. Bern who'd pulled the trigger on Sid Hatfield. He'd done so because the answer would have put him where he was right then. Running and hiding and shooting.

"You got a gun?" the girl asked.

"Go on back to bed," Lively said.

Running and hiding and shooting, Chicky thought. It was time to drop one of the three forever. Two of them were necessary still, but one was not. He lowered the derringer and stepped to the back door. He watched the little girl called Alice who had caught him at his worst, saved him from becoming what he'd once been. When he stepped off the last porch stair, he turned and ran.

Johnnie Johnston was leaving on the 7:30 westbound. Chicago was his destination. He'd never have guessed that Chicky Gold the harmonica man would be sitting next to him, breathing heavy from having almost killed a man, stinking of rotgut whiskey, and trying again to forget everything he'd ever known.

CHAPTER TWENTY

YOU CARRIED WHAT YOU COULD

The suitcase was black, split cowhide with silver hardware. The key that worked its locks was no bigger than a junebug. Inside, it was all double silk, gray. Fine quality stitching. All those compartments necessitated such. Four cylindrical housings meant for a lady's toiletries, sewn tight to the frame. There was a series of snap-down lashes for securing vanity mirrors. And, in addition to the normal inside pockets of such a suitcase, there were those of the hidden variety, small and useful.

It was perfect for a man in need of carrying seven harmonicas, two flasks, a lockbox filled with newspaper clippings, a change of clothes, toothbrush, shaving razor, comb, and hair tonic.

The Civil War backpack had seen its last re-stitching efforts fail in the fall of 1947. It had finally gone rotten beyond repair. Chicky Gold, living in a one-room apartment on Chicago's West Side, had been unable to throw the old pack out. It had been with him for too long. He cut the best pieces from its holey exterior and made from them a belt to hold up his trousers. The buckle he fashioned from the dismantled derringer parts. He'd smashed the little gun to pieces with a sledgehammer the second night he'd called Chicago home in 1946. It was the same night he'd found the little apartment, the same night he'd sworn off firearms for good. If he couldn't give up the drink, he could sure give up the gun.

Two blocks from his place, on Western, was a pawn shop called Iffy's, and about the time the pack went rotten, the toiletry suitcase went on window display. With the money he'd been bringing in for gigs at nightclubs like Pepper's and Sylvio's and the Fickle Pickle, Chicky could buy a suitcase if he wanted to.

By late fall 1952, he could have bought a car with the money he'd made blowing harp all over Chicago. He was a lonely white musician among the likes of Howlin' Wolf and Sonny Boy Williamson and Willie Dixon, all of which he'd played with at one time or another. He'd even recorded some in the studio with Dixon, which meant folks could hear him, though they'd not know his name, playing harmonica on all those thick Chess 78s lining stores downtown. But Chicky had found Arly Jr.'s words to be true, for though he made music with the best of them, he was never friends with a black man or woman in any genuine way. But he'd come to a place in life where he wasn't friends with anybody, no matter the stain of their skin. And his one true friend, Arly, was a man he made himself forget. A man on the run has to forget.

He kept mostly to himself between gigs. When he played St. Louis or New York, he always went ahead of the others, by train, for he'd kept his vow to never sit inside a moving automobile again, even if he could afford one of his own.

Johnnie Johnston had left for St. Louis in 1949, after the initial success of The Homesick Dynamite Boys, the band he'd formed with Chicky and a bass player named Bones Watts. Watts went with him,

Chicky had stayed.

On Halloween night, 1952, Chicky keyed open his suitcase behind a makeshift red velvet curtain covering the stage at the Stuck Pig on Roosevelt. He put the key back in the inside pocket of his black suit coat. The coat, along with matching black pants, patchwork belt, white shirt, and black tie, were the only digs the man would ever be seen in. He was clean-shaven. Short-haired.

That night he chose the 12-hole Echo Vamper. He unsnapped the long harmonica from its housing inside the case. It was a B Flat night, he could feel it, and he'd bent the reeds of the Echo Vamper earlier that evening using toothpicks. He'd give them something they weren't used to for All Hallow's Eve.

Chicky sipped from the gun-less derringer flask covered in etch marks of time. He nodded to the other three men behind the curtain. He could hardly see them through all the smoke. Somehow they fit a stand-up piano and drum kit back there, with enough room left for Chicky and Hubert the singer to get around a little. Hubert nodded back. He was young with conked hair, and he liked Chicky despite his whiteness. The same couldn't be said for the other two, thrown together at the last minute for this show, but they respected his playing ability just the same. If Chicky wanted to take off on a solo, blow his harp with his noseholes like he was known to do, nobody would cut him short. It meant asses stayed in chairs, and asses in chairs put drinks on tables, and drinks on tables put money in a musician's pocket, and pocket money put booze in veins, roofs over heads. Money converted everything.

They all wore black suits and ties. The curtain was pulled and they went straight into the first number, Muddy Waters' "I Be's Troubled." Hubert's voice was low down deep when he sang that he'd never be satisfied. In front of them, the audience sat in unmatched side chairs pulled up to wobbling, squared-off tables covered in Schlitz bottles and half-empty rocks glasses. People smoked and tapped their feet and closed their eyes and swayed. Behind the band, the cracks in the brick wall crumbled a little with each stomp of the foot, tap of the keys, beat of the bass drum. A sign hung from twine and paperclips. It read, in black paint on white butcher's paper: *Happy Halloween.* There was a neon Budweiser sign in the window and a clock behind the bar, nothing else. Up above, exposed conduit snaked the ceiling and waterpipes were wrapped in towels.

White folks had taken to coming to shows here and elsewhere on the West Side, and it was unusual for Chicky to be the only one in the place. That night there were two white men, sitting front and center, looking too sober and clean cut for anybody's liking.

Before the break, Chicky let loose a solo. He bent notes hard and laid on the vibrato. Tongue-blocking it like nobody else could, he stood, rocking at the waist like a metronome. He never sat when he played, always held that microphone in his cupped hand so that the sound assaulted the ears, amplified. He got exercise up there, jumping around and flexing to keep himself young.

When folks thought he had finished, Chicky began to sing into his harmonica, all throat wobble, filtered and loud. "Well, lovers is you right?" he sang. "Oh, yes we right. Bluefield women read and write, Keystone women bite and fight." No one, not the native Chicagoans or the migrants up from the Delta, knew what the hell this all meant, but they clapped anyway.

As the band went to break, Hubert introduced his bandmates. When he said, "And on harp, Mr. Chicky Gold," one of the white men bent to the other and whispered something. Chicky noticed.

He took his suitcase with him to the bathroom.

He never came back out.

It turned out that they weren't really there for him. Hubert was a draft dodger, evading those Far East orders to Korea. An overly ambitious F.B.I. agent had asked his police officer buddy to accompany him to the Stuck Pig that night on a tip that Hubert would be performing. The F.B.I. agent had gotten a warrant from the judge to arrest the young singer, and he aimed to do so. While Chicky listened from the bathroom, they cuffed Hubert for his non-patriotism and asked the other two, "Where's that Chicky Gold gone to?" That was all he needed to climb out the window.

What the cop friend had whispered before the break was that the name "Chicky Gold" rang a bell. That before he'd moved north for work, he'd spent some time in West Virginia, mining coal. That a man had used that name as an alias, a man who'd been involved in a Bolshevik plot of some sort against those who might make a little money in this life. It was all a little unclear to the cop, but he gave the F.B.I. man his take on things. "That harmonica man is a fugitive from way back. He came out of hiding, then disappeared again a few years ago."

The next morning, Chicky was on the ten a.m. train bound for St. Louis.

As Chicky had discovered for himself upon re-entering civilization, the telephone was a truly magnificent invention. Between Halloween and Christmas of 1952, it was used near to death by lawmen in Chicago, calling up other lawmen in West Virginia. There weren't many energetic folks around from the mine wars of the 1920s, but those who were around got hot under the collar. Especially the Crews brothers. And Sheriff Frank Dallara. This Chicky Gold, this one-time Trenchmouth Taggart, murderer in cold blood, had resurfaced to bury his mama, then disappeared again. Now, more than five years later, according to the F.B.I., he was a bluesman in Chicago. But his apartment had come up empty. He was running again.

There were men who aimed to catch him, and they had the latest phones and guns.

So it was that Chicky Gold went west, and on a special Christmas Eve show at the Cosmopolitan Club in St. Louis, sat in with the house band, The Sir John Trio. Sir John was his old piano man Johnnie Johnston, who was doing well enough. But not well enough to quit his job at the steel mill. That night, his sax player had the flu, so another newcomer was sitting in. The replacement was named Chuck Berry, and he had his own kind of hillbilly flair. Chicky was drawn to it, and the two traded solos on stage as eagerly as they traded flasks of whiskey behind it.

They played an improvised duet involving the exchange of shouts: "Chicky!" "Chucky!" "Now Chicky!" "Now Chucky!" and so on, the crowd roaring in between. It was big city, hillbilly, holy hell blues, and nobody who saw it forgot.

Chicky had no idea that Chuck Berry was to be the first of two famous music men he'd meet in a week's time. One was on his way up. The other, his way out.

When the same jar-headed F.B.I. man showed up in the crowd during the final number of the night, he had Warren Crews in tow. Warren Crews had aged, but the look in his eyes was the same as it had been that day playing Mumblety Peg. There was hate there.

Chicky was on the run again. In the parking lot, he slashed the F.B.I. man's tires. He said to his friend, for the third time in six years, "Be good, Johnnie," and, in the middle of a blackout, did something he said he never would again. He got inside an automobile, the Cadillac Series 62 convertible Chuck Berry had on loan.

The smell of the law and the sight of Warren Crews had gotten

Chicky thinking on the past again, and he had to double up on the drink to keep from busting. But he was fifty years old, and his liver was giving out. The binge he started with Chuck nearly broke him.

He rode in a car and blacked out for three straight days.

When he woke up on December 29th, Chuck Berry was nowhere to be found. Chicky was alone on the cheap linoleum floor of an illegal bar in the back of an abandoned barn. He tried to lift his head. His face stuck to the linoleum. When he pulled it free, it was quickly evident that his own dried blood was the adhesive. His mouth throbbed.

When he put his fingers to it, he winced. The gums were ragged, swollen like they'd never been before. The gold was gone. Arly's words came back to him. "They'll pry em out of your head for pawn."

Four top, four bottom, all pulled with the pliers now sitting in the corner wearing the steely crimson fingerprints of a cold-blooded unknown man. Chicky retched twice. There was nothing left to come up. He'd let go all a man could and still live. It was everywhere around him. Blood, vomit. Whoever had done it had left his black wool overcoat hung on a nail in the wall. The suitcase was gone. The seven harmonicas, including his daddy's Marine Band. All gone. But across the room, broken open, its contents still there, was the little lockbox. The Widow's saved newspaper stories. Nobody had need to steal stories. They were still his to carry.

Looking at the room, all he could surmise was that he'd been poisoned, finally, by the drink. Poisoned enough to lose three days and sleep through a tooth extraction. He tried to get up but couldn't. A fever was on him. He pulled at his clothes to let the winter air on his skin.

Then he did something he had never before done.

Lord, he prayed to himself, shivering hot. *Get me through this one and I won't take another drink.*

He lay there, burning, unable to lift his head. He watched the dried blood and vomit swirl in patterns on the linoleum next to his face. All went red. Glowing red. Then nothing.

When he was able to get up, Chicky washed up in a creek, gargled over those gums though it nearly killed him to do it. The wool coat they'd left him kept the winter wind out of his bones and he clutched the lockbox as if frozen. He saw a sign on the road, and his best guess was that he'd somehow ended up near Cape Girardeau, Missouri. He hopped and rode an empty freight car east. It wasn't long before he hit the Kentucky line.

By the time he got into southern West Virginia in the pre-dawn morning of December 31st, 1952, all Chicky Gold wanted in this world was a drink of liquor for his pain. He jumped off the slow moving freighter, hit the deck hard, and scrambled back up. He ran in earnest to the only place he could think of where a fugitive might procure the strongest shine known to man.

It was ridiculous to think that a jar of the Widow's moonshine could still be inside Mary Blood's hollowed out tombstone after all those years, but he dug down just the same. He found the chute and the canister, opened it. He'd never felt the kind of relief that swept his bloodstream when he saw that canning jar, its murky contents sloshing. But before he unscrewed the lid to swallow, he saw himself, as if from above, on his knees in the sloped Methodist cemetery, digging in the dirt of the dead. It seemed then that he'd always been digging. Digging holes to bury clay marbles and Indian Head pennies. Climbing up hills and digging out holes to hide away from the world. Digging holes to shit into. Digging up the dead. Now he dug again, and if he drank what was unearthed, he'd no doubt die himself. On top of it all, he'd made a promise to a God he wasn't sure could hear.

Chicky slipped the full jar into his coat pocket and ran for the railyard.

As the hours passed on that New Year's Eve, and as the rain turned to sleet, Chicky's thatched home in the high hills above Bluefield called to him. It struck him that he'd lived there almost a quarter century of his life, alone, and off the booze. He'd thought he was sipping it all that time, from the magic flask, but he'd found out different. There was no magic in life. Only crazy.

Robbed of his teeth and damn near his life, he knew that crazy and alone on a mountain was better than what was left for him down there. More running. The past catching up.

At half past ten, he stood out back of a service station in the dark, pacing. He had freight-hopped to the outskirts of Bluefield by then. His plan had been to make a trade with the attendant inside, moonshine for provisions. But the more he paced, the more he became paranoid that the attendant would recognize his face, call out the F.B.I. For all he knew he could have been in the papers again.

Out front, a baby blue, rag top Cadillac pulled up to the pumps. The driver, no older than eighteen, stepped out and stretched. His breath turned to condensation in the cold air. He looked at the tall, thin man seated in the back. "You want somethin to eat, Mr. Williams?" he said.

"No. Just want to get some sleep." The man stepped out. His cheeks were sunken and he wore a center-dent, white felt Stetson. He stretched as his driver had done. The cowbell on the station door jingled as the boy went inside.

Chicky watched the tall man. He estimated the fellow couldn't weigh more than 130 pounds soaking wet. There was something familiar about him. Without knowing why, Chicky approached.

Each sized up the other, hunched a few feet apart to keep dry under the overhang. "Evenin," Mr. Williams said, nodding.

Chicky nodded back. His gold teeth gone, he was re-perfecting the art of silence, of hiding his mouth like he'd done for so many years as a child.

"You look worse than I feel, Mister." The accent was deep south. Alabama.

Chicky didn't answer. He looked in the back of the car, the guitar propped on the seat.

The attendant came out and starting pumping gas one-handed. With the other, he drank an RC Cola. Chicky watched him and felt his stomach lurch. If he didn't eat, he'd be sick. If he ate, he'd be sick.

Mr. Williams stepped around his Cadillac and stuffed his hands in his pants pockets. He breathed in and looked at the hills surrounding them. "Pretty country," he said. The attendant didn't respond. He finished filling up and went inside.

The boy emerged with two sandwiches, chips, and two RCs. When he tried to give one to Mr. Williams, the man stood still, then took it and looked at it. "Let's go," the boy said. He got in the car.

Before he climbed into the backseat, Mr. Williams handed Chicky the sandwich. Pimiento cheese. "You look like you could use this more 'n I could," he said.

Chicky took it. He knew it was the last food he'd eat for a while that he hadn't trapped or picked off a bush. "Here," he said, without opening his mouth much. He pulled the last existing jar of the Widow's mule-kick from his coat pocket and handed it to the man. They nodded goodbye and went their ways, one to a mountaintop, the other to sip and sleep and never wake up again.

As he climbed, revelers welcomed in the New Year with drink and dance. None of them knew he was to be taken, again, by the wilderness. And Chicky Gold did not know that down below, in a week's time, he'd met both the man who'd kill the blues for rock'n roll, and the man who'd kill himself with corn liquor, taking country music, real country music, with him.

Chicky Gold didn't even have a harmonica to blow. No gun, no knife, and no liquor. He had a pimiento cheese sandwich and the clothes on his back. He had newspaper stories.

CHAPTER TWENTY-ONE

WIDE VISION RUNNING

It was to be a bad winter. Signs foretold it. Beavers built lodges with twice the logs and the screech owls cried like a woman. August had been foggy. Tree bark grew thicker on the north side of a tree, wild onions had six layers, and acorns came in double cropped. So, Chicky Gold gathered all of the acorns he could. Alongside the drying parts and pelts of opossum and raccoon and black-tailed jackrabbits, he stockpiled chicory root and spruce needles and wild onion bulbs. Two decades in the woods as a relatively young man had taught him some of this, but his second go-round had taught him more. He'd come to the wilderness with nothing this time, and he'd made it through. New Year's Day 1958 was three months away, and if he made it through the winter, he'd have spent five more years of his life alone on a mountaintop.

He awoke to an October sunrise, curled like a baby, on the side of a trail. He'd been night tracking a cougar until two a.m. Most folks thought mountain cats weren't in these hills, but Chicky knew the track to be genuine. The Widow had shown him one as a boy.

Four paws, retracted claws, and a three-split pad. Tracking a cougar could fool a regular man into thinking the animal walked on two feet—when it picked up its front paw, the back one came forward and landed smack in the front's impression. A single register of its path.

Chicky could smell the cat's scent piles from a quarter mile off. He had ground to cover, and he traveled light despite winter moving in. He'd converted his Bostonian shoes into moccasins when the soles ran out, replacing the bottoms with tanned animal hide. He'd used the old favorite raccoon penis bone as needle, rabbit sinew as thread. In this way he was able to fashion clothes for all seasons from what he killed.

His hair had grown long and his beard reached his chest. Both were gray.

He found the cougar's freshest scent pile and relieved his own bladder on top of it. Then he was back to fast-tracking, wide-open running. He unfocused his eyes so that he had peripheral and wide-reaching sight. He landed silently on the outside balls of his feet and rolled inward. He became the cat he tracked.

Twenty yards from the edge of a mountain stream, where clearing met with thick woods, Chicky ceased his stalk to wait. To ambush. He knew the area, knew that he was less than a half mile from the mountain bald where Clarence Dickason and Rose Kozma had made their home. He'd passed the spot on his way back up five years prior, and even then the place had been deserted for some time. It was in ruin. The outhouse had caved in under a tree limb. He'd never find out what became of Clarence or Rose, and often he wondered about little Albert, and especially little Zizi. At weak moments, out there alone, he longed to hold the baby. To soothe her.

From his crouch behind a tulip poplar, he saw the cat. Its shoulder muscles rolled and piggybacked each other as it walked diagonal.

When it bent to drink at the water's edge, it stopped and Chicky watched those ears move independent of one another, forward, back, sideways, listening for him. When its tongue touched water, he stood, feet planted. Keeping his spear close to his body, he drew back slow and let go fast. The animal heard the short range intruder and turned. Cat-backed and claws out, it jumped from the creek's edge and howled. The spear had missed and now the man faced the animal. For a moment, he wanted to howl back, to hiss and yowl like he had as a boy when Fred Dallara kissed Clarissa. But he watched the cat instead. After several seconds of the standoff, it ran.

He'd not mastered the spear like other weapons. The sinew and hide slingshot he'd made easily knocked foxes and raccoons silly. He had the bones and pelts and full belly to prove that he'd never forgotten the slingshot lessons Frank Dallara had given him. And the four bait-stick deadfall traps he moved once a week and reset had harvested squirrels and rabbits to keep him fed through winter. But when streams froze over and his trident spear could catch no fish, when the cold moved in so bad that he holed up inside his hut for days at a time, he wished he could figure out how to get the big game without a gun. Once, he'd dropped on top of an eight-point buck from a hickory tree branch, stabbed away at the animal's throat with a flint-rock knife while it tried to buck him off. But this had been a slow, awful kill. He'd dry-preserved it, eaten from the deer for months, but he never hunted that way again.

The cougar had escaped him for two years running.

That night, he used his bow drill to make a fire. When he'd done his sit-ups, jumping jacks, and push-ups, he ate. When he'd eaten, he boiled the inner bark scrapings of an oak tree in water. It cooled some, and he swashed it over his emptied gums and spit. It dulled the pain. So did the spruce needle tea and chicory root coffee he made over the fire. He had rituals. He had drinks to nullify his aching mind and body. It wasn't whiskey, but he'd promised God that he'd not sip that drink again, and he aimed to keep his promise.

He'd never prayed again in the years since that morning on the Missouri linoleum. He mostly kept his body busy to stay out of his own head. Fishing, trapping, hunting, picking root, these things could fill a man's days. Nights were when he got himself in trouble. Memories came at night.

On that particular October night, he did what he always did to keep from going crazy. He pulled out those newspaper clippings the Widow had saved for him. He'd read those stories until they fell apart. He licked his thumbs and patched them back together. The words blurred, disappeared in spots. He'd memorized their every word so it didn't matter much. He read of coal mine wars and world wars. On the backsides, there were parts of fluff stories with no real purpose, like the one from 1932 about a zoo animal: *$6000 hippopotamus in the Cincinnati, Ohio Zoo chokes on an indoor baseball and dies.* Police Blotters told of folks *loitering in houses of ill fame,* driving while drunk, assaulting, and, of course, *possessing un-taxpaid whiskey.*

There were two stories that he'd read most often, both from a newspaper out of Richwood called the *News-Leader,* both written by a man named Jim Comstock. This man rose easily above the others. He could write a bluestreak, and his subjects were real there on the page. Mountain people who'd kept the ways of old. Or their children, who were used up by World War II and coal mines and sent home minus limbs. These stories got Chicky to writing his own. He put down the ways of the Widow. The cure-alls for ailments, the hunting knowledge, and the philosophies on how to live right. At first, he'd used the charred black ends of kindling to write on scrap pieces of tanned hide. But this was impractical. Soon, he'd again found a use for the raccoon penis bone, of which he possessed a multitude. Sharpened and dipped in a mixture of ash water and animal blood, Chicky carved his stories indelibly on the stripped and soaked basswood and black cherry skins he procured daily. It was beautiful paper, thick but pliable. Able to be rolled into a scroll and quick to soak in stain. He marked his homemade paper with frequency. One story was titled, *The Woman Could Cure Ailments*. Another: *Frank Dallara Fashioned a Tool*. He'd become a sort of warped, lonely version of the newspaperman the Widow had wanted him to be. And he never felt as good as when he wrote.

In April 1958, they came up the hill in a team. Most of them were city-footed. A geologist, a government man in charge of zoning, an engineer. Experts from the university in topography, cartography, and economics. There was a state man for land rights and another from the U.S. Forest Reserve. They spoke on surface mining. Underground was a thing of the past. Stripping a mountain top to bottom was cheaper and easier and required less men. Some in the group had ideas on taking the whole mountain top off to get to the seam.

They stopped to eat lunch and looked upwards at the incline that eventually led to Chicky's hidden home on high. All they saw was bituminous gold.

He heard them when they were still a half mile off. At first he moved quick in the sound's direction. Wide-vision running toward the only human echo he'd encountered in five years. Then he slowed, stalked the men from above. In thick red, they painted symbols on trees. They set up tripods and pressed small buttons on small machines. They laughed while they worked. It was easy to laugh when the earth could yield so many dollars.

Chicky was packed by midnight. He burned his thatched hut.

Inside the hides of raccoons and foxes, he rolled up dried meat and plants and the stories he'd written. All of these he bound with sinew cordage and strapped to his belt.

He was northeast-bound by three a.m. Richwood was the place he had in mind.

He'd stayed inside the Appalachian's upper range folds for the most part. As best he could figure, he'd hiked north of Hinton, then south of Oak Hill, on up into Nicholas County, a part of the state he'd never ventured before. To a tourist, the terrain might have seemed the same as the highlands above Bluefield. But to Chicky, it was like a new world. Mid-May, he found himself on jutted rock, 4,000 feet in the air, stairstepping with his arms out like a trapeze artist. An hour later, his footing was moss-covered. Birch and hemlock trees abounded, and he'd never seen so many deer. On a single day, he counted three turkeys. He descended into a valley and came upon pasture after pasture. Then, a spongy type of earth unlike any he'd felt before. He was convinced he'd come across swampland in West Virginia, though he knew this to be impossible.

Twice he heard human voices, and twice he hid.

When he heard the unmistakable sound of water running, he followed it. These rivers and streams were clearer than any in southern West Virginia. The trout were quicker. They tested his speed and accuracy with the trident spear he'd strapped to his back.

On a particularly sunny mid-morning descent toward where he imagined Richwood to be, he picked up the sound of water running hard. He tracked it. It was further than it first called out, and as he got closer, its volume confused him. When he finally came upon the source, he understood. Standing atop the smooth rock edge, he grew dizzy looking down. Forty feet below, the water hit the churning pool and kept going. It was the only waterfall he'd ever seen.

He followed the river down the mountain further and came upon another waterfall. Then another. The third was nosebleed high. Eighty feet or more, he estimated. The sun came through the canopy and lit the locomotion of water like crystal. Chicky made it to the bottom and looked up, shading his eyes with his hand. He stripped himself of packs and belt and clothes and moccasins, braced for the cold, and walked into the frigid pool. He screamed something awful when that ice water enveloped him, but he pushed on. He wanted to feel that waterfall power come down on his skin. It was to be the most memorable of his outdoor bathing experiences. He held steady under the barrage of the waterfall though it knocked him down. He stood back up and hollered, though he could hardly hear himself over the rush of it all. His skin grew red and swollen. Pounded to numb. He raked through his hair, his beard. Let the force of the water wash it all clean. Eyes closed, ears roaring, he opened his mouth and let the water cleanse his ravaged gums.

He was like this for twenty minutes.

When he emerged, there was a group of people watching him from the makeshift trail above. Chicky pulled himself from the small pool and stood upright, in his altogether, to face them. He twisted his hair and his long beard, wrung himself out like a wet towel. The lone woman in the group turned her back. One man laughed himself silly, another snapped photographs. The one who seemed to be leading them, a slender man with a graceful gait, told the laugher to be still. He raised a hand and waved at Chicky.

He knew the group was not surveying for coal seams. They didn't have that arrogance of presence. That greed about them. But they weren't tourists either. He decided not to wave back. He stared at the slender man a little, noticed that he carried a small notebook in his shirtpocket, a pencil in his ear. Chicky put his clothes back on, re-lashed his gear, and climbed up the opposite incline as they watched him, before descending to the bottom of the falls themselves.

When Chicky had disappeared up the ridge, the man bent to where he'd dripped dry. While the others in his party discussed the viability of clear-cutting a path into the falls for tourists, their organizer took out his notebook and wrote on the mountain man, his demeanor and dress. The way he scampered up a hill. He didn't know that the same man would walk into his office two days later.

Looking down at the lights of Richwood past dusk, Chicky had thought about a shave and a haircut. But he didn't know Nicholas County barbershops. They may not take a man such as himself off the street for a cleanup. And he had no money to his name. His trident spear had broken, his dried food supply had run out, and the sight of human beings had changed him.

He walked into Richwood on a Monday morning in late May. It rained, and folks stared at him from inside their cars.

The street sign told him he was on Oakford Avenue. There was a little restaurant with a neon sign above the door reading *Ritzy Rae Diner*, and without thinking much, he walked in. A lone man sat at the counter chewing a toothpick. He regarded Chicky and put down the fork he was using to cut his eggs over easy. He blinked more than normal. Behind the counter, a woman stood up from where she had been unstacking supplies. She went still when she saw him, the silver napkin holders in each hand seemingly balancing her, keeping her from falling down. "Can I help you honey?" she said. She was pretty, brunette.

"Yes ma'am," Chicky said. "I'm looking for the offices of a publication called the *News-Leader*. A fella by the name of Comstock." He dripped where he stood, careful not to step from the welcome mat.

"*News-Leader?*" the man said. He frowned and looked past Chicky, through the pane glass behind his head.

"Honey, that paper ain't been around for ten years or more," the woman told him. "But Jim Comstock runs the *Hillbilly* out of his office over on Main Street." She almost smiled. "He expectin you?"

"No ma'am," Chicky said.

"You hungry?"

He didn't answer. If he hadn't long ago perfected keeping his mouth securely tight-lipped while conversing, he might have smiled at her. To a man such as himself, she looked more beautiful than anything nature could offer. And she'd offered to feed him.

"I make biscuits and red-eye gravy you wouldn't believe," she said.

"I appreciate your generosity. Thank you for the direction." He nodded to her, then to the man with the toothpick, and stepped back into the rain.

The glass window front of the small building on Main Street read the *West Virginia Hillbilly: A Newspaper.* For the second time that morning, he almost smiled. He pulled the door open and stepped inside. The front office was unoccupied, but the phone on the desk rang loudly. From the second office, behind a half-opened door, a voice hollered, "Dorothea, you mind gettin that?" The phone quit, there were some mumbles from the back office, and a toilet flushed inside a closed door to Chicky's right. He gathered it was Dorothea in the john, Comstock in the back, and he didn't wait for her to emerge. Instead, he shook what water he could on the mat and walked directly to the man whose writing had kept him going on so many nights when nothing else could.

He knocked, then entered. When the swivel chair came around to face him, Chicky saw the same slender man he'd seen at the waterfall two days prior. This, for some reason, caused him finally to smile, full on. He revealed the empty spaces of his mouth, the strangely healed gums. For most, such a sight as this would be cause for alarm. Chicky was, after all, a grizzled, animal-hided, toothless man. But Jim Comstock only smiled back and said, "Mornin."

Chicky nodded.

"Or maybe I ought to say 'hello again.'"

Chicky used the wide vision so expertly honed all those years to get a feel for the place. There were piles everywhere. Books, papers, more books. A mess of what some might call junk, others treasure. The man himself was well-groomed, near to handsome, and he wore a shirt and tie, semi-pressed.

"Mr. Jim Comstock?" Chicky finally spoke.

"That's right. What can I do for you sir?" He held his spectacles in between two fingers, touched the earpiece to his chin.

"Wellsir," Chicky said, "My name is A.C. Gilbert." He stepped forward and the two shook hands. "I think you're a very fine writer, and I'm lookin to get into the newspaper business myself."

CHAPTER TWENTY-TWO

WRITING CAME NATURAL

It was as it had been before. Re-entry into civilization. This time he dubbed himself A.C. Gilbert, a name he had never forgotten from childhood. The original A.C. Gilbert had invented the Erector Set, and in doing so had stolen a boy's hidden hobby. This new A.C. figured it was fair give-and-take to use the moniker.

His haircut and shave were professional this time, paid for by Comstock. The barber in town loved cutting hair, and A.C.'s would be a worthy challenge. "He'll make a ring around your eyes and set the brush on fire," Comstock had said. "He'll set your ears back just right." It was after he'd read the tree skin scrawls left for his perusal that Comstock offered the grooming and the purchase of a suit, hat, and shoes. A visit to the dentist, Dr. Pinkerton, was arranged for working on those gums, though teeth were not in the budget. Comstock also agreed to staff A.C. as a feature writer. His first month's rent for the one room space above the *Hillbilly*'s office was an advance on more to come. A.C. wanted cash under the table, and Comstock was happy to oblige. It wasn't everyday that he came across such writing as the mountain man's.

There was a kitchen faucet and a claw-footed bathtub in the little apartment. Two-burner gas stove, electrical outlets for lamps. A.C. came to enjoy all of it. A man accustomed to wilderness survival was suspicious of modern conveniences, but he was equally drawn to their capabilities. Their boastful claim to invention.

His first few stories for the paper were done with ink pen on yellow legal pad. Dorothea typed the copy and Comstock edited. One was an ode to the raccoon penis bone. Its uses as a toothpick, writing utensil, and sewing needle. Another story was on sassafras tea, instructing to use only the red roots. Then there were ramps. Jim Comstock had a thing for the little, garlic-like plant growing all around Richwood. He sent A.C. to gather, cook, and eat the plant in as many ways as he could, then write what he wanted about all of it. He was glad to. They kept him young.

Comstock busied himself with the business end of things, and writing about politics, religion, literature. Folks were taking notice of the spare but sharp weekly out of West Virginia. Folks in New York and Chicago, among others. The subscription blanks in the back of each issue started coming in faster than Dorothea could handle the checks and dollar bills inside. Somehow, she found time to instruct A.C. on the art of banging Underwood typewriter keys.

He typed one phrase over and over in those days. Dorothea found it to be the best finger training for a novice newspaperman. Sitting in his apartment at night, the old Underwood on his kitchen table, A.C. typed, hundreds and hundreds of times, *Now is the time for all good men to come to the aid of their country. Now is the time for all good men to come to the aid of their country. Now is the time for all good men to come to the aid of their country.*

Everyday, A.C. had his breakfast and lunch at the Ritzy Rae Diner.

He made acquaintances there, if not friends. Though Jim Comstock never did, other folks asked A.C. where he'd come from. "Wheeling, thereabouts," he'd answer. It was left at that, because here was a man for whom uncomfortable questions of the past were imposing and plain rude. His eyes and his weathered skin told would-be-conversationalists to pick a new subject. Like the weather. Or the difference between rainbow, steelhead, and brook trout.

He'd told everybody in town he was born in 1916. That he was forty-two years of age. It seemed the truth, because despite the obviousness of having lived hard, the man had the build and the presence of a fast, young type. Like a prizefighter just past his prime. And folks around Richwood were accustomed to men and women looking older than their years. It had always been that way.

One day at lunch, A.C. was drinking his third cup of the mud black coffee Rae served up. A man in town to hunt was at the countertop beside him, asking after where to buy wooden turkey calls of the hand-held variety.

"I don't truthfully know," A.C. told him. "Never was much on turkey. But you can use your mouth just as well, I reckon."

"Your mouth?" the man said.

The cowbell on the front door handle rang out. A woman in a sharp white top and gray skirt walked in, as out-of-place as out-of-place could be. People kept up their conversations, one-eyed and eared. The woman walked toward the lunch counter and stood beside A.C. The turkey hunter was bug-eyed. She was an olive-skinned, pulled-back hair, big city beauty. She carried a black leather portfolio under her arm.

Rae asked if she could help the woman.

"Yes, thank you. My name is Cynthia Webster. I've just come from Mr. Comstock's office. I'm a writer for the *Saturday Review*, here on an interview about the *Hillbilly*. Mr. Comstock said I might find Mr. Gilbert here, the local feature writer." It was fast speech, and very proper.

"Well," Rae said. "He's settin right here in front of you."

Ms. Webster turned to the turkey hunter. He seemed the obvious choice. The stitching in his leather outdoorsman jacket was sophisticated in its placement. He wore expensive spectacles. "Mr. Gilbert," she said, and held out her free hand.

"Nope," the man said. He was playing disinterested now, had learned that doing so, combined with removing his wedding ring, attracted single women.

Rae poured more coffee. "Next one down the line, honey," she said.

Ms. Webster regarded A.C. cautiously but apologetically. It was natural to assume his unimportance. Despite the suit, he was a local with lips that told of the absence of front teeth. "Pleasure," she said. They shook hands. "I'm down from New York just this morning. I wondered if I might interview you briefly. Your paper has caused quite a cultural interest in this region's unique customs."

A.C. nodded and thought how glorious it was to see such words emerge from perfectly-formed lips. He found that he could not carry on with a lady of this magnitude in such a claustrophobic arena. "Why don't we go for a walk?" he proposed.

They did. And Ms. Webster got her interview, which ran the following month. Readers of the *Saturday Review* fell in love with the two-man staff of the Appalachian newspaper then, and subscriptions kept coming. A.C. had charmed Ms. Webster, and she often called him at the office to talk about city customs and country ones. Flat versus hill. She even spoke on a return visit, or the other way around. On him coming to the city that never slept.

＊ ＊ ＊

On April Fool's Day, 1960, A.C. sat at his wide oak desk opposite Dorothea, practicing his copywriting skills. Mostly he was preoccupied with thoughts of Cynthia Webster. For almost two years, she'd flown in every couple months, at first under the guise of professional work, later personal. She kissed him on the third visit, despite his attempts to turn cheek. She loved him, and looked past the superficial, the mouth that had plagued him all his life. On the fourth visit, she stopped booking a hotel room.

He was proofing a piece Comstock had written called "How to Make Your Own Drinkin' Likker." It was, as usual, pristine and devoid of grammatical error. But A.C. couldn't help but find fault in some of the moonshining advice. The fire under the mash seemed too high by this account. The suggestion to use parsnips instead of potatoes if it came to it rang false for quality. When Comstock had asked him to proof it, he'd eyed A.C. strange. Almost like he knew the man had himself brewed up mule kick. It had been another of their moments when it was evident that the country editor suspected his new employee had seen some things. Done some things. As always, both let the moment pass.

Articles on homebrew, like articles on coal mining or the race issue, had caused A.C. to consider offering his own expertise and experience. Maybe he'd write something about the new mining technologies, the surface or strip variety that put men out of work and killed whole mountainsides and the streams that ran there. He thought about a piece on Moundsville, on men like Arly Jr. But, to write such material would open things he'd closed tight. To do so would risk uncovering what he'd worked hard to cover. It would risk

U.S. Marshals and the F.B.I. and sons-of-bitches like Fred Dallara and the Crews brothers. He had no idea if such folks were still interested in tracking him, or if they even lived and breathed. He was not ready to find out. He stuck with writing on mustard poultices and walking sticks and boiling up poke greens.

The phone rang and Dorothea picked it up. She signaled him and excused herself for lunch. A.C. walked over and found his sweetheart's voice on the other end.

"It's official," Cynthia Webster said. "Kennedy will be in Charleston on Tuesday. They say he's planning to campaign hard." John F. Kennedy had finished up his primary in Wisconsin and most folks thought he'd skip West Virginia for fear of too many stubborn Protestants.

"Hot damn," A.C. said. "You comin to town early then?"

"I booked a flight this morning. I'll be there Sunday evening."

"I'll scrub the floors and clean out the ashtrays," he said.

She laughed. She knew him now better than most, though he'd never told her his true identity. She forgave his mistrust of the automobile, his dislike of the big city. She did not find it unfair that he'd never come to New York. "A.C.," she said. "Bill Simpson over at the *Times* got me an inside track to Kennedy's primary plans. I think I can get you and Jim an interview. Apparently, he's familiar with Jim's work."

"Hot damn," A.C. said.

Cynthia spoke with the man from the *New York Times* later that day and got Bobby Kennedy's number on the road. He told her his brother would be glad to sit down with a man like Comstock, that he could ride along a little if he wanted. By Saturday, the news had spread through Richwood. The Catholic rich boy was willing to ante up.

On Sunday, A.C. took the early train to Charleston to wait for Cynthia's arrival. They'd agreed to meet at the train station at six. At 6:30, when a fat lady in the coffee shop started hollering before she fainted outright, he was still waiting. He'd have to wait forever. On approach, the DC-8 had lost altitude fast and exploded against the side of a mountain.

The ABC store was thirty-seven steps from the train station. He'd counted them after the news came in about the crash. People cried and gathered around televisions. But A.C. just kept quiet and walked out of the place. When he got to the liquor store, he cursed the blue laws while at the same time thanking them for keeping his hand from the bottle. But they couldn't keep his hand from the loose brick protruding from the building's façade. He pried it out and readied himself to throw it through the glass windowpane. To re-unite him with the best friend he'd given up so long ago, the liquid friend who could ease his pain like no woman ever could. Now that he'd lost another woman, he figured he'd let it rip. But his knees buckled before he could throw the brick. His behind hit the pavement and his vision went red as it had so many times before. The blurry crimson came again with jumbled visions. Mountains crumbled. Automobiles and jet planes were ignited in fireballs. The high-pitched, vibrato howl roared through all of it.

A.C. came to and stood up. He dropped the brick, walked back to the station, boarded the 8:00 to Richwood, and holed up in his apartment. He curled on his mattress and wondered if everything he ever loved would forever turn to shit.

CHAPTER TWENTY-THREE

KENNEDY HAD A WAY

Jim Comstock didn't wait long to fix things. He had a key to the apartment upstairs, and though he'd never have done so otherwise, he used it when his knocks went unanswered. It was past noon on Tuesday. He had news.

The door's catch clicked behind him, and he could see A.C. under the thin white sheet, still balled up. Comstock knew the place smelled like Ajax on account of Cynthia's perceived arrival two nights prior. He walked over to his friend. "I don't know what to say about it, so I won't say anything other than I'm sorry. Truly sorry." He cleared his throat. "Anyway, I reckoned you'd let me pound all day, so I let myself in. Got news."

A.C. had never been one to sulk or show weakness in the company of others. He sat up. He was still in his undershirt, slacks, and socks. Before he said anything, he loosed a Chesterfield from its pack on the bedside table and lit it. Smoke in the lungs could halfway right the ship this early. "News you say?" He was forcing out meaningless words, like a character actor.

"News. You know ol Doc Pinkerton's had an eye on those gums since you got here."

A.C. eyed him sideways.

"I never have paid you enough to even think about a dentist, I know that. But Dorothea's the action type. In time of sorrow especially. She's been around the last couple days taking up a little here and there."

"C'mon, Jim." He held the cigarette with his lips, pulled his shirt on.

"Now just listen. You know he made that wax impression when you went in. He's over there finishing up a set of temporaries right now. I believe he called them 'immediate dentures.' Somethin new."

A.C. stood. He had the movements of a man about to give up. Too tired to really argue. "Jim, false teeth ain't going to fix what's happened."

"I know that. But work fixes anything that's broken. And I'm putting you to work. The dentures is just so you don't send young Kennedy running for Spruce Knob."

"How's that?"

"I've got something that's come up. I've got to go to Hinkle tomorrow. Personal business." He cleared his throat again. "Anyhow, he's speakin at the capitol tomorrow noon. I've got you on the six a.m. back to Charleston. You'll follow him around like a dog for as long as you can. Sniff out the Catholic."

"Jim, I'm not interested in—"

"His brother Robert knew Cynthia a little I guess. He said nice things. Said for you to come on."

A.C. sat down on the bed again. He dragged, inhaled, exhaled, and shook his head. "I wasn't even goin to New York for the funeral, Jim."

"Well. That's alright."

"I didn't even know her goddamned people, her kin." He clapped himself hard on the back of the neck four times.

Comstock was through talking. They exchanged a look.

"Teeth," A.C. said. "Goddamned teeth."

They hurt and they were hard to talk with. He'd practiced all the way on the train, gumming rubber and tonguing porcelain. He read aloud all the newspaper reports Jim had saved about Kennedy's primary thus far. In Wisconsin, the Catholic issue had blown open even wider. The waves reached all the way to Senator Bob Byrd, now back home, with his fiddle in one hand and Bible in the other. He was stirring folks that hadn't thought to be stirred, playing to the crowds at backroads churches. A Catholic was coming to sell West Virginians on what they couldn't afford to buy, he said.

A.C. couldn't have cared less about religion. About a rich boy from New England. He just wanted to work so he could forget her. He couldn't drink and pick a fight just to taste his own blood, so work was the next best thing.

There were close to five hundred people on the steps of the Charleston Post Office that day at noon. John Kennedy moved back and forth among them with a microphone gripped tight in his left hand. He had a way about him that told questioners to bring on the Catholic stuff. To have at it. "I am a Catholic," he spoke loudly. "Does that mean that I can't be the president of the United States?" Folks listened to him. "My brother was able to give his life, but we can't be president?" A.C. already had death on the brain, and listening to this young man speak on his own brother's death allowed some clarity on the subject somehow. A.C. had seen plenty of death, and he'd come through okay before. He nodded as Kennedy hollered to the listeners, "Nobody asked me if I was a Catholic when I joined the United States Navy. Nobody asked my brother if he was a Catholic or Protestant before he climbed into an American bomber plane to fly his last mission."

The New Englander had gained the quiet attention and respect of the West Virginians. He was scrappy, and when he spoke, the words became truth somehow. The words were not manufactured. They were honest. They were real. A.C. pulled his notepad out and wrote down all of them.

After the speech, he spoke with Kennedy's campaign chairman, a fellow named McDonough. McDonough told him to come on to Huntington that evening. He set up a six o'clock dinner interview, assuming A.C. was willing to follow them. "I don't carry in automobiles," A.C. told him.

This confused McDonough, who only said, "Jim's Steak and Spaghetti, six o'clock," then walked away.

A.C. hotfooted it back to the train station to check the Huntington schedule.

The United Mine Workers favored Hubert Humphrey, not John Kennedy. In the space labeled *Periodicals* at the Huntington Public Library, A.C. read on this and other things. Some bothered him. Miners and railworkers didn't back the young senator from Massachusetts, for one. But other things impressed A.C., like the man's service on a Torpedo Boat at Guadalcanal. Kennedy had saved men. He'd survived when others might not have. To do what he'd done, to swim for miles like that, it was something. And, A.C. thought, to see those coconuts on that faraway island, John Kennedy was liable to have possessed the power of wide vision.

A.C. looked at the clock. It was ten to six. He'd gotten stuck reading and thinking on wide vision. He walked out the doors and down 5th Avenue to the restaurant.

When a man in a black suit directed him to a large booth against the right wall, Kennedy still hadn't sat down. He was glad-handing and posing for photographs. McDonough stepped in. "Jack," he said, "this is Mr. A.C. Gilbert, writer for the *West Virginia Hillbilly*. I spoke to you about him."

"Yes, I remember," Kennedy said. He shook A.C.'s hand and looked him in the eye. "I like your paper's name. How do you do?"

"Evenin," A.C. said.

They sat down. Introductions were made to Frank Roosevelt, FDR's grandson, and to a man named Sorenson. The waitress had an accent that said Logan County, if not Mingo. She wore all white and her hair was pulled back. She was nervous and she reminded A.C. of Clarissa. The other men ordered, all of them spaghetti. A.C. got a little hitch in his throat from the waitress's looks. Clarissa had got him to thinking about Cynthia and he had trouble speaking. "Cheeseburger," he managed to say. His upper denture came loose. He bit down, clenched the upper hard against the lower. Kennedy looked in his direction while he drank water, fast.

A.C. shifted in his seat. Air wheezed from a rip in the green naugahyde. McDonough cleared his throat. They were all tired. The day before, they'd campaigned from 4:30 a.m. to 1:30 a.m. "Well," McDonough said. It had almost become awkward.

"Mr. Gilbert," Kennedy said. "I heard from my younger brother of your colleague and lady friend, Ms. Webster. I'm very sorry for your loss."

"Thank you," A.C. said, and he meant it. It occurred to him that another man might have forgotten such a thing on little rest and long hours and rough hill towns and speech upon speech to strangers and reporters. Or, even if he remembered, another man might choose not to say it.

"Would you like to ask me some questions for the *Hillbilly*?" For some reason, A.C. laughed when Kennedy said this. It may have been his accent, the way he said his A's. The way he spoke the word "hillbilly." Whatever it was, he'd showed his false teeth.

Kennedy laughed right along with him.

"Well," A.C. said. "I reckon you've heard about every question you'd want to hear on mine workers and our fine state's slow descent into poverty." The waitress brought out coleslaw and he smiled at her, making sure to keep those straight pearly whites pressed tight against each other. He worked the salt shaker while he spoke. "And I know you've heard enough on religion to last you on up through the Second Coming." They laughed some more. He'd awakened the men. He took a bite of his coleslaw, careful to chew with his back molars. "Why don't we get fed a little. I can ask questions when they come up." They ate.

A.C. spoke on West Virginia having a dozen Congressional Medal of Honor winners. On having more vets per capita than any other state in the union. He complimented Kennedy on his bravery in the Solomon Islands, and Kennedy thanked him for it.

They spoke on vote-buying and how the slate system meant everyone bought votes, in one sense of the word. "I've never handed a man a bottle of whiskey or a twenty dollar bill to make a mark on paper ticket," Kennedy said.

It was important to him not to speak poorly on the character of Humphrey, no matter what the man said on *him*.

In the middle of a discussion on Senator Byrd and his anti-Catholicism, Kennedy said, "This is the most unusual spaghetti sauce I've ever tasted."

The man who would be president fueled up on the strange, thick sauce that night. He put his arm around Jim Tweel, the restaurant's owner, for a picture. He told A.C., who'd written down little of what was said, "Why don't you come along to the mines in Logan with us tomorrow morning?" They were going to greet miners at six a.m. Comstock had given him a little extra for incidentals, hotel fare.

A.C. met the campaign team outside the number three mine at six the next morning. He took notes on how the senator asked the men questions, genuine questions, about their equipment and hours of operation. Kennedy said little about himself or the election. One miner, an old, stout man with a Kentucky Cheroot stump stuck in his teeth said, "Senator, what I want to know is, is it true you're a millionaire's son and never done a day's work in your life?"

"Well, I suppose it is true."

The man slapped Kennedy's back then and smiled. "Well, that's just about alright," he said. "I'll tell you somethin. You ain't missed a damn thing."

Everyone who heard it laughed. Kennedy the hardest of all. He nearly bent double.

Later that morning, they drank strong coffee together and John Kennedy told A.C. that he'd had the opportunity to see some of the state. "It's not right how some of the people are living down here," he said. "If we make it, I'm going to do something about it."

It was these words, more than the others, that would stick with A.C. after that day. He spent nearly a week with John Kennedy, on and off. He'd almost come to think of him as a friend. But something about the vow to "do something about it" worried the mind and troubled the soul. Kennedy had called West Virginians "forgotten." On the one hand, A.C. wanted Washington to start remembering. His people needed money more than most. But with money came other things, expectations of change from on high. He remembered the studies of Mr. Estabrook, the eugenicist. The Widow had said such men wanted to change what they found in the hills, erase it maybe.

A.C. remembered what Arly Sr. had told Arly Jr. all those years back. "When they look down at you, start em to lookin up."

He had found, in work, exactly what he needed to keep going after Cynthia died. Thought. Real thought. He followed its paths while he rode back to Richwood. He watched the dark mountains pass outside his window slow, none the same as the other. When he got home to his old Underwood, he put down words unavailable to the meek-hearted masses among us who think they have something true to say.

CHAPTER TWENTY-FOUR

DISCOVERY HAD ITS WAY

He made it to New York City after all, a year and a month after Cynthia died. The story he wrote on Kennedy, entitled "Hill People Found a Man to Reckon With," had run in the mid-November issue of the *Hillbilly*, days after the man had been elected president. The *New York Times* picked it up and ran it front page the following week. In April, A.C. got the call that he'd won the Pulitzer Prize for Local Reporting.

The story had taken no easy sides. It had spoken truths so simple that they'd become invisible in the face of assumptions. In part, it read:

Senator Kennedy never handed whiskey to a woodhick. If any of his people did, he didn't know of it. The same went for paper money. West Virginians, by virtue of our topographical isolation, among other things, could use money more than most. We are often called 'forgotten' by those who live far away from here. So, outsiders come. They study. Once, a supposed scientist named Arthur Estabrook visited here and measured

*our heads and wrote a load of horse manure and called it a book. In
many ways, it is folks not unlike him who have alleged that our votes for
president can be purchased. But any vote-buying here happens in places
like Logan County, in elections for offices like sheriff. It's been that way
for years, and if you can fix it, come on down and start studying.*

*It is true that we have a slate system for presidential candidates, but
until that is made illegal, until critics understand its workings, I'll not
fill the page with more words on that system's inequities. No, John F.
Kennedy did not need to buy our votes. He won them outright with his
gumption. He looked us in the eye, not from a steep angle down the
bridge of his nose, mind you, but straight on. He asked us questions about
poverty the likes of which he, as so many who profess to fix it, had not seen
before. He shook our hands and made us a deal. It was a deal to forget
all that which goes on in the papers and in the television box nightly.
Massachusetts means this, West Virginia means that. Catholic means
that over there, Protestant means this right here. Hogwash.*

*The truth is that we West Virginians will never be ruled by one religion
or another. We are calm pew sitters, tongue-talking snake handlers,
rapture- awaiting born-agains, and ear-to-the-Pope chest crossers. We are
all shades of black, tan, and white. We come from Scotland and Ireland,
Hungary and Sicily. We come from Africa by way of Georgia. And if our
own fine senator tells us not to vote for a Catholic, we might just remember
that he still conversates cordially with men who wear hoods over their
faces and show us just how ugly humans can be. West Virginians elected
John Kennedy president of the United States of America, and a man to
be reckoned with such as him, well, we reckon he'll do right by us.*

A.C. stayed at a tall, fancy hotel in Times Square, along with Jim
and Dorothea. It was important to him that they both be there, as he
felt they were just as responsible for the story as he.

On the day of the Pulitzer awards luncheon, Jim and Dorothea accepted the morning ride offered by the editor of the *New York Times*. He was taking them by the *Times* offices for a tour before heading to Columbia for the awards luncheon. A.C. had said no thanks at dinner the night before. "I'd just as soon walk," he said. On his way to the university, he almost took off the new pair of shoes he'd bought for the occasion. He almost walked barefoot through Manhattan. Blisters were coming on. His new suit and tie were black, like the ones he'd worn as Chicky Gold the Harmonica Man in Chicago. And he felt a little like Chicky again as he crossed 110th Street. Harlem reminded him a little of the West Side spots he'd played in Chicago, and when he walked past an underground club on Amsterdam, he stopped and stared. He nearly went inside. It was 11:30 a.m. The thought of the university a few blocks away, and all those intellectuals with too many forks, it was almost enough for a change of plans. From inside the little dark club came the smell of corn liquor, soaked in from the night before and oozing out through pores. It no doubt covered the floor in sticky glory in there. It was on the shoe soles of whoever it was inside, tapping and blowing that harmonica in the key of G.

He'd tried not to think of the harmonica since Missouri. But he'd heard things here and there about Chuck Berry, rock and roll. The little of the music he'd heard, he did not care for. But that morning in Harlem, outside that club, his mouth watered and threatened to pry loose his new, properly fitted dentures.

A.C. made it to the luncheon. He was seated at a table with the president of the university, and he sipped good coffee and smoked and was cordial to everyone who congratulated him. To each, he introduced Jim Comstock and Dorothea, being sure to mention each time, "She taught me how to type."

The big check was much appreciated.

One man stood out from the rest that day. He was a staff writer at the *New Yorker* named Joseph Mitchell. Originally from tobacco country in Robeson County, North Carolina, his accent comforted A.C. somehow inside that room. A.C. had read a copy of a story he'd written in the forties called "Professor Seagull." Comstock had given it to him as homework, and it was some of the finest writing A.C. had ever read. He told Mitchell so that day.

"Well, I don't know about that," Mitchell said, looking away. He had a friendly face and a genuine smile. "I've actually been a subscriber to your weekly for some time, and would say the same about your work."

"Well, I thank you," A.C. said. They both looked down at their coffees, sloshed the stuff around.

"In fact," Mitchell said. "And I hope this isn't too presumptuous, but if I may bend your ear?"

"Shoot," A.C. told him.

"Well, I've been re-reading all of what you've written in the last couple years, and after a visit back home recently, and a light bulb idea of sorts, I spoke with my editor about the possibility of a job for you at the *New Yorker* . . . should you be interested." He smiled, lit a cigarette.

"Is that right?" A.C. said. "Well." He couldn't think of what to say. The sound of the harmonica from inside the club on Amsterdam echoed in his head. His coffee suddenly smelled like whiskey. "Truth is, Mr. Mitchell, I could probably set up camp in New York City for a while." He almost swayed while he spoke. The words came out before he'd thought on them. "I could bang away at it. But at some point, I suspect I'd go crazy from the discovery nobody in this room can speak to." He didn't elaborate.

"Discovery? How do you mean?" Mitchell laughed nervously.

"Well, I think you know if you consider real hard. Those stories you and I write about people, their places. Far as I can tell, we get em about as real as they can be in ink on paper. Follow?"

"I think I do."

Somebody dropped a glass on the floor. The hum of conversation was deafening. "But every real story loses a little of its truth as soon as you type it. And as soon as somebody reads it, it loses a little more. And then, important folks call it special, give it an award. They write stories *about* your story, and it loses more of its initial truth. You follow?"

"Yes, I do." It was the best and the worst conversation Mitchell had ever had at a luncheon.

"So," A.C. went on. "At some point, you got to say to hell with it and hang up your typewriter. I'm not saying I'm there yet, but if I move to New York, I'll sure be a hell of a lot closer in a hurry." He finished the rest of his coffee in an unsophisticated gulp and put the cup down hard on a bus tray next to them. Then he leaned in close to Mitchell, whispered in his ear. "All this around us," he said, "it ain't real. And as much as we try to find the real and put it down on paper, it can't be done. There ain't no real when it comes to writing." He stepped back and smiled at the other man, who wore a look of confusion.

A.C. lit a Chesterfield, inhaled deep and laughed as he blew it out of his noseholes and mouth simultaneously. He fought the urge to spit out his teeth. "But you come about as close as anybody, I reckon," he said. He shook Mitchell's hand and excused himself for the men's room. Expensive coffee had a way of going right through.

A.C. thought for a short while on Joseph Mitchell's offer. It was easier to consider once back in Richwood, with all the talk about the F.B.I.

upping their investigation of vote-selling in the primary, of mafia connections. There was talk that an agent was coming to interview A.C. He knew what this meant. Background checks. Digging for dirt. It wouldn't be long before the fellow who chased him from Chicago to St. Louis would get wind, maybe even Dallara and the Crews boys.

He went to the bank and cashed his big check.

On a glorious June morning in 1961, Jim Comstock went upstairs when A.C. didn't show for work. The door to the apartment was wide open.

There was some rent money, plus more, on the bed in an envelope. The sheets were tucked and smoothed out, almost as if they'd been ironed. The window was open and the place smelled like Ajax. There was no note of any kind. No written word to explain where the man had gone to or why. Comstock had some idea. He'd been forming it for two years, as he was a man adept at figuring folks, their pasts. But he didn't think any about it that particular morning. He sat on the thin little mattress and sighed. He stared at the Underwood on the kitchen table, its scuffed off marks of measure and the forever stuck-down margin release key. He almost cried a little when he thought of lunch at Ritzy Rae's without his friend, of going downstairs to tell Dorothea the inevitable had come to be. But he just sighed again instead. He thought of how he might word a goodbye column to A.C. Gilbert. Then, he thought otherwise. He'd not attempt such a feat, for it was impossible to capture some things in life.

BOOK THREE 1989–1993

If the truth was known, we're all freaks together.

—Jane Barnell

CHAPTER TWENTY-FIVE

THE TRI-STATE DUMP

Zizi and the Kozmanauts were an old-time bluegrass gospel band. Four piece. Dale Price on stand up bass, Everett Harrah on banjo, Flunky Cy Ray on drums, and on vocals and theremin, the beautiful Zizi Kozma-Townsend. The band was to have reached their pinnacle of stardom as the headliners of a concert on Saturday, May 29th, 1993. All of their friends and family would be there for support. It was to be a magical evening.

Zizi Kozma had first played the Theremin at age twelve when her older brother Albert sent off to a hobby magazine for one and built it. In 1968, when Albert was twenty-five years old, he was killed in Vietnam. Zizi was in the Ph.D. program in Music Education at West Virginia University. A virtuoso on the cello who still played the theremin at parties. She was married to a young history professor by the name of Sam Townsend who would later publish a book on the disaster at Buffalo Creek. After Albert's funeral, Sam and Zizi disappeared. There was much abuse of drugs and alcohol. They were among those who dropped out of a world that seemed to them to be ending. They ended up on a hippie commune of sorts near Berkeley Springs. In 1974, Al Townsend was born to them. A big boy. Healthy. His mother had given up the psychedelics and the drink to carry him. His father followed suit.

On a warm fall night in 1975, the theremin hooked into a generator belonging to a heroin-dealing biker from New Jersey, Zizi played and sang simultaneously. The communers swayed in the mountain marijuana haze. She did a song she'd grown up with, "All that Thrills my Soul is Jesus," then an oddly morose version of "Put a Little Love in Your Heart" by Jackie DeShannon. She matched her soprano-high voice with the melody of the theremin, controlled by the movement through air of those delicate cellist hands. In the crowd gathered, there was an older man who'd wandered in from the hills that afternoon. He called himself only "Ace." When he heard the vibrato sound of that instrument, that voice, he nearly fell down. It was what he'd heard so many times before. Under the ether in Bluefield, in the hallway at WHIS, and outside the ABC store after Cynthia died. He'd finally tracked that sound.

When Zizi finished, he approached her. "Zizi Kozma?" he'd said. She nodded. "Daughter of Clarence Dickason and Rose Kozma?" She nodded again. He smiled. Didn't have his false teeth in. "I used to hold you when you had the colic."

From that night forward, he held little Al, another screaming child. And, like his mother before him, the boy would only quiet in the evening hours if he was placed into the still-strong arms of a man who'd walked in from the woods.

Sam Townsend was a good man whose white family had not approved of him marrying a mixed breed woman. He was an amateur carpenter as well as a doctor of American history. He loved

his wife, and he'd built a beautiful, cherrywood housing for her re-
furbished Wurlitzer theremin as a wedding present. For four years
on the commune, he appreciated the help Ace brought with him,
in spirit and in work. The old man, 75 by then, still did his push-
ups, sit-ups, and jumping jacks daily. He could swing a splitter axe
with the best of them, and once, when a Baltimore hippie tripping
on acid had tried to touch young Al in an improper fashion, Ace
knocked him on his tailbone with one right cross. Sam especially
appreciated Ace's help raising little Al, who was a spirited boy, much
like a young Trenchmouth Taggart.

And one night over sassafras tea, when Ace revealed to Zizi and
Sam his identity as Trenchmouth Taggart, Sam became enamored
of the old man. He'd studied a little about the rotten-toothed
sharpshooter, his struggle. Most in Sam's profession thought Taggart
was a myth for empowering the underdogs among us, but Sam had
always believed. His father had been a miner in Marion County.

They were sworn to secrecy.

So it was that in 1979, when the Townsends re-entered society,
they took old Ace with them. They settled in Huntington, in the Tri-
State valley, where Sam took a professor job at Marshall University
and Zizi gave music lessons. Ace had occupied the garage apartment
ever since, and he spent his days watching television, reading the
paper, teaching young Al how to box and be a man, and playing
the occasional harmonica with Zizi and the Kozmanauts at revivals
and picnics.

A man named David Pace over at the *Huntington Advertiser* paid
Ace a hundred dollars a week, under the table, to write the Police
Blotter. Pace was the one who'd later dig a little in the obituary
archives at Ace's request, inform him of the 1964 prison death of
a man named Arly Scott Jr. Ace dug himself to find the 1932 burial

date of one Mittie Ann Taggart, criminally insane inmate of the Home for Incurables. He went to visit the grave site, but never made it past the front entrance, where he spat and turned around and walked away.

It was in 1984, the same year he got his dog Yellow, that Louise Dallara showed up at a Kozmanauts revival concert at Beech Fork State Park. She was 61 years old, married to a 70-year-old mandolin player named Larry. They still lived in Mingo County, Williamson. Larry was a former coal miner whose first wife and two children had been killed at Buffalo Creek. Since then, he'd held first the post of president of the West Virginia Black Lung Association, then director of the War on Poverty program, and finally vice president of Save Our Mountains. The latter position he still held, and he and Louise played concerts in front of bulldozers and landmovers, doing what they could to slow down strip mining. That, and the newest thing, mountain top removal.

When Louise saw Ace on stage playing that harmonica with his nose, she knew who he was. In a sea of Pentecostal folks lining up to get baptized in Beech Fork Lake, she walked up to him and said, "West Virginia Shine Guzzlers, WHIS Bluefield, Saturday night." They hugged and laughed, but when he asked after her mother, Louise looked down at her feet. Clarissa had died in 1971, a year after Fred.

Now there were two more, Louise and Larry Blevins, who knew Ace's true identity as Trenchmouth Taggart, as Chicky Gold. And in 1988, when Larry bought a house down the street from them in Huntington so he and Louise could recruit college students for the anti-surface mining movement, Ace told them all some more. Around the dinner table, Albert having excused himself, Ace told

Sam, Zizi, Louise, and Larry about his days as A.C. Gilbert. About President Kennedy and the Pulitzer Prize. He brought out the newspaper clippings to prove all of it. "My Lord, Ace," Sam said. "You ought to make this known. You're famous. You ought to write a letter to Governor Caperton. He'll champion a man like you, give you a pardon on all that back in Mingo."

Ace had looked at Sam then like he'd better shut his mouth. At 86, the old man could still put a fear in others, still had that presence, that muscle and quick tendon of a younger man. Sam had looked down at his food. Ace said, "So anyhow. I trust all of you to keep this to yourselves. I just couldn't hold it shut up no more. Not now that we all ended up here together, dumped in the tri-state." He spoke on the mystery of fate, of past friends and family finding themselves together again. Of old time music's power to heal. When Ace talked liked this, as when he talked of tracking and trapping and surviving on nothing in the winter-coated wilderness, folks generally listened.

Ace walked into the garage with a chrome measuring tape in his hand. "Wingspan," he said. The older he got, the less words he used.

Albert lifted his arms, straight out from his sides. Behind him, Ace pulled the tape and locked it shut. It was getting to be so he almost couldn't reach anymore. It was 68 and a half inches all the way across. "Twenty-six, thereabouts," Ace said. "Going to start calling you Stretch."

The boy put his arms down. He was six feet even at fifteen years of age. But he was bone and muscle. 128 pounds. In his nine years of public school, he'd passed for white and black and neither and both, but at fifteen in the West Virginia summertime, he was black. Ace looked at the words on the back of his T-shirt. *Boogie Down*

Productions: Criminal Minded. There was a picture of the rappers and their pistols. Ace flicked Albert in the back of the neck—his signal to straighten up posture. Albert stuck his chest out, his behind in. "What do you know about criminal minded?" Ace said.

"Huh?" Albert sat down on the milk carton and started wrapping his hands.

"Your shirt."

"It's music, Grandpa." He'd always called him this.

"That ain't music.

"You going to tell me what is now?"

"Don't sass." The old man walked to the workbench and picked up the punch mitts. He put his fingers in the holes. The hands had started shaking a little in the last year, but only in the middle of the day. Every time, it was a reminder of coming off the drink, a feat he'd never reneged on. Ace smacked the flat, split fronts of the mitts together. This meant Albert needed to hurry up and wrap. Get up and punch. He did.

When the boy was twelve, long since used to throwing punches, Ace had started surprising Albert with love taps to the cheekbone and chin. Zizi had seen it from the kitchen window. She came out, said, "Ace, I don't remember there being anything about *you* hitting *him* in this training regimen you spoke to me about."

"That's just a love tap, Z. The mitts is padded."

"It's just a love tap, Mom," the boy had said. Ace had liked that about him. That, and how when they woods-walked he never complained about being thirsty or his feet hurting or how they had to sometimes sit and not move for an hour at a time.

In the summer of 1989, they didn't go for walks in the woods any longer. Albert was fifteen. They lived on 12th Street near the viaduct, close enough to his friends over between Hal Greer and

20th Street that the days of woods walking with Grandpa were over. It had whittled down to boxing, three times a week if he was lucky. Albert's days meant basketball at the Lewis Center, his nights meant hanging out on porches. But only until 9:30, when Sam waited for him on his own front porch.

Ace knew from working the Police Blotter that on some of those other porches where Albert hung out, someone might have cocaine in his pocket, cooked and baggied, fresh down from Detroit City. And if someone had that in his pocket, he probably had a pistol too. It was what confounded Ace most. These boys were as different as different could be from T.T. Stinky. They had drugs and he had moonshine. They were black and he was white. They were city and he was country. But, when it came to guns, they were all the same. There wasn't anything in this world better than a gun for a boy trying to be a man.

Albert stuck out that left two quick times and pivoted his back right foot to bring the straight right. Pap pap, poom. Again. Pap pap, poom. Yellow Dog moaned from his spot in the corner. He didn't care for the noise. Ace circled around Albert and Albert followed circle. When he started throwing combinations without moving his head, without snapping his guard back fast, Ace counter-punched him. Stomach, then nose. He put a little more on his love tap that day. He couldn't help it. The boy was slipping away from him and he'd never told him who he was, what he'd done. It occurred to Ace that he'd never told Albert much of anything. He hit him in the nose again, then lowered his mitt on purpose under Albert's straight right, just to feel that old sting again. Just to let the boy know what it was like to be on the sending end. Albert smiled and let out a little laugh after he connected. "You got me," Ace said, smiling back, his teeth out as they always were those days.

* * *

Sam Townsend was trying desperately not to sleep with one of his Post-1877 U.S. History students. She was tan and leggy, from Wetzel County, and she'd failed the course in spring just to take it over again in summer. Sam was forty-seven, she was twenty. He'd never cheated on Zizi.

On Tuesday morning, she shut his office door behind her. There were no windows, just stacks of books and cheap furniture. She sat down on the edge of his desk so that her knee touched his. He swiveled his chair away. "So, I was askin you about that recommendation letter for the departmental scholarship?" She wore a green shirt that matched her eyes and showed her bra straps.

"I don't normally write recommendations for students who fail my courses," Sam said. He laughed a little, looked at his trilobite fossils, six of them. Paperweights.

"I don't normally fail classes. Just yours." She smiled and bit her lower lip with her teeth.

Sam knew that teeth-on-lips move. It was like so many others. It meant something. Everything meant something. "Alright," he said. "I've got to get out of here for the day."

"What about office hours?"

"It's summer." Truth was, the knee brush and the teeth-on lips had gotten his pecker to stand at attention a little. He had to get up and get moving to be at ease.

It was the same as the first time Ace saw Zizi sipping vodka. A travel-sized purple lotion bottle, no doubt scoured of lotion trace years prior. This time though, she was in her own house. In the kitchen. The time before, in 1986, had been backstage after a sold-out show at Ritter Park Amphitheatre. Ace hadn't said a word to her that time, or after. Not even after seeing her testify and cry at her regular A.A. meetings. He'd gone along once or twice. But standing outside the kitchen window that day in August, taking old Yellow Dog out for a poop walk, he hollered. "Hey!"

Zizi threw the plastic bottle into the sink and turned her back on the window. On Ace. She stood very still there in the kitchen, middle of the day. Ace walked in calm through the back screen door. "It's alright," he said. "I ain't sayin a word to anyone, if that's your worry."

She looked at him out of the corner of her eye. Then she started crying. At forty-three, Zizi was still the kind of woman who looked pretty even when she cried. She put a product in her hair that made it shine and hold still. No gray. Her teeth were straight and white and mild scoliosis had never bent her a bit. "I just . . ." She couldn't think of what to say. She was caught.

They sat down in the TV room. It was on like always—*All My Children*. Zizi stood back up, ran the sweeper across the rug. She watched the soap opera while she did it, though you couldn't hear a word over the roar. She switched it off and sat down again. They both lit cigarettes and she ran her fingernails through her hair. Ace just sat and watched and waited for her to put the words together. "I just . . . I used to do everything, you know. Acid, mushrooms, coke. So, somehow I thought bringing back just one of em, here and there, you know? Who's it hurt? Let me ask you that, Ace. Who has it hurt in the last four years? Who even knows about it cept you?"

He watched her go from caught and scared to mad and accusatory. Five seconds. It was something. "Nobody I reckon." He put out his cigarette in the big green ashtray on the coffee table. "Like I said, you don't have to sell me on nothin. I ain't judging you. I been through too much with that drink to pretend I can preach on it."

"Thank you," she said. She was all worked up then. "Thank you. See . . . I wish more of em in A.A. were like you. I've been working the program . . . I say the words, I read the Big Book, you know. I try to believe they're right about the great obsession, control and enjoy. I memorized all of it." She picked up the remote control and turned it around in her hands. "But I pulled into the lot at the ABC over on 3rd one night, and there you go." She dragged on her cigarette, put it out next to his, then looked straight at him while she talked. "And I did it. I know it sounds crazy, but I am *the one*. Maybe there's more of us, but I have been able to take a drink, after lunch, after dinner, before bed, since 1983, Ace. Christmas 1983."

"That's the only times you do it?"

"Only times." The television had gone to commercial. An African tribesman put on a pair of Nike gym shoes and said something in his native tongue. At the bottom of the screen was the subtitle *Just Do It*. Ace and Zizi both half-watched. "Well," she said. "And sometimes before a big show, maybe right after if it went really good. But only eight ounces, you know? That shampoo is only eight ounces."

"Uh-huh." He thought it over. Nodded his head and looked blank.

Zizi stood up. "Hey, we got a show up at the mall on Sunday evening. You sittin in?"

"I don't care for the mall. It's what made downtown the way it is."

"It's a *mall*, Ace. It's not the devil."

"Uh-huh."

She forced a laugh and walked to the basement stairs. She didn't teach music in the summer, was always doing laundry. Doing something in that basement.

Ace thought about following her down there that day. He knew she was going to change whatever hiding spots she had for those pints and half pints of vodka. They were flat and made of plastic, could be hidden in small spaces and would never break. It had gotten easier for the alcoholic since his days. Invention. That old vodka of hers may not have been untraceable to the nose like the Widow's shine, but it was damn near odorless.

Ace could hear her through the floorboards below him, shuffling things.

CHAPTER TWENTY-SIX

MAN ATTACKED, MAN ROBBED

December 23rd, 1991, marked the end of Ace's seventh year at the *Advertiser*. Nobody said a word about it.

He met Officer St. Clair at the police station like he did every Monday at eight a.m., just like Wednesday, Friday, and Sunday. Used to be that the cops scared him, worried him on his past deeds. But he played up the old man angle and did just fine. That Monday was like any other. St. Clair handed over Xerox copies of his arrest reports from the nights prior. Outside the evidence room, he and Ace drank coffee from styrofoam and spoke a little about the football squad without Major Harris under center. "You can forgit bowl games," St. Clair said. They had to hide in the break room to talk Mountaineer football. Every other officer was a Marshall fan, and they'd lost the Division II championship to Youngstown State a couple weeks prior. St. Clair shook Ace's hand and said what he always said. "Stay out a trouble."

"Will do."

In his no-window office on the half-empty basement level of the

Advertiser building, Ace used an electric typewriter to bang out the Blotter for that day's press run. St. Clair's arrest reports were the usual. Assault. Robbery. Always drinking involved. Ace chose which crime would lead, then started thinking up headline titles to match it. "If I had a nickel," he said out loud. If he did indeed have a nickel for every time he'd typed the words *Man Attacked* or *Man Robbed* in his seven years on the job, he'd have laughed to the bank. *Man* began most of the headlines in the Blotter section because it was mostly men who did the crimes and men who got done. *Woman* ran occasionally, but it was almost always a victim lead.

People were poor and people were drunk. Angry sometimes.

Ace had always been good with titles. He'd saved his favorite of the *Advertiser* stories, flat-pressed between pages of the same book inside which he kept a few of his stories from the *Hillbilly*—Mr. Samuel Clemens' *Follow the Equator*. The Blotter pieces weren't as colorful, but there were classics just the same. *Man stuffs wigs into pants, walks out of store* was a favorite. It was a costume shop, broad daylight. *Man knocks self out after girl's parents turn him away.* They wouldn't let him court their daughter so he bashed his motorcycle helmet against his own head until he dropped in the driveway. *Husband tells wife to 'fight like a man.'* He'd backhanded her after she burned him with the curling iron. Wanted to see how much she had in her. *Man attacked with rusty machete.* The blade was dull. Minor lacerations. He shouldn't have bedded another man's wife.

Indecent exposures were Ace's favorites. They came around four or five times a year. They were most enjoyable to write up when they involved multiple crimes, as in *Naked man steals purse, woman takes it back.* He took it from her while in his altogether at 2:14 in the a.m. He didn't think she'd give chase to get it back, but she did. While he ran, he pulled off the used condom hanging from his pecker and threw it at her, but she was a persistent one. *Naked man arrested trying to enter church service.* He wore only a sheet around his neck at 10:30 in the morning. The ushers at 5th Avenue Baptist held him down until the police got there. They booked him on "disruption of religious worship," a misdemeanor.

Ace never laughed or scratched his head as much as the time he wrote *Man finds home burgled, hair and pornographic magazines scattered.* The owner had been in Myrtle Beach for the week. It wasn't his pornography, and it wasn't his hair. Ace had wondered what Jim Comstock would think when he'd typed *It is believed that someone broke into the man's home, shaved off his or her pubic hair, scattered it throughout the apartment and then slept in his bed. Nothing was found to be missing.*

Dorothea had trained his fingers to be semi-quick back in Richwood, but he figured there weren't many who could type as fast as he the words *Larceny, Burglary, Robbery, Armed Robbery, B&E Auto, Battery, Malicious Wounding, Vandalism, Fleeing,* and *Destruction of Property.* David Pace didn't even proof the Blotter before he ran it.

More and more, Ace found himself typing the phrase *possession with the intent to deliver a controlled substance.* And, more often than not, the substance was crack cocaine. The possessors were usually young and black and resided increasingly closer to the street where Ace and the Townsends lived. December 23rd marked the third time in the last two years he recognized one of the names. Friends of Albert's, who, at seventeen, had quit hitting the mitts in the garage. He'd quit showing up to meet his father on the porch at curfew. Sometimes, in those days, Albert didn't show up at all.

Yellow Dog had to be twenty years old. When he'd shown up at Ace's open garage door on a spring morning in 1984, half his right ear bit off and scabbed black, Ace had set his coffee on the ground and kneeled. "C'mon," he'd said. Yellow wagged his tail and came on. They'd been roommates ever since.

But, by the looks of him on that first day, even after a bath, he was past ten. His hips hurt him. His muzzle had gone to white. Especially his eyes, encircled perfectly with the color of age. He was a mongrel, but there was no doubt yellow lab in there. "Fat Labrador," was what Ace said when folks inquired as to the breed.

On New Year's Day, 1992, they did what they always did together by then. Watched television. Ace had given in to the moving picture box a couple years after coming to town when Sam was going to throw an old one out. Within a year, he'd grown tired of the poor reception. He gave in to the cable soon after. He ran it illegal from the splitter on the neighbor's box, which had also been hooked up illegal.

Inside the TV, Bob Barker had yet to go gray. Every day, Yellow and Ace watched *The Price is Right*, and this day was no different. In the showcase, a girl wearing a mohawk couldn't get the big wheel spun all the way around. "Put some elbow grease in it," Ace hollered at the screen. Yellow lifted his head from the green carpet between his front paws and woofed. He looked around him confused. Certain noises, inflections of Ace's voice, caused him to do this sometimes. Ace rubbed his ears. "It's alright Fat Boy," he told him. The dog put his head back where it'd been. He wasn't as fat as he once was. Couldn't eat like he once could.

During the commercial, Ace turned to CNN. It was the same. The Soviet Union kept collapsing. The boys who went to the Persian Gulf kept coming home as men who were collapsing somehow themselves. If you watched it too long, you'd think the world was ending.

He changed the channel when they started rolling footage of oil-coated ducks sticking to the earth again.

Sally Jesse Raphael was on. Thirteen year old girls were dressed like street-walkers. One of them hollered, "You cain't tell me what to do. I'll do what I want to. I get paid." When they started bleeping out her words, Ace changed the channel again, but it was too late. The bleeping sound always got Yellow going. He was up on his front legs then, barking. Each time he barked, he whimpered, because it hurt his insides to do it. But he kept it up anyway. "Simmer, Fat Boy," Ace told him. He rubbed his old dog's head, massaged him between the ears. "Simmer."

Only four showed up. Four college students interested in stopping surface mining's ruination of West Virginia's hills. They could have fit more in the wide living room at Louise and Larry's house, but it was a place accustomed to emptiness. Louise and Larry spent most of their time at the house in Mingo. They'd asked Ace to come for his historical expertise. They'd asked Zizi and her bandmembers to come for a pledge to play a show. Sam they wanted for his construction skills. He hadn't known that one of the Marshall students would be Brandie, another of his history undergraduates with legs and eyes and ways that meant things.

"How many are here because you saw the fliers on campus?" Larry asked.

Three of the four raised hands.

"How many know what mountain top removal is?"

Two of the four. Louise came back in from the kitchen carrying a tray. On it were lemonades and a plate piled high with dried beef rolled around cream cheese. The floorboards creaked when any of them moved.

"Well," Larry said. "Massey Coal, among some others, has decided to push on, in the face of all the protest, over sludge reservoirs and poisoned water, among other things." Larry always said "among other things." He rubbed at his unkempt mustache between sentences. "They say they keep blastin because they have to meet the demand for low sulfur compliance steam coal, but the land just doesn't bounce back like they say. It just doesn't."

He might as well have been speaking another language. Brandie made eyes at Sam who tried to be nice to Zizi despite suspecting her of drinking again. Zizi wondered how long till she could have her next drink. The band members looked like they'd shared a joint on the ride over, and Ace was missing the Showcase Showdown portion of *The Price Is Right*.

When it came time to commit to a trip down to Mingo the following Friday, folks had spring term final exams and family illnesses all of a sudden. Only Ace gave a definite yes. Louise was about to express her disappointment when a car drove past the front of the house slow. Bass beat out of it like static thunder. Everyone looked. Cutlass Sierra. Black with black windows, barely open. Ace could see two tops of heads inside, and he thought one of them was Albert's. He was supposed to be in school.

The band cleared the beef log plate like it was a contest. "Mrs. Blevins," Flunky Cy the drummer said. "These beef logs is savory."

On Friday, May 1st, Ace boarded the Amtrak Cardinal passenger line headed to Matewan. It gave him a stomach ache to do it, but it was time to go home. Have a little look. Larry and Louise had promised he'd be fine, no police troubles.

He'd put in his teeth for the occasion.

What drew him there most was the house he'd grown up in. It still stood. The coal company wanted the land, but Louise had fought them off in court. The Widow had left it to Clarissa, who kept the place up, had the roof repaired a little, and left it to Louise. She had the deed, the property rights, to prove it.

That Friday, when the protest was a bust due to bad weather and a no show by the earth mover operators, Ace, Louise, and Larry went for a hike. Up Warm Hollow. It was a welcome change from Main Street Matewan, what folks had started calling "Mate" Street. Even if he'd been able to stomach walking on paved ground he'd once shot men upon, Ace didn't want anything to do with the mess they had down in town. It was all torn up to build the new flood wall. Matewan was not the same. Houses and roads gone. People. It was enough to make an old man think about crying.

Up Warm Hollow, the air was breathable. He could still side-step up steep, rain-slicked inclines with the help of a walking stick he'd snapped off a dogwood tree. "Slow down, youngin," Larry hollered from behind. They laughed. Across the ridgeline, he could see the spot where he believed his first hideout may have been. Caved in upon itself no doubt.

They reached the top of Sulfur Creek Mountain and looked south, along the Tug Fork. Ace couldn't believe his eyes. The spot where his second hideout would have been was gone. All of it was gone. The entire top of a mountain range replaced by flat, red-brown workroads and levelled expanse. "It looks like the surface of the moon," Ace said.

Louise breathed heavy, sat down on a rock. "Been like that since '88," she said. "No re-growth."

All around the massive, planed blank was green. Bright, swirling green encircling the dull void like an unfinished puzzle. "Flush as a pool table, isn't it?" Larry said. He pointed to a faraway spot, a steep grade just under a flat top. "See that?" Where he pointed, there was a pile up of junked cars—a rusty, dead traffic jam on the side of the mountain. "When they take off the top of a mountain, why shouldn't folks roll their junkers off the side? It's already gone to shit. You heard of wrecking yards, there's your wrecking hill."

Then, nobody spoke. And again, the old man came close to crying. It all seemed too much for a moment, so he turned around and quit looking.

They came down the other side of the mountain and walked up to his boyhood home. The barn was gone, the outhouse. Part of the cat-and-clay chimney had broken off so that it stuck up from the roofline like a blood-red fang. Ace stopped and looked at it all. He could see himself young, running. Always running and climbing and digging. He saw himself there in 1946, standing outside the door with Clarissa, their mother pale and lifeless on the bed inside. He turned to Larry and Louise, who had stopped a few paces behind him to give him space. To give him a moment. "I thank you all for bringin me here," he told them.

It seemed so small to him, dwarfed by the hills around it.

Inside, he climbed the ladder to the loft and laid down on the half-rotted boards. He breathed and pretended others breathed with him. When he came down, he put his hand to the old cook stove and laughed a little to himself. Shook his head. "The way we used to live," he said.

"You know Ace, it's still underground mining they're doin up thisaway," Larry said. "Louise kept this place outright, judge ruled it. We think it'll stick and keep those blasters out, for a while at least. Till we can get some legislation passed, some folks fired up."

"I don't know that folks get fired up about such things nowadays, Larry," Ace said. His voice had lost a little of its usual weight. "Everybody's got a price. Everybody gets bamboozled."

Louise frowned. They watched Ace, his hand on the stove top, looking out the thick, warped window. The panes had broken off. There were holes in the molding. When the rain picked back up, it blew inside, dotting Ace's cheeks and collecting in his eyebrows. But he stood still. Staring.

Out beyond where the garden had been, past where staked tomato plants had once grown head high, Ace saw a figure. It was hard to make out through the rain, but it was no doubt a man. A stooped one, old like him. The man stared back, soaked through. Then he walked into the woods.

Ace could smell it as soon as he stepped inside the garage. When he opened the door to his apartment, he saw. Vomit. Everywhere. It was the bile type, yellow and brown. There was blood in some. Yellow Dog had stepped in it in places. On the cheap vinyl kitchen floor, his tracks showed. Four-pawed. On the green carpet, it had soaked in deep. They were like little islands across the length of the place, and he couldn't help but think back to his own bile islands on the Missouri linoleum.

Ace tracked his own dog and found him in the bedroom, wedged between the bed and the wall. He was panting hard. His ribcage showed through.

"It's alright fella," Ace said, bending to him. He got on his knees and hugged Yellow, whose breath carried the stench of an animal on his way out of the world. "That's my Fat Boy," Ace told him. He rubbed his hands down the length of the dog, slowing the pants for the moment.

He went to the kitchen for water, but thought better of it. The dog would not hold it down.

He left the garage for the main house. Sam was no doubt in his study. Ace put his hand on the screen door and stopped. He thought better of this too. Sam would advise a trip to the veterinarian's, and Yellow Dog would not want that.

It was getting dark out.

Ace helped his dog up from his spot between the bed and wall that evening. He carried him to flat, open ground outside the garage and set him down. Eight years back, he'd shown up licked, but on his own four legs. He'd walk out that way too. Ace made sure of it.

Yellow's hips gave out at first, but he hefted himself back up. Ace hugged him, kissed his white muzzle, and watched him walk away. He knew where the dog was going. Fire had taken a two-story apartment building down the block two years prior. When the rubble was cleared, only the thick front hedges remained. Behind them, the city had let the brush grow wild. Weed stalks and goldenrod grew tall in there, and people walking by dumped their trash.

It was as close to the woods as Yellow Dog would find.

Ace knew it to be a private, peaceful thing, this walk toward death. But he went to the front of the house just to be sure he was right about the destination. To make sure Yellow got there okay. He peered around the side of the porch and saw the dog, his bowels giving out freely by then, walking into the wild brush of the abandoned lot. In there, he could lie down and breathe easy.

Ace waited till morning. Then he collected Yellow Dog and buried him in the backyard.

That night, he didn't see anyone in the main house to tell them what had happened. Albert didn't much live there anymore, and there was trouble between Sam and Zizi. The puke needed cleaning, but Ace was out of Ajax and had gone in to ask for some of theirs. He'd slept a little that day, watched TV through the stink as long as he could.

Mansour's, the family-owned store down the street that stocked

Chesterfields just for him, was closed. Ace was a little sore from his Mingo woods-walk with the Blevinses. He put on his comfortable shoes and his fedora, took two twenties from the still-thick Pulitzer roll stuck inside his mattress, and set out for the big supermarket on 1st Street.

He'd never shopped there before. Always Mansour's, always the same list. Inside Kroger's, he couldn't find a damn thing. And when he found something on his list, there were twenty varieties to choose from. He'd never seen so many sardine tins. All colors, fancy names. Where were the cigarettes? Where was the cream chipped beef? There were no store employees in the aisles. Music played, a bad excuse for country, and when the water jets cut on over the produce, he jumped from the spray.

Ace kept looking down at his fingers, gripping the cart handle. All that black dirt under the nails. He'd been digging all morning. It seemed to him that he'd been digging his whole life. "Dig to goddamned China by now," he said under his breath. A woman with a baby in her cart looked at him funny. He smiled, tried to look like an old man should, but he didn't care. He'd buried his dog that morning.

He walked to an aisle under a sign that read *Brooms, Mops, Dish Detergent, Laundry Detergent, Bleach, Furniture Polish.* He couldn't find Ajax. There was Mr. Clean. Windex for glass and Lysol with bleach. Pine Sol. Pledge. Goo Gone. It was the language he'd heard spoken for ten years on television, one he'd never understood. Standing there, he knew that all around him, the people pushing their carts past one another without saying hello, they understood. They all spoke the language of the commercials. They fed their kids Pop Rocks and Lucky Charms and all manner of foods that made noise and glowed neon.

Ace thought to himself how West Virginians had elected Kennedy president in 1960. How, like he said he would, he'd done something about the state of things, the state of people. Now, they were the same as everybody else.

Ace left his cart sitting in the middle of the cleaning supply aisle. He walked to one of the twelve checkout lanes, brushed past a skinny man unloading his handbasket, and said to the checkout girl, "Could you point me in the direction of Ajax, Miss? I'd appreciate it."

"A-what?" she said.

"Cleaning powder."

"Aisle nine."

"Yes ma'am. I been in aisle nine for a while now, and I can't place it."

She grabbed at the CB box in front of her face and spoke something unintelligible into it. Whatever it was she said cut off the bad country music and crackled across the place.

"Thank you," Ace said to her.

An hour later, after he'd used a scrub brush and water bucket to work the Ajax into and out of all seventeen vomit piles, Ace opened the big window of his second story apartment. The place needed to air out. He walked to the television, bent at the knees, and lifted it, sidestepping across the small room. He perched the brown box on the windowsill and caught his breath. Then he gave it a push, stuck his head out, and watched it split and scatter on the blacktop down below.

CHAPTER TWENTY-SEVEN

GODDAMN SON OF A BITCH

Sam was in his study again. He was always in the study, reading or writing or drawing rough plans for stage backdrops. Ace knocked at the door. "It's open," Sam said.

"Sam." Ace nodded.

"Ace." Sam leaned back in his leather chair and put his feet on the desk. He looked tired. Eyebags and stubble. "Have a seat." He motioned to a small couch against the far wall.

"How's things?" Ace preferred a hardback chair to an upholstered one. He tried to get comfortable.

"Good, workin on a book."

"Ain't you already written three of em?" Ace laughed. Sam joined him. "Look, Samuel," he said. "Officer St. Clair said somethin this mornin about the Task Force whatever. The drug busts. Sweep comin through this week sounds like to me."

"What are you telling *me* for?"

Ace cleared his throat. He took a minute to figure how that last question was meant. "I'm tellin you because when a net scoops up, things likely get caught in it."

"So Albert is a *thing* in this metaphor?" It came out louder than Sam intended. For a couple weeks, he'd been having trouble staying bottled up.

"Samuel," Ace said, and he gave Sam a look that reminded him of who he was talking to. "If you're going to do your fake talk, you can head on over to the professor's lounge at the supper club. They fall for leaky cases of verbal diarrhea over there."

Sam sighed and put his feet on the floor. "Point taken," he said.

"There's going to be some acquaintances of Albert's, maybe friends. You just got to make sure it ain't him."

"I know." He looked through Ace, at nothing.

"Alright, buddy," Ace said, and stood up. He shook Sam's hand and reached across the desk to pat him on the shoulder. On his way out the door, he turned and said, "And why don't you get out of this goddamned son of a bitch once in a while. Stinks in here like assholes and oregano." There were a few utterances from his past, utterances like this one, that would not be wiped from memory.

Out in the living room, Zizi sat on the dented yellow sectional with the band. They were supposed to be practicing. Flunky Cy had brought over a videotape copy of the 1970 movie *Little Big Man*. It had just started. A very old man spoke on the film. "I am a white man and never forgot it," he said.

"How old is that man?" Ace asked.

At first they just ignored him. Then, Everette the banjo player said, "It's Dustin Hoffman, man."

Ace had liked Everette since the time he first let him hold his banjo. The tone ring on it had been made by a Detroit friend of his out of an aluminum torque converter ring from a 1956 Buick transmission. It was pretty. "The hell it is Dustin Hoffman," Ace said.

"It's him, Ace. They've got him in makeup." Zizi wanted it quiet. She hit rewind, then play again.

Ace leaned in over the back of the sectional and squinted his eyes at the old man on the screen. He'd never seen a body so old, so wrinkled and splotched. It was a real fella. He'd be damned if it was Dustin Hoffman in makeup. He straightened back up. "That ain't no Dustin Hoffman," he said. He waved the whole room off and walked out the screen door toward his home in the garage. On the back stair stoop, he said, "Goddamn son of a bitch television." He'd been meaner ever since he'd thrown his own out the window. He'd never tell anyone how much he missed his friend the television, but oh, how he did.

CHAPTER TWENTY-EIGHT

BOYS SHOULD HAVE GOTTEN
THEIR EDUCATIONS

Albert did not get caught in the net that weekend in August of 1992. It was in October, the day after Halloween, that Officer St. Clair handed Ace the police report Xeroxes with a funny look on his face. "Could have been a lot worse, Ace," St. Clair had said.

Ace didn't have to type the words *possession with the intent to deliver a controlled substance* after Albert's name. He was thankful for that. It was only *fleeing and underage possession of alcohol*. Still, Albert got twenty hours of community service.

Ace went with him to Presbyterian Manor on Thanksgiving. It was a nursing home, and it was a place every young, misdemeanor type of kid went to work off community service. Helping to write cards to family members and bussing dinner trays. Some of the staff didn't care for the visits, but generally they were on holidays.

They followed a good-looking young nurse down a hallway to the indoor recreation area. Ace knew he was older than some in the place.

But at 89, he could still pass for 70. He whispered to Albert, "Don't let them keep me here, you little turddropper." He wanted to try and get the boy back from where he'd gone. Sam and Zizi were evidently unable to do it.

"Watch out for Mr. Overby," the nurse said. She stepped aside for an old man, pushed in a wheelchair with oxygen tubes in his nose. Albert and Ace stepped out of the way.

The old man looked up at Albert as he passed. "Navel?" he said. The fat man pushing him kept going, but the old man craned his neck to see Albert. "Navel?" he said again.

Albert looked at Ace, who laughed a little. "Guess he thought you was Navel," Ace told him.

In the rec room, Albert sat with a woman from Wayne County and wrote out the addresses of her people still back there. Her hand was too shaky. Her name was Mrs. O'Brien and she had cards, dozens of them, all with birds on the front. "This one here, now I said this one is a Dusky Lory. And this one here, now I said this one here is a Pink Ring Neck Dove," she said. Before every phrase that parted her lips came the words, "now I said."

In the corner, Ace fed a pop machine quarters and pushed the button for grape soda. He looked at the book spines on the shelves. He'd never heard of a one. Picked one off called *Voyage of Vengeance* and put it back on the shelf after a couple sentences. It was no *Follow the Equator*.

Albert finished addressing the last of eight cards for Mrs. O'Brien. He smiled and shook her hand. At this, she began to holler, "Oh my. You are a cracker jack today!" Evidently, she found Albert to be handsome and charming. "He's a cracker jack today," she called out to the room of old folks. "He's a cracker jack today." Albert nodded and patted her hand softly until which time he could pull his own away.

She gave one last tug and he leaned in and kissed her on the cheek. This quieted her down and she wore a dreamy look then that might have put her at fourteen were it not for the cataracts in her eyes.

Albert said "Alright, Mrs. O'Brien, you take care of yourself."

After he'd bussed some trays, Albert and Ace made eye contact and nodded toward the hallway. Smoke break.

They hotfooted it down the hallway.

Through the open door to a room, they saw and heard an old, bearded black man saying, "Get out. Get on out," though there was no one in there.

In the lobby was Mr. Overby. Still with tubes in his nose. He looked out the glass panes at the traffic going by on Veterans Memorial. When he saw them headed to the door, each pulling a pack from his shirt pocket, he spoke. "Navel. Navel come over here."

Ace wondered if they'd come on a bad day. Plenty of the old folks were sedate, tranquil even, but the percentage of shuffled decks was high.

They could do nothing but walk over to the man. He had a blue wool blanket across his lap. The fat chair pusher was reading a magazine and watching TV in the corner. As they approached Mr. Overby, Ace whispered to Albert, "Before I start to seeing people that ain't really there, I'll walk out to the woods of my own accord, just like Yellow Dog, and I'll lay down under a hickory tree at the top of a mountain."

"What did you whisper to him?" the old man said to Ace.

"Told him I thought you had mistaken him for another man."

"Oh. Well, *are* you Navel?" He looked Albert up and down over his spectacles. Hair grew wild from his nose and ears and he breathed with his mouth wide open.

"No, I'm not Navel."

"Well, what do you know about it?" the old man said. "Give me a cigarette."

"Don't do it," the fat man in the corner said without looking up from his magazine.

"Maybe next time," Ace said.

"I know you too." He looked at Ace wild. "You know me. I went to grade school up in Mink Shoals. We was in grade school at the same time. Boys should have gotten their educations."

"Nossir," Ace said. "I believe you have me mistaken with somebody else." He was perfectly willing to give an old man his time, but, for obvious reasons, this recognizing from the past conversation had never been his favorite.

"Navel," the old man said. And then he got a confused look and started to cry a little bit.

"Alright now," Ace said. He patted the man's hands, tucked under the blanket. He waved over the fat man. "Sir," he said. "You might want to . . ." he nodded at Mr. Overby. The fat man understood without ever looking up from his magazine. He stood, dropped it on the couch, and walked over.

"Alright, Mr. Overby," Ace said, and he and Albert exited Presbyterian Manor.

Outside, it was cold for November. "Damn," Albert said. He held the cigarette in his lips, didn't have a lighter.

Ace lit his Chesterfield and held out the flame to Albert, cupping it as he moved. "That's just how it goes," Ace said.

CHAPTER TWENTY-NINE

EWART SMITH SPOKE IN A DREAM

"Harla harla ha na na na atta hoo hay om idayayamana," she said. But it wasn't that way. It was the Wurlitzer theremin, on the spritz, humming like it had lips. Ewart was in among all the people somewhere. They danced like marionette puppets. Above all of it, Ewart was saying, "Glove box baby. Thirty-eight. Glove box baby. Thirty-eight." There was the smell of anointing oil and poison and flesh on fire. There were serpents. Ace let one ride his arm, on up into his mouth like he had as a boy. But he gagged and retched when the cold nose hit the back of his throat and tried to keep going down. It clogged his esophagus with its head, opened its mouth wide once in his throat.

Ace sat up while he still slept. Choking air, he went to the kitchen, knocking his right kneecap on the doorframe. Still, he did not wake up. Not until he had the Ajax canister in his hand, held up above his head. Only then did he open his eyes. He looked at the cabinet in front of him. He couldn't remember opening it or grabbing the Ajax. He breathed deep and heavy and wondered at his sleeping intentions. If he had to put money on it, he'd have bet he was about to pour scrubbing powder down his throat to scare off the snake that had clogged it.

"Ace," somebody yelled outside. "Ace!" His heart hadn't slowed and he was yet to catch his breath. He cracked the kitchen window.

In the driveway, Zizi stood shivering, holding a cordless phone. "It gets static out that far. Come take it in the house."

"How's that?"

"Phone for you."

In that moment, Ace could not recall having ever once received a phone call in the thirteen years he'd lived there. He slipped on some shoes. It was cold out.

He took it from her and sat down on the back stoop. He took another deep breath. "Hello?"

"Two words for you?" a man's voice said.

"How's that?"

"Two words for you? Self-defense? That's all ol Charles Lively had to say to keep you from killin him? I thought you was cold-blooded. Thought you could drown a glass a water."

Ace tried to do some math. He couldn't figure who'd still be alive to speak to him that way. Lively had to be long dead, way he lived.

"Mouth too rotten to talk?" the voice said.

"Now you look here."

"No, you look here." It was Warren Crews. Ace had heard it in that enunciate of hate. Real hate. "I wasn't even going to mess with it no more. But then you come on to town with the cocksuckin tree huggers. You go on over the hill to your shithouse and walk around inside of it. They'll put a feller our age in the penitentiary, don't matter his state."

Ace stood up, yelled into the phone. "You been in there Warren? You just get out? You listen to me you goddamned son of a bitch—"

Warren Crews hung up the phone.

Ace jumped up and down on the stair then. He rubbed at that

knee he'd knocked, cursed in an unknown tongue. He had on a holey T-shirt and boxer shorts. Wingtips with no socks.

Zizi watched him out the window. She opened the back door. "What in the hell is going on Ace?" she said. She shivered in the open doorway.

"Oh, just go on back in to your eight ounce bottle, Zizi."

The skin on her neck drew in. She looked behind her to see if anyone had heard, then thought better of that. Albert hadn't been to the house in a month and Sam slept in his sealed off study. Zizi cracked the screen door and took the phone from his hand. She looked at Ace, then away from him, and shut the door.

He went back inside and ran a bath of Epsom salts.

In the tub, he gargled and spit salt water. Swashed it over those sore gums. The pain had come back in recent days, the old ways of the mouth. He knew that mouth was what brought the dreams, what put him in a foul mood. The throb brought all of it down on him. He'd let himself say something he never should have to Zizi. And it wasn't just the once. He'd been saying things to Sam too. Things he shouldn't, like, "You're a goddamned professor and you don't even push your boy at college?" It was as if the words came out before he thought of them these days. The throb in the gums caused it. But he'd not see a dentist. He'd not go under that gas again.

He thought how nice it would be to just stop talking. To just sew his mouth shut and clog up his ears with cornbread crumbs.

He got out of the tub and into the bed.

It was Yellow being gone.

It was the boy being out in the streets.

It was the television thrown away.

It was winter. He'd just have to get through winter and things would be all right.

CHAPTER THIRTY

A MAN TOOK IT ALL TO THE STAGE

It was Saturday, May 29th, 1993. Memorial Day weekend. Ace got up at 7:00 and swashed antiseptic mouthwash until it burned too bad to hold. His gums still throbbed when he laid down his head, but the swelling had shrunk since winter. He pulled on his white dress shirt and buttoned it slow. In front of him on the bureau were his teeth in a dry highball glass. He'd quit putting them in, even for work.

Ace looked at the dentures and thought to himself, "This is the last time you'll see those teeth." He left them where they lay. Sitting down on the bed, he pulled back the sheet, and fished his arm in for the money roll. This time, there was no peeling of bills from the Pulitzer round. He took the whole wad out, unrolled it, and folded it flat under his right shoe insert.

Inside the main house, he called Louise and told her to bring the property deed papers to the show that night.

"Why?" she asked.

"Just bring the papers," Ace said.

He sat at the electric typewriter in his *Advertiser* office rubbing his tongue over his gums. He looked down at the police reports St. Clair had given him that morning. *Larceny. Battery.* He put his fingers to the keys of the electric typewriter, but he didn't feel like writing any of it. It was the Saturday of the big event. The sun was shining outside. The whole family, all souls dumped in the tri-state, were meeting at six at Camden Park for a concert. Camden Park was of the amusement variety, run-down rides that spun you sick. Six bands scheduled from all over, including the Kozmanauts. Some called it a revival, others a carnival.

He pulled a folded paper from his back pocket. On it, he'd written in inkpen the made-up Police Blotter he'd been working on since he took the job in 1984. It was just what he did sometimes. Made up things to write about when the real stories became too much. Over the years, he'd crossed out parts and re-written them. But until that morning, he'd never typed them out at work.

He loaded a fresh piece of paper and put down the headline. *Outlaw rides off, leaves city dwellers for sunny Mexico.* He tested his typing skills. Ninety-year-old fingers could still get the job done if they'd been trained by Dorothea. He really banged it out. He knew when he turned it in later, Dave Pace wouldn't even look at the thing.

At the end, he'd stopped, still not having written what he truly wanted to say. It couldn't be done. Like he'd told Joseph Mitchell that day in New York City, "There ain't no real when it comes to writing." He pulled his hands back, then put them on the keys again and typed, *Now is the time for all good men to come to the aid of their country.*

Sam had been in the Camden Park parking lot since six a.m. He'd loaded his Volkswagen van with the unassembled backdrop pieces and three student volunteers. Gary, Jason, and Brandie. All morning and afternoon, they staple-gunned and nailed together and painted the mountain scene. The mountaintops had been shaped with a variable speed jigsaw and a detail sander. It was beautiful, painted green. Deep green. Sam had done something to be proud of.

He drove the last nail at five. At five-thirty, the opening band set up, and at six the Stetson-hatted singer said, "Welcome everybody, we're Nehemiah's Blowtorch." They opened with "Sweet Home Alabama," only they replaced the state's name with "West Virginia."

At seven, Sam looked at his wristwatch. Albert still hadn't showed. Zizi was too happy to be cold sober, and the rest of the band had walked out the main gates and disappeared inside a patch of trees across Route 60. They were scheduled to play at nine.

A section of the parking lot the size of a football field had been cordoned off for the event. Folks were filling it up.

Ace walked up to Sam. He'd heard something from a Kentucky harmonica player that confused him. "Sam," he said. The sun was lowering behind Ace, bouncing off the worn top of his fedora, reflecting off the chrome cars of the Big Dipper coaster as it rattled in the distance. "I gather you had a chance to meet most of the musicians this afternoon?"

"Most."

"You meet a band leader from Fairmont named Hambone?"

"Yes." Sam took bites out of a ketchup-smeared pronto pup between words.

"He say anything about a famous fella sittin in on piano this evening? Fella from Fairmont. Johnnie Johnston?"

"Did this piano player used to be with Chuck Berry?" He scraped his teeth over the stuff stuck to the stick.

"I'll be damned," Ace said. He shook his head and laughed. He wasn't looking at Sam then or any one of the folks gathered around them, some dancing to the music, some not. He rubbed at the stubble on his jawbone. "Well, bring it on, I reckon," he said.

At eight, he found Johnnie behind the stage, smoking and waiting to be called up for two songs with Hambone and the Virginia Slims. "Johnnie," Ace said, walking up to him. Johnnie Johnston looked good. He wasn't overly wrinkled or fat for a sixty-eight year old man. He dropped his cigarette on the pavement and cocked his head at Ace.

"Yes? Who is asking?" But he thought he might know. He just couldn't say it out loud.

"Chicky Gold the Harmonica Man of the West Virginia Shine Guzzlers," Ace said. He stood as straight up and down as he could. Had his muscles flexed under his clothes.

"Sheeeeeeeeeeeeee-it," Johnnie said. He smiled and they hugged, clapping backs hard.

When Johnnie got carried away with the back-clapping, Ace said, "Watch it now. I'm a cold-blooded old son of a bitch."

Did they ever laugh then until Johnnie got called up to twinkle keys on Ray Charles' "Georgia." Ace watched him from the front row of the three hundred or so in the crowd. Johnnie played beautifully. Out among the sweaty, couples slow danced while the sun hung orange, then dropped behind the hills. The drunk ones among them played grab ass.

After "Georgia," Johnnie called Hambone over to his piano. He whispered to him and Hambone walked back to his microphone. "We have another special treat for you folks. Mr. Chicky Gold the Harmonica Man will be joining Mr. Johnston for this next number." He looked down at Ace. "Mr. Gold," he said, waving him toward the stairs.

Ace didn't speak into the microphone when he replaced Hambone at the stand. He pulled it from its holder, and stuck it to his Hohner. He was checking for feedback, wrapping his long skinny fingers around the whole deal. He looked back to Johnnie, who had just finished telling the stand-up bass player, "Walking twelve bar, C." Johnnie and Ace nodded to one another and the rumble came down. Then the piano, then harp. Johnnie sang the first verse, Ace the second. Both closed their eyes and moved in the spasm sway. On the chorus, they harmonized:

> Well, I'll drown a glass a water
> And I'll hang a rope
> The devil he done come to me
> Took away my hope
> Well, I'll put that stick a dynamite
> Right on under your nose
> Cause I done seen the worst a man can see
> That's just how it goes

When it was through, those in the crowd who had seen some things in life clapped their hands over their heads hard and howled like dogs.

Louise came up to tell Ace how good he'd sounded. Ace thanked her, took her to a roped-off section housing junk behind the stage. The sun was being halved by the trees encircling the park. The hills would block it out before long. They sat down inside a retired purple Dodge'em car. Ace said to Louise, "Did you bring the papers?"

"Yes." She'd gone pale.

"Let's have a look."

Louise pulled them from her pocketbook and spread the creases.

Ace looked, then bent and took off his shoe. He took from what was under its sole, handed Louise three thousand dollars, in hundreds. "I'd like to buy my house from you," he said.

She teared up. Then she nodded okay. It was the right thing to do.

"I'll die before I let them blast up there," he told her. She nodded again. On the back of the papers, they wrote up a little contract, signed it. Louise looked at her money, Ace his deed. She kissed him on the cheekbone, and he thanked her.

Back at the stage, Zizi came up to Ace with a smile on her face not possible without liquor. "You were unbelievable, baby," she said, draping herself on him.

"Thank you sweetheart," he said. He held her there against him while people knocked into them filing toward concessions. He rubbed her backbone and she was still. Then, Zizi straightened up and ran off, barefoot, ready to hypnotize, harmonize, and praise the skies with the stuff she called Theremin Good Time Music. She had somebody to see first. Ace watched her go. As she ran out the gates and across Route 60, he could see that the bottoms of her feet were tar black.

Nine o'clock came and went. Flunky Cy, Dale, and Everett had taken their positions in front of the twelve foot wooden mountains on stage. They stood wide-eyed and swallowing hard, dumbfounded as to the whereabouts of their star. Her Wurlitzer glowed under the spotlight. The metal rods hummed electric. Somebody had switched her on already.

The crowd mumbled and whistled with their fingers in their mouths. It was dark. Some with kids went home.

Sam looked at his watch and shook his head. He opened up his Volkswagen van and crawled into the back. Pulled the curtain.

Louise and Larry took the stage impromptu. While Larry tuned his mandolin, Louise moved the microphone away from the theremin. She spoke, amplified. "This one's called 'The Ballad of Trenchmouth Taggart,' and it's the truest tale you'll ever hear."

Larry could pick that mandolin. It was something. The crowd

listened to the words, stood still. Louise sang holier than Hazel Dickens.

> Miners stayed poor loading that coal
> Till Trenchmouth Taggart come to save their soul
> He stood his ground and took his stand
> An eye for an eye with that green-fisted man

A few rows from the stage, Ace nodded a thank you to Louise, daughter of his first and only love. She nodded the same back.

When Zizi still did not show, Ace climbed the stage stair for the second time that night. A few folks applauded. Everett unfolded a beat-up chair for him, and Ace sat down, put the microphone to his lips, and closed his eyes again. Though he could carry a note, he wasn't known for his singing. He'd never attempted a cappella. Not until then. "Well, lovers is right?" he sang, low. He opened his eyes and leaned back toward Everett. He whispered to him, "Get on the other mic and answer me, 'Oh yes we right.'" Everett did as he was told.

"Well, lovers is you right?" Ace sang. It carried across the quiet crowd with the weight only old men possess. He watched Brandie get into the Volkswagen.

"Oh yes we right," Everett sang.

Ace dropped right in, "Daddy killed a rabbit brought it home, children got choked on a rabbit bone. Shake it to the river boys, shake it to the river."

After a couple verses, he'd waved the crowd into answering.

"Oh yes we right," they called out softly, a little ugly.

"Newborn baby born last night, walkin talking 'fore daylight. Carry to the mountain boys, carry to the mountain."

Johnnie Johnston leaned against his Cadillac backstage, touching his handkerchief to his eyes.

Ace had brought it all to the stage, and before he pulled out his harp to blow until he was sapped, he leaned his head back and sang out one last verse: "Tri-state women read and write, Mingo women bite and fight. Carry to the mountain boys, carry to the mountain."

When he finished his harmonica solo, having played two and a half minutes of it with his nose while standing and dancing a stomp, the crowd roared for him. It was then that Zizi ran up on stage. She stubbed her toe on the last stair and fell. Caught herself with her hands and stood back up. A couple people laughed.

"You alright?" Ace rubbed her back again as she moved the mic stand back by the theremin.

"Fine," she said. Her laugh had a bad sound to it. Like quiet hysteria.

"I'm Zizi Kozma!" she yelled at the people.

The Kozmanauts played two songs, "A Charge to Keep I Have" and "He Will Meet Me at the Portal," both poorly.

The band called for an early break, but Zizi wouldn't get down. She wanted a solo.

People filed away as the theremin virtuoso stood before her machine and stroked at the air with those delicate fingers. It was "Amazing Grace," and she harmonized along with the electricity, soprano-high and lonesome. None there had seen anything like it before, and they stared.

Ace heard somebody say "Police" behind him. He turned and saw the cruiser inching folks away, parting them. On stage, Zizi and her theremin belted out, simultaneous, "He will my shield and portion be."

Ace walked toward the cruiser. On his way, he watched Brandie step from the side door of the van. She was mad, pulling strands of her hair out of her mouth and screaming, "You fucking pervert." Inside, Sam shook his head and wondered at how nothing ever meant anything.

Officer St. Clair put it in park and stepped out. "Now hold on Ace, the boy is okay. He's fine," he said. He pushed down on his gun belt, picked at his crotch.

Ace's mouth had things to say that his brain hadn't thought of yet. "*You* hold on, now. I know he's fine. I ain't worried about Albert. I got something to tell you."

It occurred to Officer St. Clair that the old man wasn't like most. He was hard to figure. "Alright," he said.

"Glove box. Thirty-eight," Ace told him.

Officer St. Clair cocked his head back. "What's that now?"

"It's my pistol." Ace's whole body hummed. "I made my mark on there."

"Did Hodge call you?" Hodge was the rookie officer who'd just arrested Albert across town. St. Clair asked the question despite knowing there was no way Hodge could've reached Ace. The bust had only been an hour prior.

Then Ace took off his hat and held it with two hands at his waist. "Listen here," he said. "Your man pulled him off driving that black Cutlass Supreme, ain't that right?" Behind him, Zizi let a note hold. She waved her arms like a perched bird, pulled a vibrato out of herself and her machine.

"How did you know that?"

"Listen." It was a wholly independent organ by then, his toothless mouth. St. Clair stared at it, watched it go. "I'm going to tell you somethin important," Ace said. Just then, Zizi finished the oddest "Amazing Grace" rendition on record and leaned against the wooden mountain backdrop sweating while the audience clapped confused. Ace spoke the words, "*I put it in the glove box. My .38.*"

St. Clair shook his head and held his mouth open. "But," he said. "But you don't ride in cars."

"Started a couple weeks ago."

"At your age? Without a license?"

"Been up to the state police's last Monday. Showed em my eyes are good. I got what you call 'wide vision.'" Sometimes in life lies were required, and sometimes real change. St. Clair laughed a little and shook his head some more. Then, Ace took a seat beside him in the cruiser and rode in an automobile for the first time since 1952 when he'd awakened stuck to the floor, half dead.

On the way to the police station, where Albert sat in a holding cell with black-inked fingertips, the lie grew bigger and more believable. The gun was for protection, he told St. Clair. He'd been planning to drive the Cutlass to Camden Park that evening. A man named Crews had threatened to kill him there, he said.

At the station, the Cutlass was still parked out front, yet to be impounded. Inside, Ace walked straight to the holding cell. He gripped the bars and told Albert to stand up and come to him. Eye to eye, he said, "It's going to be alright. But you've got to right your ship, you hear me?"

"Yessir," Albert said.

"Ace, come on away from him," Officer St. Clair said from behind the desk. He was trying to locate Hodge, who'd gone for McDonald's.

The little office smelled like mildew. It had flooded in April and the surveillance system was still down. The camera in the corner collected dust. White paint chipped off the brick wall in pieces the size of half dollars.

It sat all wrong with Ace, seeing the boy in a cage. He'd not allow it to proceed.

A female officer who'd been watching Albert asked St. Clair what was what. She'd never spoken to Ace when he'd come around for the arrest reports, but he'd always noticed her yellow hair, the way it stood up stiff, thick with all that spray.

"Ol Ace here says it was his .38 in the glove box."

"Can prove it too," Ace said. "I etched my mark in it with a raccoon penis bone."

"What?" The female officer laughed from the belly up. "Raccoon what?" she said. Her seated posture was poor.

"Ace, I'm going to get the firearm out of evidence for you. See about this mark. You sit tight right here." St. Clair walked down the hall, pulled a key from his spring-loaded rollaway, and unlocked the evidence room. When he was in, Ace turned toward Albert and winked.

There were flies humming around the place. Some butted their heads against the windows, the lights.

Ace walked over to the coffee pot and poured himself one in styrofoam. He took a fistful of sugarcubes from the glass bowl beside the creamer and kept them in his hand. At the female officer's desk, he said, "Miss, you ever seen the magical world of the fly and the three sugarcubes?"

"Boy you are full of em, aren't you?" She had a condescending way toward old folks that resulted from a poor self worth.

Albert watched from his cell while Ace lined up the cubes right to left on yellow hair's desk. Before he set down the third one, he licked it without her seeing. "Now watch those close," he said. She did so. "The fly will land on the far left one if you concentrate on it hard enough." Ace pointed to it and stepped back from her desk. Then, he stepped back again. Albert watched him move out of her sight range and down the hall to the evidence room.

She never took her eye off that cube. When the fly landed on it, she said, "Well, I'll be a—"

The phrase did not finish. St. Clair hollered something unintelligible from the evidence room and the yellow-haired lady officer stood up scared.

Hodge, aged 20, came in the back door carrying a cardboard coffee holder balancing two full McDonald's bags. It took both hands. "McRibs," he said. Then he looked around himself and froze.

Ace was walking back from the evidence room. He held St. Clair from behind by the wrist. With his other hand, he pressed the .38 to the man's head.

"Hodge," St. Clair was saying. "Hodge. All you have to tell me is that you emptied it before you checked it in. Understand?" They'd been short-handed since budget cuts. No double-checkers on staff when every able body works Saturday patrol.

Hodge was a statue with that stack of fast food, balanced and unmoving. Albert was to his left, yellow hair to his right. She had yet to draw her gun, but she'd undone the button.

"Hodge?" St. Clair said.

"Everybody easy now," Ace said. He kept the pistol pushed hard to St. Clair's temple. Let him know it wasn't going anywhere.

"Hodge?"

"I can't remember," Hodge said.

A look swept St. Clair's face. He didn't know whether to shit or go blind.

Albert's mouth had gone dry and he licked and swallowed and tried to breathe normal.

Ace said, "Now I am saying right here to all of you that this weapon is mine. I own it, not the boy. I put it in the glove box this morning."

Hodge still did not move. Yellow hair still did not draw her sidearm.

"Lean over and get the keys off the desk," Ace said. St. Clair did so, the .38 sticking to him. "Drop em in." St. Clair reached his free arm back and felt for Ace's pants pocket, dropped in the Oldsmobile keys. "Now," Ace said. "Listen all of you. I am going to leave here with *my* gun. You ain't going to give chase, hear? Albert is going to walk out a free man because you got nothin to hold him on. Albert?"

"Yessir?" Albert straightened his posture, chest out, behind in.

"You get you a public defender if it calls for it. They can't convict you on a single charge without evidence. Hear me?"

"I hear you Grandpa."

Of all the names he'd ever been called, this one he liked the most.

"Now St. Clair knows me to be a fair man. I'm askin you all not to give chase, not to make any more of this here tonight. When I leave, I'm going to Mexico to die in the sun. Don't want no trouble along the way. Once I'm gone, that's the end of all this here. Are you willin to do that?"

Nobody spoke and Ace pressed the barrel harder.

"Yes," St. Clair spit out. "Ace has been an acquaintance of mine for years now," he said. "I give my word on this being the end of it."

It was quiet again for a moment. "You called me acquaintance, I noticed. Not friend." Ace smiled and the two officers who could see the open mouth shrunk back into themselves for fear. "I like that. Ain't never known but one officer of the law to be a friend. You all don't mix too well with outlaws." He backed down the hallway with the gun trained on St. Clair for the length of the place. Then he was out the door and on the road.

There were six in the cylinder. Hodge had never unloaded the weapon.

They kept their word. There would be no chase. Albert walked out, free and easy.

Ace drove fast to Mingo, so fast he couldn't believe it himself. As it turned out, driving an automobile was easy. He put ninety miles of dogleg behind him in two hours.

He bought groceries, a backpack, a plastic tarp, and a shovel at an all-night super store in Williamson. Then, he tracked Warren Crews and put a bullet between the old man's eyes while he slept alone on a bare box spring. He dragged him to the car and hefted him into the tarp-lined trunk.

He drove to his boyhood home. Next to where the outhouse had stood, he dug a grave. He rolled Warren Crews down into it, spit in his eyes for Arly Jr., and covered him up with dirt.

He drove the car to Sulfur Creek Mountain, pulled to the top of what Larry Blevins had called "the wrecking hill." He left it perched on the drop off in the dark, a present for a lucky worshipper of automotive invention. He was not one of their kind.

It took Ace an hour and a half to hike back to the house up Warm Hollow. The backpack's weight caused him to feel his age.

The sun rose about the same time he laid down in the loft, the property deed in his shoe with the remaining five hundred dollars. He closed his eyes as folks all over the tri-state opened theirs to the Sunday edition of the *Advertiser*. They called each other and read in wonder the words of the Police Blotter:

Outlaw rides off, leaves city dwellers for sunny Mexico
An outlaw left town yesterday after residing in the city for more than a decade. Any other crimes committed were deemed unworthy of punishment, and prisoners were let free from their cages.
The Outlaw recognized the uselessness of most things considered useful

today, and the demise of most things once considered grand. He'll miss
little of your fair towns, only the friends and family left behind. To them,
to you, he shouts from on horseback:
   Now is the time for all good men to come to the aid of their country.

Somehow, in the days, months, and years following, the people
in those hills knew to leave be the man in the old log house. Men,
women, and children stayed clear of him. The coal company found
another fill for their uprooted earth.

   The old man worked on the house, patched its drafty sills and
seams and populated it with furniture built from trees.

   One day, he found a rusted tin box under a rotten floorboard in
the loft. Inside were the letters of young Clarissa, letters addressed
to a boy named Trenchmouth but never sent because he lived in the
same house. These yellowed, cracking papers marked in longhand
spoke of love never tried, because in this life, trying was always
met with heartache. The old man read the letters with a joy and
a sorrow more palpable than any he'd ever felt reading newspaper
stories. Afterwards, he rested. He closed his weary eyes and pictured
Clarissa, writing all those letters to him in secret. The floorboards
warmed. He could hear her breathing beside him. He matched his
own to hers and nearly let the music of such breathing lull him into
the sleep of the dead.

   He sat upright instead. Then he did his push-ups, sit-ups, and
jumping jacks. He decided to live a while longer, to go into town every
now and again, procure things like chipped beef and Chesterfields.
He decided he'd no longer speak. The rotten hole in his head between
his nose and his chin no longer had words to utter.

EPILOGUE

The old man finished telling his story to the reporter from *Time* magazine. He rested. Worried that the saltwater-rated fishing line hadn't held through all the talking, he put his fingers to his lips. There was nothing there. No fishing line at all. Just the old, cracked lips circled in beard stubble, the empty, rotten gums inside. "I'll be damned," he said. He looked to the reporter for answers.

The man across the kitchen table from him was someone he'd never seen before. A sort of blank man, no particular features at all. He moved his hand across the table to the voice recorder and pressed his thumb to a button on the tiny, steel machine. The red light went out.

The old man grabbed at his ears, for a ringing had overtaken then, sudden and loud. "Put your light back on," he said.

"Take your makeup off," the reporter said back over the howl. Then he stood up. The sound ceased. He said to the old man, "I don't know what name to call you by."

It was safe to take his hands away from his ears. He spoke through the confusion. "Call me as the first ones did. Call me

Trenchmouth," he said.

"Alright, Trenchmouth." The man's voice had changed somehow, become recognizable. "What do you say to those who claim your story is fabricated, not real?" His body seemed to wobble while he talked, the pitch of his voice along with it. "That it is stolen from a history book published twelve years ago by a Marshall University scholar in the field of Appalachian mythology?"

"Come again?" the old man said.

"Sir," the reporter went on. He looked at some papers he held. "What do you say to this record of the infanticide death of an Early Taggart in February of 1903 in Mingo County, West Virginia?" His mouth opening grew smaller and smaller as he spoke, until he was talking only from a small, pursed hole.

"Why are you speaking like that?" the old man asked.

"In tongues?" The reporter did a little dance then. A twitch jig. While he shook, he sang, "Newborn baby born in town, Devil talkin, mama got to drown." It was the song of the birth mother in the voice of the birth mother. The song went on in the voice of Hob Tibbs and Arthur H. Estabrook and J.B. Smith: "Devil's got a hold on God, boy. Pretty as you please, boy. You seen red, heard that howlin sound? That's steel invention, diggin you underground."

It occurred to the old man then that he had no memories and may have never lived at all. That he may have been sitting in silence for days, watching a red glow on a tiny steel machine. Listening to its gears howl electric.

But that was hogwash. He lit another Chesterfield and shut his eyes tight. "I know what's real," the old man said.

When he opened them up again, he was alone in the house. Had the reporter been there, had he not been an apparition, a sign of having lost all mental faculty, the old man would have told his guest that he'd seen and heard his kind before. The bamboozler. No more than a salesman of eugenics, a prophet for a fake God. A man such as him could no better speak on what was real than a New York newspaperman dropped in the bloody Mingo hills. "I'll not be bamboozled," the old man said. It came out muffled.

He touched his lips again. The saltwater-rated fishing line was there. He ran his fingers over it. "I'll be damned," he said. When he lowered his hands to the table, he found his old Underwood typewriter resting there, his fingers on the keys. It scared him, and he stood up quick, knocking his chair over with the backs of his knees.

"Well," the old man said to himself. "That's just how it goes." He'd finally lost his mind, he figured. Finally started seeing things and people that weren't there.

What came next was easy to figure.

There was ice on the kitchen window, inside and out. But he did not take his wool coat from the rack. He limped to the front door and took up his sassafras walking stick from where it leaned against the jamb. With his free hand, he took the doorknob. He stopped. Didn't turn it. Out there, all was liable to be red and crumbled, leveled forever. Out there, everything was liable to be gone.

He felt something pressing against his behind. He reached into his back pocket and pulled it out. The derringer flask. It held no scratches to mark time's passage. Instead, it shone silver, as if spit-shined. He read the mark etched with skill on its face:

Bottomless

&

Never-ending

He unscrewed the cap, put it to the hole, and swallowed all he could. It warmed his bones and righted his ship.

The old man wore a smile then, as much as was possible with a sewn-shut mouth. "Well," he said, and he turned the knob, walked outside. It was cold, but he moved through it, past where the outhouse and the barn and the garden used to be. He came to the edge of the woods. He stepped into them and carried to the mountains.

That night, the 108 year-old man known by many names climbed higher, and all the crying babies who lived in those hills went still. He tossed away his walking stick and side-stepped the incline. He used his arms for balance, like a trapeze artist.

When he got to the top of Sulfur Creek Mountain, he smiled again, this time wide enough to tear that stitching from his mouth. He did not mind the discomfort. For stretching out before him, as wide as his vision would reach, he beheld it.

It was not the surface of the moon, nor the wrecking hill, nor the great colorless void, flush as a pool table. His vision did not blur to red and his ears did not howl electric. The mountains had never buckled. They were there before him, real and true.

He felt the Widow all around him. He thanked her aloud for trying. Then, he found a suitable hickory tree and lay down beneath its limbs. It was as if no war had ever bloodied the ground beneath him. As if the world was a proper place.

Everything had come back. Everything was as it had been.

ACKNOWLEDGMENTS

I am grateful to so many books by authors who have tirelessly put down the history of a people not to be forgotten. I owe a debt of gratitude to *Best of Hillbilly* by Otto Whittaker, *The Battle of Blair Mountain* by Robert Shogun, *Thunder in the Mountains* by Lon Savage, *Mountains of Music* by John Lilly, and *The Foxfire Book* by Eliot Wigginton. I am also indebted to the CD *Work & Pray*, which reflects the work of Dr. Cortez Reece. I'd like to thank the *Williamson Daily News* archives, *Wheeling Register* for its early reporting on the penitentiary at Moundsville, and the late Joe Chambers for the videotape transcript of his father's words about May 19th, 1920. For assistance with President Kennedy's 1960 primary campaign in West Virginia, I consulted *An Unfinished Life* by Robert Dallek and *John F. Kennedy: A Biography* by Michael O'Brien.

I would be remiss if I did not acknowledge the first place I came across a version of the expression "hang a rope and drown a glass of water," which grew, in Trenchmouth's world, to be an anthem of sorts. "Diamond Bob" first uttered those words, and I thank Jerome

Washington, a writer who knows better than me what's real, for listening and writing.

Thank you to the folks at West Virginia University Press for all their help. Thanks also to the writing programs that assisted me financially over the years, and especially to the writers they employed to teach.

For giving me time to write, and for so much more, I wish to say thank you to my wife, Margaret, without whom I would be completely lost. And to Reece and T-Bird, I say thank you for being the boys and the best friends that you are. I am grateful to my parents, Carol and Maury Taylor, who hail from Marion and Mingo Counties, respectively. From the beginning, they have given support in all its forms. My father is particularly worthy of acknowledgment, as he inspired in me, through his own genuine interest in remembering his people and their place, a similar interest. I could never thank him enough for that, for such interests are rare these days.

M. Glenn Taylor was born and raised in Huntington, West Virginia. This is his first novel. His stories have been published in literary journals such as *Chattahoochee Review, Mid-American Review, Meridian,* and *Gulf Coast,* among others. He teaches English and fiction writing at Harper College in suburban Chicago, where he lives with his wife and two sons.